Loverboy

Ben Tomlinson

ANDERSEN PRESS

First published in Great Britain in 2025 by
Andersen Press Limited
20 Vauxhall Bridge Road, London SW1V 2SA, UK
Vijverlaan 48, 3062 HL Rotterdam, Nederland
www.andersenpress.co.uk

2 4 6 8 10 9 7 5 3 1

All rights reserved. No part of this publication may be reproduced, stored in
a retrieval system or transmitted in any form, or by any means, electronic,
mechanical, photocopying, recording or otherwise, without the
written permission of the publisher.

The right of Ben Tomlinson to be identified as the author of this work has been
asserted by him in accordance with the Copyright, Designs and Patents Act, 1988.

Copyright © Ben Tomlinson, 2025

British Library Cataloguing in Publication Data available.

ISBN 978 1 83913 519 4

Printed and bound in Great Britain by Clays Ltd, Elcograf S.p.A.

Maya

Prologue

When Alfie woke up and saw a missed call from Maya, his heart soared. It always did when she called or messaged. Then he looked more closely and realised there were six of them. All left around three a.m. Now he was worried. What the hell had happened? He wanted to check if she was OK. He phoned her immediately.

Twenty minutes later he was outside her house, calling again.

'I'm here,' he said as soon as she answered.

'I'm not there!' said Maya. 'Go down the alley!'

'What alley?'

'The one at the end of the road! I'm on the sofa.'

'*Sofa?*'

He hung up and hurried along the passage, pushing past overgrown bits of hedge and bramble, until the path opened out into a small green. Maya was sitting on a battered black leather sofa that someone had apparently dumped, tapping on her phone. She wore a bow-knot dress with puffy sleeves. On the floor by her feet was an open suitcase. Inside lay a half-used pack of tissues on top of a mess of clothes. Her thick black hair was tied into two shoulder-length ponytails and her pale skin and spotty cheeks were caked in white make-up. She had full lips that were painted blood red, pale grey eyes bloodshot from crying and mascara ran down both her cheeks. She looked beautiful and ridiculous, like she was sitting on a stage set that someone had dressed, just for her.

'What?' said Maya, catching him staring. She patted her suitcase. 'My plane takes off at one! I'm about to go to the airport!' She pointed to the cushion next to her. 'Try it. It's actually comfortable.'

He crossed the green and sat down next to her.

'I can't believe you left your warm bed, just to see me for five minutes!' she said.

Alfie smiled sheepishly.

'I was totally harassing you,' continued Maya. 'Sorry about that. I was freaking out and very, very drunk.'

'I was asleep, so it didn't exactly bother me,' said Alfie. 'Plus when I called you back, you were blubbering. Of course I was gonna come.'

'Aww, Alfie, I really appreciate it,' said Maya, patting his arm. She managed a smile before tears welled up in her eyes. 'He cheated on me, Alfie!'

'Ovi?'

'Yeah!'

'Last night?'

'Yeah!'

'Your boyfriend cheated on you while you were with him *at his own party?*'

'I know! That goth girl! The one with the cleavage.'

Alfie remembered. She was following Ovi round all night.

'Ovi's cousin's friend from Germany,' continued Maya. 'She's over for the summer. I walked in on them. In his bedroom. She was all over him! Seriously! I had a massive go at him. He tried to deny it. He said he was trying to push her away.'

4

'And was he?'

Maya held up her palms, held them over her chest and made a squeezing motion.

'Jesus Christ,' said Alfie.

'I know, right? Unbelievable! Rule one of Ovi's parties. Something crazy always happens. Except this time it bloody happened to me!'

Two tears ran down her cheeks. She picked a fresh tissue and wiped them.

'Sorry, Maya. That's really, really, shit.'

Was it shit? This was big news! The truth was, Alfie felt … excited.

Maya smiled and then her bottom lip wobbled. 'And now I've got to spend two weeks in Greece with no Wi-Fi and nothing to do but feel like a piece of dirt. I mean, what must he think of me to *do* that?'

'Hey! You are not a piece of dirt. *Ovi* is a piece of dirt. He's worse than a piece of dirt.'

'You think?'

'I think? I *know*! His only redeeming feature is that he holds great parties.'

Maya looked startled. 'Have you always thought that?'

Alfie squirmed. He probably shouldn't have said that.

'Well, I *have* spent the whole summer listening to you moan about him.'

'Why didn't you say so earlier?'

'It's not that easy, is it? You were really into him,' said Alfie.

'You should have said! You should have stopped me.'

'How could I, Maya? You were unstoppable!'

'Argh! You're right. I was. What was my problem? Why did I

get so into him? He always made me feel like I'm too intense. And I only put up with it cos he's stupidly good-looking. And I stupidly hoped it would change. Ugh, it's so humiliating.'

More tears ran down her cheeks, and she grabbed more tissues from the box.

'Hey. Hey,' said Alfie. 'Listen. Maya. Maybe it's a good thing. It might be hard now, but I promise you, it'll feel ... like a weight off your shoulders. That boy does not deserve you. You'll get with someone else. Someone better. Someone who appreciates you. Someone who sees how beautiful and special you really are.'

Maya looked up at him as if she was taken aback at his comment. Alfie was taken aback too. Where had that come from?

'Alfie. That's really kind of you. Thank you,' she said. Her phone rang. Alfie looked at it. 'Just my dad stressing about getting to the airport. Ignore it,' she continued.

Maya stared at him for a moment, before resting her head on his shoulder. She'd never done that before. They sat there in silence. Happy tingles fizzed around Alfie's legs.

'Do *you* think I'm too intense?' asked Maya.

'Well, you *do* get this dressed up just to go on a plane. Everyone else would cry about their ex in their room, but you have to do it out here.'

'My dad was driving me nuts!' she said. 'He gets really anxious when he flies. I didn't want him to hear me sobbing through the wall. No one comes here and I needed some space. It's actually the *best* place to cry.'

Alfie laughed.

'We've basically spent every single day of this holiday

6

together,' he said. 'Do you think I'd do that if I thought you were too intense?'

Maya lifted her head.

'Seriously?'

'Yeah!'

'Have we really spent *every* day together?' she said.

'Not *every* day. You did see Ovi *sometimes*. And sometimes other people were there. Like when we watched all *The Lord of the Rings* films in one day. And the day that security guard in Tesco thought Jack was a shoplifter and chased him down the street.'

'And the day we all went to Canvey Island and we thought Gwen drowned. And the day we did the London graveyard tour.'

'I can't believe you dragged us round a bunch of graveyards.'

'I can't believe Jack and Lily tried to shag in that one in Hackney!'

'Oh my God, that was so inappropriate!'

They both laughed.

'Seriously, Maya. I love spending time with you.'

Maya sat up, turned to him, grabbed his hand and squeezed it. Her eyes sparkled.

'Really?'

'Yeah!'

'It hasn't been all bad, has it?'

'No!'

'Oh my God, I've just realised I spent more time with you this summer than my actual boyfriend. Sorry, *ex*-boyfriend. That should have been a sign, right there.'

A sign of what? That Ovi wasn't right for her? That Alfie and

Maya were right for each other? She just said *ex-boyfriend*. So she was definitely, officially single now?

'It's just . . . natural,' he said. 'Isn't it?'

'Yeah. It is.'

Maya's fingers interlocked with his. Her thumbs made small circles round and round on his palm. She was sitting up now, facing him, her knees pushing into his thighs.

'Maybe it's cos of our mums,' said Maya. 'We find it easy to be around each other cos we have a shared life experience. I guess it's harder for you. You actually knew your mum. You had a close relationship. You had something to lose. I never even saw her face.'

'Mine wasn't exactly Mum of the Year though, was she?'

'Isn't something better than nothing?'

'I actually think I would have preferred nothing.'

'Listen, Alfie. What I'm trying to say is . . . you *get it*. Me and you . . . *we get each other*.'

Maya held his gaze. It was like Alfie could see the cogs whirring, she was having the realisation, in real time, right before his eyes: *Have I been going out with the wrong boy? Is the right boy here, sitting next to me? Now?*

Suddenly, Alfie was terrified. He liked her, he really, really liked her! He'd been trying to ignore it but it was too damn strong! And maybe she liked him too? His one big obstacle, Ovi, had gone. Did he have to do something about it now? Right this second? Things were moving fast. Maya had been single for less than twelve hours!

'I spend five minutes with you and I already feel better,' she said. 'I don't wanna go on holiday, I just wanna stay here with you.'

Alfie panicked. Was this the right moment? What if she was on the rebound? What if she was still drunk from last night? Vulnerable and sad and desperate for anyone? What if deep down she still liked Ovi and would get back with him and dump Alfie at the first opportunity? Wouldn't it be better to wait until he was certain she was over him? Her eyes were still red from the tears, for Christ's sake. His throat was so dry it was painful to swallow.

'Me too,' croaked Alfie. Dammit. That didn't even make any sense!

Her eyes looked down, towards his lips. Her head dipped forwards, her eyelids closed . . . She wanted him to kiss her! She did! Right now! On the lips!

Alfie tried to move. His body refused. He tried to bend his neck but his muscles were paralysed. He was made of rock. He watched her lips hover there in painful slow motion, expecting his to touch them. Her face grew confused. Then disappointed. She let go of his hands. He slipped them round her back and they hugged.

OK. Hugging was nice . . . She wasn't letting go . . .

Maya yelped and stood up abruptly. Her dad had appeared at the end of the alley.

'What the hell are you doing?' he shouted. 'Close that suitcase and get in the car! We're gonna miss our check-in!'

Alfie turned and ran his hands through his hair guiltily.

'Oh, hi, Alfie!' said Maya's dad, suddenly bright, waving at him.

Alfie smiled and waved back. But he felt sick to his stomach. He knew in his heart that that had been their moment. And what had he done? He'd blown it.

1

Two weeks later

'How much?' said Nan.

'Fifty,' said Alfie.

'*Fifty?*'

'It's gone up.'

'How many lunches does fifty quid get you these days?'

'Two weeks.'

'Two weeks? That's restaurant prices! Who's cooking, Gordon Ramsay?'

Nan wore her pink night-time onesie, her short grey hair sticking out at different angles, eyes bloodshot because she'd just woken up.

'Nan. It's like, five quid for a meal. It's cheap.'

'It didn't used to be that much.'

Alfie sighed.

'It's outrageous!' said Nan.

'Just give me your debit card, OK?'

Nan pushed past him into their narrow kitchen, where she stopped, hand on hip, scratching her head. 'How can one bowl of cereal result in so much mess?'

'I'll sort it out later.'

'Ah yes, leave me here, living in filth.'

Alfie stood by the living room window, listening to the bangs and clunks of plates being stacked, the tap gushing, the pop of the tea jar opening, the kettle roaring, the teaspoon clinking around a mug. He pushed back the net curtains, revealing their tiny balcony and his old, rusted, too-small bike, chained to the railings, as if someone was going to steal it twelve floors up. Down below, a stream of blazered children walked towards his school; beyond them the green expanse of the Brent playing fields, the tired old roofs and endless satellite dishes of the Brent Estate. Then, on the horizon, the giant tilted arch of Wembley Stadium.

One of those satellite dishes belonged to Maya. Alfie squinted. Was that her?

Nan ambled in, mug of tea in her hands, followed by Bailey, their sausage dog, who struggled to keep balance on the slippery laminate floor.

'Now you have to wait for walkies. Yes, you do. You're a very naughty doggie.'

'If I don't top up Parent Pay, I won't get any lunch!' said Alfie.

Nan took a big slurp of her tea and walked towards her bedroom, stopping outside Alfie's open door. 'At least you ironed your clothes. I thought you'd come running to your nana. How does this strange machine work? Where am I supposed to put it? Why is it hot?'

'Ha. Ha.'

She went into his room, picked up the iron and yelped. 'It's still on!'

'Sorry.'

'You could have burned the whole bloody block down!'

'Sorry!'

She unplugged the iron and stepped back into the living room, face fierce, fists clenched.

'How many times do you want me to apologise?' said Alfie.

He didn't tell her that he'd spent an hour thanklessly ironing his shirt, twenty minutes slicking back his big curly hair with gel, cleaning his teeth twice and spraying Lynx all over his body. He didn't *need* to tell her the last one. They could smell it, now, stinking up the place.

Nan tutted, went into her room and returned wearing her thick brown-rimmed glasses and holding her handbag. She stopped, put the bag down and placed her hands on her heart. 'Oh, Alfie . . .'

'What?'

'I can't believe it! You're a handsome young man!' Nan wiped her eyes. 'It seems like yesterday I was reading you *Horrid Henry* and you were too scared to sleep with the light off.' She waved her hand in front of her face. 'Where does the time go?'

'Nan!'

'It's not every day your grandson starts A levels!'

She gestured for Alfie to stand by the hall wall, picked up her phone where it was charging on the sofa and handed it to him.

'For God's sake!' said Alfie. He stretched out his arm, twisting his wrist to find the right angle, leaned his head against Nan's, and took the picture.

'Stunning!' said Nan, gazing at the screen. 'Look at those big blue eyes!'

Alfie winced.

'*Someone's* going to break a few hearts . . . The most eligible bachelor in Brent. How can they resist?'

'Nan!'

'It's about bloody time you found yourself a girlfriend.

13

Even that Jack managed it! Didn't see that coming. What's her name again?'

'Lily Chen. Her parents are Chinese. She's a swimmer. She wins competitions and stuff.'

'Oh.'

'Plus she's very annoying.'

'Thick as thieves, you two. I used to sit on that sofa and listen to you laugh in your bedroom. Lovely sound. I actually miss having him around.'

'Yeah, well ... things have changed.'

'I just hate seeing you mope ... staring at that screen, listening to that dreadful music. If *he* can get someone, then surely there's hope for you!'

'One, I am not moping. *Football Manager* is the greatest game ever. Two, it's not dreadful! It's Jōnetsu. I love them. Me and my friends are gonna see them in November. They keep me alive. Literally.'

'It's just noise!' said Nan, as if that was the end of the matter. She opened her bag and rooted around the tissues, mints, a comb, vouchers ... 'I won't be upset if you don't like girls. I may be old but I'm not—'

'Nan. Please!'

Nan produced a shiny new purple debit card. Alfie snatched it, picked up his laptop from the sofa, opened it and logged into Parent Pay while Nan sat at the table and drank her tea.

'Some people are just unlucky in love, I suppose,' she said. 'It's a family curse. I was like that. Your mother was certainly like that. Falling in love every five seconds. Hopeless romantic ... Goodness me!' She went quiet. Her whole body seemed to shrink. 'She'd be so proud if she could see you now ...'

'She's not gonna see me now.'

'I wish she could—'

'She's not gonna see me.'

'I wish you'd reply. It's only an email, it'd take two minutes. Am I allowed to say that?'

'Is she allowed to dump her seven-year-old son in the school playground? Leave me sitting in the office, freaking out? Disappear and never come back? Is she allowed to do that? Can she just expect me to say, *Ah well don't worry about that, no bother, you prefer crack to your son, that's fine*—'

'Not crack—'

'Crack, heroin, what's the difference!'

What was Nan doing? Bringing up all this personal stuff! His mum! His love life! She didn't get it. Why couldn't she cut him some slack?

He saw that the transaction had been processed, slammed the laptop shut, and handed the card back.

'How do you know what's happening in my love life anyway?' he said irritably.

'I don't. You never tell me anything.'

'What if I said it's going well? What if you don't know about it cos I keep my private life private?'

'*Is* it going well?'

'It might be.'

'Can I meet her?'

'Stop nagging me!'

Alfie opened the front door and stepped into the hallway then turned back to Nan.

'I am *not* unlucky in love!'

2

'How's it going, dude?' said Jack.

'Good, man,' said Alfie.

'Long time!'

'I know!'

'Really long time!'

The smell of over-boiled vegetables filled the hall as the students streamed in, clutching their trays, filling up the green-and-white Formica seats laid out like a chequerboard. Jack and Alfie had grabbed their usual table in the corner, next to the windows, by the strip of blown-up photos from the school prospectus that ran the circumference of the room. In front of them were two plates of wafer-thin slices of roast Halal chicken, carrots and peas so soft you could crush them by tapping them with your fork, and a couple of supposedly roast potatoes with no crispy bits, all covered in watery gravy.

'Things are more than good, *actually* .. .'

Jack mashed up a potato, balanced it on his fork, and shoved it into his mouth.

'There's been some ... developments ...' Alfie added.

'With what?'

'Me. And Maya.'

Some bits of potato flew out of Jack's mouth onto the table in front of them. 'Developments?'

'Yeah! That's what you get for not replying to my messages, bro.'

'Sorry, man. Me and Lily were housesitting for my granny in Bexhill. I wasn't checking my phone, if you get what I mean.'

Alfie felt irritated. Jack was always rubbing it in that he was no longer a virgin.

'So Ovi cheated on her and she dumped him ... you know that, right?'

'Yes!' said Jack. 'Lily told me this morning.'

'Rule one of Ovi's party, never leave early,' said Alfie. 'And then, the next day—'

Alfie jumped as a tray clattered down opposite him. A Year Ten boy, with a mop of shaggy black hair and a bum-fluff moustache, sat down.

'You can't sit here,' said Alfie.

'Yes, I can,' he said.

'No,' said Alfie, 'you can't.'

Jack stood up, his whole, hulking six-foot-three frame, his wispy beard, his tied-back ponytail, new charcoal suit and bright red tie making him look like a Hell's Angel bouncer.

'OK!' said the boy. He picked up his tray and left.

'I love how people who don't know you find you scary, but anyone who talks to you knows you're a wuss,' said Alfie.

'Shut up,' said Jack. 'And get to the point.'

'OK, so we had this heart-to-heart about Ovi. Obviously she realised that he wasn't the man of her dreams. Then she said that being around me made her feel better. Then we spoke about how close we'd got over the holidays, how we really get each other. *Then* she held my hand. *Then* she stroked my hand. Then she told me she didn't wanna go on holiday, she just wanted to stay with me, while like, looking deep, deep into my eyes.'

'OK . . .' said Jack.

'I mean . . . I always thought she was fit. That's obvious. Two, we get on really, *really* well. We both have the broken-home-absent-mum thing.'

Jack nodded.

'We're both obsessed with Jōnetsu. We make each other laugh. We spent all summer together. We're basically the same height. Me and her dad support Arsenal. But there was always Ovi, right? Boom! Ovi's out of the game! And now she's giving me *the look* . . . she's *puckering up* . . . *Kiss me Alfie, Kiss me!*'

Alfie was distracted by Raheem, who tried to put his tray down next to Jack.

'These seats are taken,' said Alfie.

Raheem frowned. 'Taken? Who by? The invisible students?'

Alfie used to play football with Raheem in Year Seven. Back when they used to be friends. Raheem always spoke to him as if they were still on the same team.

'Am I not cool enough for you?' continued Raheem. 'Only heavy-metal Satan worshippers allowed on this table? I thought you and me had a centre-back right-midfield psychic understanding.'

'Raheem, just because we listen to guitar music, doesn't mean we're Satan worshippers.'

'I've heard your music. Play it backwards! Tell me you don't get messages! Direct from the Dark Lord himself!'

Maya, Lily and Gwen turned into the main hall, trays in hands, roast chicken and veg piled on their plates. Gwen and Lily hung back to talk to Samira. Maya saw Alfie and waved brightly, before stopping to join the girls.

'They're taken by them!' said Alfie, nodding towards Maya.

18

Raheem eyed Maya. 'Oh. OK.' He shook his head. 'I get it! Yeah, baby! Yes, big boy! Eh? Eh? You sly fox!'

He backed away, smiling and nodding, and Alfie felt himself go red.

'Dude!' said Jack. He grabbed Alfie's arm. 'What? Happened? Next?'

Alfie glanced across at one of the blown-up prospectus photos, thirteen-year-old Maya sitting cross-legged in the main quad, big baggy blazer done up tight, wearing glasses and reading a book, then back to the girl who was laughing with Samira. She wore a white blouse (top two buttons undone) and pencil skirt (as short as she could get away with).

'Please tell me you're going out with Maya!' said Jack.

'No!'

'No?'

'I'm gonna ask her out today!'

'You kissed her, right?'

'No.'

'No?'

'You didn't kiss and you're not going out?'

'It turned into a hug.'

'She was *puckering up* and it turned into a hug?'

'I froze! I've never actually kissed anyone I care about before. It was scary. It made me realise, though. I really do like her.'

'How did she react?'

'Um . . . kind of disappointed?'

'Disappointed?'

'Why are you making me feel bad?'

'You had Maya throwing herself at you. Maya! Throwing herself! At you!'

'I know! Do you think I haven't spent the last two weeks beating myself up?'

'Why didn't you call her up?'

'I wanted to do it face to face. Plus she got on a plane and said don't bother cos the data is crazy expensive in Greece and her aunt doesn't have internet and they have to go to the village to use an internet café or the Wi-Fi in a bar.'

Jack's eyes were bulging. 'Are you sure she doesn't think you're not interested?'

'Dude! She sent me this message when she got back to England, with like, six kiss emojis! *Six* kiss emojis! Do you send six kiss emojis to your "friend"? I was gonna surprise her before school but Nan made me late. I'm going to put things right! I'll ask her out today! Face to face!'

Lily interrupted them, plonking herself on Jack's lap. There was an awkward silence before Maya sat down, playfully bumping her shoulder into Alfie's.

'Hey,' she said, smiling coyly.

'Hey,' said Alfie, his voice cracking and disappearing into the din of the lunch hall.

Maya smiled. Alfie smiled back. His heart fluttered. His palms were wet with sweat and he rubbed them on his trousers. He glanced at Jack. Jack was scowling.

'Maya . . .' said Lily '. . . was telling us a story . . .'

'Oh yeah?' said Alfie.

'Oh my God, it's so exciting!' said Lily.

'Guys!' said Maya.

'C'mon!' said Lily.

Maya rolled her eyes.

'Something happened in Greece,' said Lily.

'This is so embarrassing!' said Maya.

'Tell them!' said Lily.

'Oh my God, do I have to?' said Maya.

'Yes!' said Lily.

Maya groaned and put her head in her hands.

'Maya's got a new man!' said Lily, squealing and clapping her hands together.

3

'Rewind!' said Lily. 'From the beginning!'

Maya picked up her fork, glanced at Alfie, took a deep breath and then put her fork down. 'I don't want to! It's boring!'

'Tell, tell, tell!' squealed Lily, clapping.

'It just ... kind of *happened* ...'

Lily continued clapping, leaning towards Maya, pressuring her.

Maya sighed. 'OK! So before I went on holiday Ovi showed us his true colours. Apparently I was the last person to realise what he was really like, wasn't I, Alfie?'

Alfie nodded and forced himself to smile. His heart was thumping, he wanted to run.

'But then I had to go to my auntie's! Soooo boring. Half-way up a mountain. Zero humans. No Wi-Fi. Costs me like, a pound to send a WhatsApp. Nearest beach, forty-five minute drive. Stupid hot. She's got a pool, which is fine if all you wanna do is sunbathe, but with skin like mine ...'

'Your skin is amazing!' said Lily.

'No, it is not!' said Maya, running her fingers along her cheek, across some heavily concealed spots. 'I would love to just sunbathe, clear it all up, but I burn in like, five seconds flat. Even one ray of sun coming through the gap in the edge of the parasol *destroys* me. Everyone's like, *You're Greek, you're not supposed to get sunburned.* I'm like, *Hello, Greeks have the most diverse DNA in the* world, I'm allowed to hate the heat, shut up with your prejudiced view of what a Greek should be and pass me the sun cream.'

The girls laughed. Alfie stared at the table. It was too hard to look at her.

'Anyway, I'm there, on the sun lounger, under the umbrella, caked in factor fifty, big fat sunglasses, old-school swimsuit, covering up, and I hear this sound ..' Maya clenched her fist into a microphone and growled into it. *'I'm your puppet on a string* ... I'm up a mountain in Greece and the next-door neighbour is playing Jōnetsu. Like, *really*? The only people who love Jōnetsu are me and Alfie. And you guys. Turns out that next door is a brand-new Airbnb and they got some new guests. Year Thirteen English boys from London!'

'Woah!' said Lily. 'Crazy!'

'I know, right? My dad went round to ask them to be quiet, and this tall guy comes out, laughs in his face, turns the volume up. My dad flipped. He tells him he's gonna punch him in the face. I'm like, *Dad! You're almost fifty. He's just some drunk boy. This is supposed to be a holiday. You're not supposed to go to prison for grievous bodily harm.'*

'You should have called the police,' said Lily.

'We did better than that!' said Maya. 'Auntie Androulla, she's had a proper hard life. She lost her husband to cancer. When I was born she lost her sister as well. She's the one who calmed my dad down when he wanted to sue the doctors. She's like, *The blood clot thing runs in the family.* She really helped him accept what happened! I'm feeling protective, know what I mean? That night I sat her down and we spent like, an hour, writing the most angry complaint we could, like we're gonna

23

get them banned from Airbnb forever. Shut down next door as well. We got well into it. She's gonna drive me to the internet café to send it. Then, next morning, no sleep, music kept us up *all night*, someone kicks a football over the fence. Into the pool. Splashes me. Splashes my book. I can't even read. This other guy, short guy, goes to the gym too much ..' Maya stuck out her forearms horizontally and flexed her biceps. '*Excuse me, miss, can I have my ball back?* You know what I did?'

Lily shook her head.

'I got up and jumped into the pool, grabbed the ball, took it into the villa, came out with the bread knife, held the ball up and I'm like, *Turn your fucking music off and stop fucking up our holiday*! Then I stabbed it!'

'No way!' said Lily.

'Yes, way! Trust me. Took a few goes, cos it was quite blunt but I totally mullered that ball.'

'Jesus Christ. What did they do?' said Lily.

'I dunno. I ran into the house and hid.'

Lily laughed.

'What am I like? I'm a psycho. I am. Ovi was right.'

'Errr ..' said Gwen, who was just sitting down now in the spare place next to Maya. 'It is a *bit* psycho ..'

'You're supposed to be my friend!'

'It's an effective way to get results,' agreed Gwen.

Maya snorted. 'Anyway, we're just getting ready to drive to the internet café. There's this knock on the door. I open it. They're all there. The whole band.'

'They're in a band?'

'Yeah! They're bandmates. The drunk one. The squat one. And the other one, the pretty one.'

'Ah, the pretty one!' said Lily. 'The pretty one makes an entrance!'

Alfie's heart thudded. He shovelled chicken into his mouth, in an attempt to numb his stress, half-chewing, swallowing too quickly.

'He's holding this big bunch of flowers. He'd got up at five in the morning, climbed the mountain and picked them. He just hands them to me, and goes, *Hi. I'm Luke. On behalf of everyone next door, I apologise for the noise. We had a really long flight and we had a few drinks. It won't happen again.* The tall guy's like, *Hi, I'm Olly, I'm an alcoholic. Sorry for laughing in your face. I can be a bit rude when I've had a few.*'

'What did your dad do?' said Lily.

'He just stands there, puffing out his chest, trying to look hard. I'm like, *You're just saying all this so you don't get bad Airbnb feedback.* And Luke's like, *It's worse than that. We spent all this time convincing our parents to let us go on holiday by ourselves, and then we book this Airbnb cos it was cheap without realising it was a twenty minute car ride to get anywhere, and we'll spend all our money on cabs by day two.* Olly's like, *Yeah, I can't read maps properly.* I'm not gonna lie, it was quite funny. And then Luke's like, *We humbly beseech you—*'

'Beseech?' said Lily.

'Yeah. He said that. *We humbly beseech you, when you happen to be driving to the shop, could we possibly hitch a lift so we can stock up on food?*'

'The cheek!' said Lily.

'I hope your dad said no,' said Gwen.

Alfie felt some hope. Maybe Luke was an idiot. Maybe it was holiday fling.

25

'Auntie Androulla is a total sucker. For flowers. For pretty-boy waifs and strays. She told me to delete the message and invite them round for dinner.'

'No!' said Lily.

'Seriously. Any excuse to feed people. She's not totally naïve though. She said, *I will cook every night, if you wash up and clean the kitchen, and do some gardening.*'

'What did they say?' said Gwen.

'Hell yeah! They loved her. They stuffed their faces. They trimmed her trees. They saved their whole food budget and spent it all on alcohol.'

'No way!' said Lily.

'What's the name of the band?' said Gwen.

'Twisted Dreamland. Metalcore. What are the chances? My next door neighbours are in the year above me in school and into the same stuff! And guess what? Cos it's an Airbnb, they had to have Wi-Fi! They had a 4G router, so I could connect! It went from the worst holiday ever to the best holiday ever – hanging out during the song-writing, watching movies on my laptop, stuffing our faces!'

Alfie felt stung. She had internet for the whole holiday? And she didn't message him?

'So, this Luke guy,' continued Maya. 'He's actually got a really good voice. And he knows how to write a song. They're actually quite good. They really ... have something. It used to be my big dilemma. Do I want to be an actor? Or a singer? Or both? I've been doing drama and musicals at school, thinking it was gonna be acting ... and then ... Me and him, at night, everyone had gone to bed – him on the guitar, under the stars—'

'*Romantic*,' said Lily.

'Oh my God . . . cos there's no streetlights, the stars there are in-cred-ib-le! And we were singing together . . . he really encouraged me . . . We wrote this song, me and him, we called it "I Wrote Your Name in the Stars". It's like this song about what happens when the person you love dies. And on the last night . . . they did a gig. Olly had his bass and Mikey – the hench one – made a drum kit from Auntie Androulla's pans. Luke sang, obviously. It was like Twisted Dreamland unplugged. And then we did our duet! Me and Luke! Auntie Androulla's like, dancing in circles and clapping her hands! I'm like, *That was incredible, we have to do it again!* And Luke's like, *Come to our rehearsals! Back in London.*'

'Oooh . .' said Lily.

'He's like, *Maya . . . When I'm with you . . . I just feel so creative . . . I feel so . . . alive!* It was one of those hot nights and the sky was all clear and beautiful . . . and we were both quite drunk . . . And everyone else had gone to bed . . . He's like, *Maya . . . you're so talented, you're so fun . . . being with you is magical!* It was like . . . I felt . . . a possibility or something . . . Like my life would change forever . . . like we had this romantic creative *thing* . . . we could be this couple in a famous band. I wouldn't have to spend the rest of my life working in my dad's café . . . I know that sounds nuts, but . .'

Maya's voice became small.

'All week this tension had been building, and then suddenly . . . he just jumped on me. Or I jumped on him. We jumped on each other.'

Alfie felt furious. He wanted to throw his tray across the room, but just like on the green that day, his body turned to rock.

'And *then* . . .?' said Lily.

'What? What do you want me to say? Use your imaginations . . .' said Maya.

Lily's eyes widened. 'I wanna see a photo!'

'Don't be so perverted!'

'No! Not *that*! I wanna see what he looks like!'

Maya glanced around the hall. 'I'm not supposed to have my phone on.'

'Photo, photo, photo!' said Lily, clapping her hands.

In one practised movement, Maya slipped her phone out of her skirt pocket, unlocked it, opened her photos app, and handed it to Gwen.

'Hot,' she said. Gwen handed it to Lily, whose eyes widened. Lily handed the phone to Jack, who glanced at it, then handed it to Alfie.

On the screen were three men. The tall one with long hair, sticking his tongue out. The short squat one making the sign of the horns. Then another, with big brown eyes, a swooping blond fringe and full, heart-shaped lips, the bottom one pierced with a ring in the middle.

'Alfie's jealous,' said Lily.

'Why would I be jealous?' said Alfie, hating Lily for seeing right through him. Of course he was jealous! Luke was beautiful. Luke was hot. Luke was better than him in every way.

Maya snatched back the phone.

'Just when I was losing faith in men . . . Luke came along . . . I can't believe it . . .'

Why had she lost faith in men? Cos of Ovi. And cos she wanted Alfie to kiss her and he hadn't. He'd pushed her into Luke's arms. Arrggggh!

'So you're definitely official then?' said Lily.

'We spoke for like *an hour* last night . . . on the phone . . . and we kind of decided yes! We're official!'

'Yay!' said Lily, whooping.

Maya was blushing, Alfie just stared at his plate. Any remaining chance with Maya had gone.

4

Alfie sat at the picnic table alone, feet on the bench, gazing into the school pond. The fountain was on, and every so often he saw the flash of a gold tail shoot across the murky depths. Students crisscrossed the quad around him, talking loudly, exhilarated by the end of the school day, and a gust of chilly wind reminded him that it was almost autumn.

'Dude.' Jack stood tall behind him, backpack on, black Jōnetsu beanie pulled down to above his eyes, earphones in, the wire tucked into his shirt.

'It's OK.'

'Dude!'

'I know! It's OK!'

Jack pursed his lips and then looked at the floor. 'You should have—'

'I didn't, though, did I?'

Jack took out his phone, paused his music and tugged his earphones out of his ear. 'You know how I got together with Lily? I went up to her and said, *I like you!*'

'I don't drink, Jack. I don't do stupid drunk come-ons!'

'Dude! You're missing the point. Lily's a teetotal athlete, remember? If anything, me being drunk should have put her off. The point is – when the moment arrived, I actually did something!'

Maya appeared on the first-floor balcony, clutching some

books to her chest with her left hand and carrying a shiny black holdall with her right. She put the bag down and waved brightly.

'You froze,' continued Jack, lowering his voice to make sure Maya didn't hear. 'Luke *jumped*! Plus he's a singer. Plus he's beautiful.'

'I know all that! Do you want me to feel worse than I already do?'

'I just wish you'd told me earlier. I could have helped you through this.'

'I messaged you. You didn't reply.'

'I'm sorry, man ... Bexhill ... We had the whole place to ourselves. Every single room was empty ... ours to use ... as we saw fit ... if you catch my drift ..'.

'Jesus, Jack!'

'What?'

'I really missed you this summer. Even my nan misses you! You totally abandoned us!'

'All we do is play *Football Manager*. Two smelly boys in a bedroom, staring at a screen. This summer would have been a whole lot different if you had a girl too. Changes everything. Trust me.'

Alfie felt furious. Why did he talk down to him? Why did he think he was better than him? Did he really think it was OK to ignore him? Just cos he was having sex? Non-stop, endless, mind-blowing, multi-orgasmic, multiple-positioned sex on his granny's kitchen table?

Jack put his arm around Alfie's shoulder and squeezed it. 'C'mon, man. Chin up. Plenty more fish in the sea.'

They watched Maya walk down the rickety fire escape.

'Soon, we'll both have girlfriends. You'll lose your virginity. Everything will make sense.'

Lily appeared from the girls' loos, ran up and hugged Jack ostentatiously, like he'd just come back from war and she hadn't seen him for years, then grabbed his arm and led him away. Maya skipped across the paving stones to join Alfie.

'Hey!' she said, kissing him on the cheek.

She sat down next to him, her shiny black shoes matching her holdall, lips glistening with reapplied gloss. They sat in silence, listening to the trickle of the fountain.

'Are you OK?' she said.

'Yeah!'

Maya gripped her textbook tighter. Alfie read the title: *Much Ado About Nothing*.

'Are you sure?'

How could he tell her? What could he say? *Congratulations on your amazing new boyfriend! By the way, I've got a massive, massive thing for you but I totally ruined it by my own pathetic cowardly lameness?* It was too humiliating.

'Yeah. Am sure.'

Maya checked her phone. 'It's three forty-five! What are we doing?'

'You're the one who's late.'

'It's not my fault Mr Davies made me do a monologue at the end of the day!'

They walked in silence, across the quad, and out of the main gate. Immediately outside the school, across the road, was Alfie and Jack's tower block, with its dirty grey cladding, tall metal fence protecting the three floors of scaffolding, the major improvement works that never seemed to finish. Across the

32

road a bus stopped, and a hundred students pushed, shoved, and jostled around the door. Alfie nipped across the tarmac. Maya hurried after him, a horn blaring as a Deliveroo moped swerved to avoid her. 'So what's the problem?' she said.

'There isn't one.'

'This feels really awkward.'

Alfie glanced up at his balcony. 'It's fine.'

'Are *we* OK?'

'Yes!' said Alfie. 'Maybe I should go home.'

'What? Why!'

'A-one. Things getting serious.'

'You study Tourism! A-one is a joke!'

Alfie shrugged.

'You tell me it's not awkward, then you tell me you wanna go home?'

'It's not awkward!'

'Alfie! I missed you. I haven't seen you for two weeks. We need to catch up!'

'I know we do.'

They walked up the road and onto the wide grass expanse of the Brent playing fields, which were covered with newly painted football pitches ready for the beginning of the season. Alfie felt a pang – he hadn't played football for ages. Another pathetic thing he'd let happen.

'Alfie. I have to ask you. Are you OK with this Luke thing?'

'Yeah. Why wouldn't I be?'

'You just looked really moody when I explained about him.'

'I always look like that.'

'Alfie!'

She'd stopped underneath the lone tree in the middle of the

park, a group of crows gathered nearby, cawing and flapping their wings.

'I just ... I thought you might have messaged me ... when you realised you had internet ...' said Alfie.

Maya's eyes widened. 'Oh my God! I'm sorry! I was so wrapped up in ...'

She grabbed his arm.

'I'm sorry. It's nothing personal.'

'It's OK.'

'I'll make it up to you.' Maya seemed relieved. 'I thought you might have ... It's just, I really value our friendship.'

'So do I!'

'Good!'

Alfie dug his heel into the mud. Could they be friends? Could they carry on as if nothing had happened?

'I didn't actually think ... I mean ... I'm not that egotistical ...' Maya became flustered. 'I didn't think you *liked* me ... it was only cos of at lunch—'

'Maya. It's fine. I'm really happy for you. He sounds amazing. You were so upset about Ovi. You deserve something good.'

'You sure?'

'Yeah!'

'It's not gonna make things weird between us?'

'No!'

'OK, good.'

Alfie pushed and scraped, creating a hole, kicking his heel down into the mud.

'You didn't leave your flat, did you?' said Maya.

'What?'

'This is the first time you've seen daylight in two weeks!

34

Ten hours a day of *Football Manager* is not good for your mental health!'

'It's the greatest game ever!'

'You should have knocked for Jack!'

'Jack thinks *Football Manager* is for lame sweaty boys.'

Maya laughed. 'He's got a point, you know. Ooh!' She reached into her holdall, producing a Tupperware box, and handed it to Alfie.

'What's this?'

'Chocolate mascarpone baklava with coffee syrup.'

Alfie frowned.

'From the bakery in my aunt's village. It's in-cred-ib-le.'

Alfie opened the box. It was crammed with layers of filo pastry drenched in some kind of delicious golden chocolatey gunk.

'For you.'

'Wow. Thank you.' Alfie felt a burst of pleasure. He liked her attention. He liked her warmth. He wanted to smile. What was happening? He was supposed to be feeling awful.

'Come to mine and we can eat it!'

'I thought you said it's for me!'

'Yeah, but you have to give me *one* ...'

'It's for me!'

'Half of one ...'

'No.'

'One bite! One tiny nibble!'

Alfie kicked a piece of mud, which flew forward, scattering the crows.

'I'm gonna lock myself in your toilet and eat them by myself!'

'So you *are* coming to mine then?'

'I didn't say that!' Alfie smiled.

'There it is!' she said, pinching his cheek. 'Ooh – Dad'll be back soon! I'll make him make sausage and mash! We can have these for dessert!'

'I've got homework—'

'You can do it with me—'

'My laptop—'

'Go and get it. I'm so in the mood for sausage and mash now! And *Stranger Things* new series on Netflix! You cannot refuse. You cannot! I haven't see you for a whole two weeks! This is me making up for not messaging you!'

She stepped towards him, clutching her book tighter to her chest, her hair swinging forwards, brushing Alfie's shoulders. Dammit! Maybe they *could* still be friends? It was still so easy . . . just being near her made him feel better . . . she was still so beautiful . . . She wanted to spend time with him . . . maybe . . . If he was patient . . . who knew what would happen in the future?

'OK!' he said. 'I'll come to your bloody house!'

'Yay!' said Maya.

She slipped her arm into his and led him across the field, out of the park and onto her road.

5

For the next few weeks, things kind of went back to the way they were. Alfie and Maya snatching hours together at her house when free periods followed lunch breaks; making sandwiches, sitting on the sofa with their laptops, blitzing their homework. Long dingy evenings with the curtains drawn, both of them squeezed onto Maya's three quarter bed, the only light the movie on the laptop screen. Maya's dad, bustling around the kitchen, fixing them omelettes, burgers, whatever Maya wanted.

Sometimes Maya went to Luke's house. She spoke to him on the phone. She went and rehearsed with him and she was buzzing afterwards. He was definitely her boyfriend. But she *still* spent most of her time with Alfie. A lot more time than she spent with Luke.

Then, one Friday night Maya had been going through a box of her old primary school stuff, and they'd ended up looking at the class pictures. They laughed at Maya's Year Four portrait, her gap-toothed girl smile, her cheek muscles stretched into a grimace so tense you thought they would snap.

'Scary,' said Alfie.

'I was cute!'

'Cute like the little girl in a horror movie.'

'You used to hide from me in the playground. You literally used to run when I called your name,' said Maya accusingly.

'I had good reason!'

She'd punched him on the arm.

In the Year Six class photo Alfie stood next to Jack, proudly clutching a football to his chest like it was made of pure gold.

'How come they let you hold it?' said Maya.

'I was captain.'

'It was a *class* photo. Not a *team* photo.'

'I begged Mr Harris. I was so proud.'

'Our team was rubbish!'

'Only cos they had to make up the numbers with three girls.'

'Oi!'

She punched him on the arm again.

'I was the best player,' said Alfie.

'You were the only player who wasn't awful. Oh my God, you and Jack were the same height!'

Maya brought the photo closer to her eyes. Year Six Jack was smaller and pudgier, with a shaved head and zero facial hair. Year Six Alfie looked the same, except his curls had now grown out into an ever-increasing mop.

Maya had looked at him and cocked her head. 'So why don't you play football any more?'

Alfie shrugged.

'When did you stop?'

'Year Nine.'

'Why?'

Alfie ran his hand through his hair. 'Basically . . . everyone grew. And I didn't. Or, I grew, but not as much as everyone else. Everyone started fouling me. Shoving me off the ball. Raking their studs down my leg. It stopped being fun.'

Maya had touched her heart. 'That's so sad!'

'It's OK,' said Alfie.

'Boys are so rough!'

'*You* can talk, football-stabber.'

'At least I don't go around kicking people.'

'It's a physical game.'

'Arsenal must have small players.'

'They get fouled too. They're just insanely skilful.'

'You're insanely skilful.'

'No, I'm not!'

'I remember, you were!'

Alfie went red.

'You were! I was joking before.'

'I dunno. I couldn't even be friends with Raheem any more. Cos me and him were at a similar level.'

Alfie pictured Raheem screaming for the ball. Alfie pinging a pass with the outside of his boot. Skipping away from a challenge. Other players shouting. The smell of mud. He loved it. He missed it. His stomach twisted inside out.

'Even Jack got a growth spurt. I'm the only person who isn't big. Being small sucks!'

'I didn't grow either!' said Maya, nudging him with her shoulder.

'You're a girl! Doesn't count!'

They'd sat in silence. Gwen's name flashed up on Maya's phone. Maya got distracted, her long black nails *tap, tap, tapping* on the screen. It was always Gwen who messaged: shy Gwen who didn't say much at school, but never shut up on WhatsApp. She was messaging for ages. Alfie felt impatient.

'She's got stuff going on at home,' said Maya. 'It's giving her anxiety. It's all kicking off with her mum and stepdad and I'm the only one she can talk to!'

'What is it?' said Alfie.

'None of your business!'

Maya put down her phone. 'And not growing enough is a rubbish reason to stop playing!'

Alfie shrugged.

'You love it! It's your passion! Start. Playing. Football. Again.'

She punched him on the arm, harder than before.

'Stop doing that!' shouted Alfie.

At ten p.m. Maya told him she was tired, she needed to crash, and led him down the stairs to see him out.

'Don't forget you're covering Nino tomorrow afternoon!' said her dad, who was waiting at the bottom of the stairs. He owned a café in Hendon – Café Delish.

'No, I'm not!' said Maya.

'Yes, you are!'

'You can't just assume that I'm gonna step in whenever you want!'

'You've been doing the job for three years! You can do it in your sleep!'

'Yeah, and?'

Maya gripped the handrail and leaned towards her dad.

'You said you would!' he spat.

'No. You told me I would!'

'Five times!'

'And each time I said I didn't wanna do it!' Maya's voice shrieked.

Maya's dad took one step up the stairs and leaned towards Maya, bringing his face close to hers. 'The café is gonna be yours one day! It's about time you took it seriously.'

Maya exploded, like one of those sudden thunderstorms,

lightning flashing, rain pounding, thunder booming. Alfie thought they might come to blows. Then, just as quickly, it was over. Maya's dad invited Alfie round to watch the Arsenal game the next day, before retreating to his bedroom.

'What was all that about?' said Alfie.

'He won't let me sing,' said Maya, suddenly calm and reasonable. 'Or act. Or do musical theatre. I used to wanna go to the BRIT school and he never let me. Do you know how many famous people went there? He's telling me it's a waste of time! It's all I've ever wanted to do!'

'What's that got to do with covering Nino?'

'He wants me to run the business. When I'm older. He treats me like I'm always on call. He won't let me do what I want. He even took the piss when I sang that song with Luke. *Don't get too carried away.* As in, *Don't think you're special*.'

'Really?'

'He takes me for granted. It's so demoralising. I lose my rag and behave like a right little cow.'

Alfie walked home, up the empty road in the hazy orange glow of the streetlights. Weirdly, he felt happy, like he'd had the privilege of seeing something private. She shared the most sensitive parts of her life with him. They'd got even closer. It was almost like they *were* together. Maybe he would get a second chance with her. They'd end up kissing. Randomly. Spontaneously. No nerves, no stress. Like Maya and Luke jumping on each other, but bigger and more romantic. And not cos of the stupid stars, cos they were actually meant for each other. She'd drop Luke like a piece of trash because she'd realise he never mattered in the first place.

He slept deeply and was woken by the front door clicking: Nan out to do a Saturday shift in the big Sainsbury's in North Finchley. He was in such a good mood, he didn't even check his phone, he just opened his laptop, and reread the email that Nan wouldn't shut up about.

Dear Alfie,

I'm writing to you cos I emailed Nana and she gave me your address. I'm going to get straight to the point. I ran away. From you. I caused you unimaginable harm. I'm sorry. I know no words can make up for it. Whatever you think, or feel about me and my actions, I take full responsibility.

Three years ago I got clean and joined Narcotics Anonymous. I live in Manchester. I have a boyfriend who's also in recovery. I'm a hairdresser. I pay my own rent and bills. I like my life. I wanted to get lots of recovery behind me before I even dared to write. I did two years clean before I even went on a date. I never stopped thinking about you. Every day. How you are. What you look like. What you love. What you hate ... I always think, I wonder what Alfie's doing right now? Every day I'm sober, I feel the shame of leaving. I want to make amends. I want to see you. I want to make up for the time we lost. I'm asking you what I can do to make that happen. I don't know where to begin, other than by writing this. I'm ready now. The question is, are you? Whatever you decide, I will accept it. I'm not going anywhere. I'm here whenever you want me. I miss you and I love you. Just say the word, and I'll come.

Mum

Bam! Mood-killer! His mum's face flashed across his mind, his chest tightened, his shoulder muscles hurt. He picked up his pillow, pressed it to his face and screamed.

Bleary-eyed, he looked up at his crumpled Jōnetsu poster. The four of them, in greyscale: Brian the bassist, Paul the guitarist, and Jason the drummer, then, Joey Silveira, the singer, with long black dreads and a black ADIDAS tracksuit with shiny gold stripes, Jōnetsu above his head in garish red letters.

Alfie connected his laptop to his battered Bluetooth speaker, and played the song 'Puppet'.

I'm your puppet on a string.
You make me do – anything!
Why don't you cut me loose?
Please will you cut me loose?
You have to cut me loose,
NOOOOOOOW!

He took a pencil, imagining he was Joey Silveira onstage in Brighton – where Alfie would be in less than two months – his eyes closed, mic in his hands, thousands of raucous faces, squeezed and squashed against the barriers, bouncing and moshing, as every word bled from his mouth. He listened on repeat, reliving the soaring, searing guitar solo, the chorus with its cathartic scream.

When the music stopped his phone pinged. Nan asking him to hang up the washing. That was when he saw the message from Maya.

MAYA:

He stuck a knife in my heart

Sent at three a.m. Then, another, ten minutes later:

MAYA:

See you on the other side

It was so unexpected, it didn't sink in. He pressed play but he'd lost the moment, he couldn't enjoy it. At the end of the song, he picked up his phone, reread the message, and called Maya. Straight to voicemail. That was weird.

See you on the other side. What was she on about? He remembered the row between Maya and her dad. That was just how they were, right? They weren't *actually* gonna come to blows . . . Were they? Maya's dad was big . . . He might have been hard . . . once . . . He wouldn't . . . Would he?

Alfie recorded a quick voicenote. 'Hey. It's me. Just checking you're all right. Call me as soon as you get this, OK?'

Alfie watched YouTube for a couple of hours but couldn't relax. He had that same nagging feeling he'd felt after Ovi's party when she'd left all those missed calls. He had to know what happened. He grabbed his coat, put on his trainers and left.

Ten minutes later he pressed Maya's bell. He waited, examining the weed-strewn crazy-paved drive, the bright blue hatchback family car, the dirty white rendering, the ageing shingle roof, listening to the permanent roar of the North Circular motorway half a mile away. Through the misty glass of the porch came the blurry shape of Maya's dad, stepping over the mess, opening the door, his stomach bulging through his bright white T-shirt.

'Alfie! Nice to see you! I didn't think you were going to come.' His face was lit up in child-like glee. 'I would have ordered a pizza! I would have got the beers in!'

'I'm not actually—'

'Come, come! I'll see what I can find . . .'

He slapped Alfie's back and ushered him inside. The football was on, the Arsenal players warming up while the commentators rambled on about *stats, assist, shots on target, take-ons, tackles, passes completed*. Maya's dad bustled about the kitchen, singing to himself. Soon he came out with a bowl of crisps and two cans of Coke. Alfie's stomach rumbled. He hadn't had breakfast.

Alfie's dad nodded to the young Arsenal player on the screen, only two years older than Alfie, with long blond hair.

'Someone needs to give him a compass so he knows which way the goal is!'

Alfie laughed. He sat down next to him. He was worried about nothing. Maya would be down in a second. He'd just watch a bit. Have some food. The game kicked off and the young blond player skipped past one, then another, before a sliding tackle took him out.

'Get up!' shouted Alfie, his mouth full of crisps.

'He looks like he's about to cry,' sneered Maya's dad.

'There's no leaders in this team.'

'Too much money. Too much, too young. It kills your hunger.'

The game was scrappy and tense, with a lot of mishits and tackles, both teams struggling to string more than two passes together. They both ate the crisps, frowning, grunting and tutting. This was nice, thought Alfie. Is this what it was like to have a dad? Is this how it was for everyone else? He suddenly felt sad.

'Where's Maya?' he said.

'Asleep.'

Alfie checked the time. He'd been there thirty minutes. It was almost one fifteen p.m. She sent the message at one a.m. A wave of anxiety washed over him. Something wasn't right.

'Do you like oranges?' said Maya's dad.

Alfie nodded. Maya's dad nipped to the kitchen and chucked Alfie an orange from the doorway. Alfie caught it in his right hand.

'Nice. You can be goalkeeper.'

'Shouldn't she be up?' said Alfie.

'Yes.'

'Should one of us wake her?'

Maya's dad sat down next to him and produced a large knife. 'Yes. You're right. I'm putting it off cos I can't face the fight. Battle to the death! She drives me crazy. I've had enough of her nonsense.'

Maya's dad carefully and expertly peeled the orange, the knife blade glinting as its sharp edge slid smoothly into the skin.

'Close him down!' he spat.

He chucked the peel, which was one long, unbroken spiral

shape, onto the table in front of him, just as a long-range shot hit the Arsenal crossbar.

'Idiot!' he barked viciously.

Knife through my heart.

Suddenly Arsenal broke, two versus two, their striker shot from outside the area but the ball skidded wide. Alfie jumped as Maya's dad hit the sofa with his fist.

Alfie felt a horrible dread. What if Maya's dad *wasn't* a nice, caring dad? He'd wanted to fight Olly, the Twisted Dreamland bass player, in Greece. He had a big knife. He was scary when he shouted at the football. He had mental rows with his daughter. He said he'd had enough. He didn't seem worried that she wasn't up and dressed. What if Maya's dad had actually stuck a knife through her heart? What if there'd already been a battle to the death? What if she was dying upstairs, bleeding out, and this was his only chance to save her?

The moment the half-time whistle blew, Alfie sprung up from sofa. 'She needs to get ready. I'm gonna wake her up!'

He was out of the room, bounding up the stairs, as Maya's dad watched, his mouth hanging open. Her room was dingy, the curtains drawn, a lumpy mountain of dress, duvet and pillows piled on her bed, clothes strewn across the carpet. It smelled of mustiness, beer and stale perfume. Make-up bottles, brushes and creams were scattered across her desk. It wasn't this messy when he left. It hadn't smelled of beer either. On the floor, next to a blood-red bra, was her phone. He picked it up. It was off. He pressed the on button. No battery.

Where was she? What had her dad done with the body?!

He stumbled around the room, running his fingers through his hair, panicking. He sat on the end of her bed, felt a hard lump under his bottom, sprang up in shock and pulled the duvet towards him.

A foot ... Then a body ... A low-cut dress with bouffant sleeves. Eyeliner smudged, eyelids hooded ... She looked like a zombie.

'Maya,' he said, fearing the worst. 'Maya!'

Her eyes opened and he screamed.

6

Alfie switched on the light, making Maya screw her face up and cover her eyes with her hand.

'You're alive!'

'What you talking about? Of course I'm alive!'

He groaned in relief, collapsed onto her carpet and lay down on his back.

Maya put her hand to her forehead, as if checking her temperature. 'I mean, I'm technically alive. I don't *feel* alive . . .' She pulled the duvet up to her neck. 'Why are you here?'

'I was worried about you.'

'Why?'

'I thought your dad had murdered you.'

'Excuse me?'

'Because of your message?!'

'What message?'

'The one you sent me!'

'Oh, no.'

Maya hauled herself up and reached for her phone. There was a painful couple of minutes while she rooted around the room for her charger, finding it underneath a jumper in the corner, plugging it in to the mains, plugging it into her phone, waiting for it to charge enough to turn on, and finally open her messaging app.

'Oh, no!'

'What?'

'You thought my dad had *murdered* me?'

'Look what you wrote!'

Maya snorted. Then sniggered. Then laughed, so deep, so hard, it sounded like she had whooping cough. She grabbed a pillow and covered her mouth, while Alfie rubbed his fingers into the carpet until his skin was red and burning.

'What I was I supposed to think?' said Alfie, when Maya had finally calmed down.

'Err . . . Not that?'

'You literally said *knife through my heart*.'

'Oh, yeah, did you think I'd just send an update message? *Hi, Alfie! Just getting murdered. Knife emoji, heart emoji!*'

'Your dad was waving a massive blade down there! Peeling oranges like a master assassin!'

Maya shrieked again. 'Alfie, I was drunk!'

'How on earth were you drunk?' Alfie stared at the zigzagging burning filament across the centre of Maya's lightbulb.

'No reason . . .'

'What, you just put on a dress and got drunk before you went to bed?'

'No.'

'What, then?'

Maya sat up. 'I went to Luke's,' she said in a small voice. 'He invited me. After you'd gone.'

'So you just dropped everything and left? At midnight?'

Maya shrugged. 'He's messaging me and I'm like, *I really wanna see you*, he's like, *Come over then*, I'm like, *Yeah, why not!*'

'He booty-called you.'

'I thought it was romantic, he really wanted to see me!'

'When you had to work the next day?'

50

'I wanted to, I missed him!'

Ugh. Luke. Of course she was still into him. Even after a whole evening with Alfie, she was gagging for him!

Maya lifted the duvet up with a sweeping motion, swung her legs over the mattress, stood and loomed over Alfie, the lacy folds of her dress blocking then revealing the lightbulb. She held out a hand. Alfie rolled over so his face was pressed into her carpet.

'Alfie, that's disgusting.'

'I'm not moving.'

'There's dust mites and hair and skin cells—'

'I don't care!'

'What's your problem? I'm the one who had the worst night ever!'

'Maaaayaaa! Alfffiiiiiieee!' came her dad's voice from downstairs.

'Oh, shit!' said Maya. She picked up her phone and checked the time. She ran to the door and opened it.

'I don't want to go!' she shouted down the stairs.

'See what I mean, Alfie?' said Maya's dad.

'What have you been saying about me?' said Maya, jabbing a finger.

'Nothing!' said Alfie.

For a moment, Alfie thought she was about to repeat the rant of the previous night. Instead, she slammed her door and sighed impatiently. 'Close your eyes.'

Alfie closed his eyes. The wardrobe door creaked, clothes hangers banged into each other, fabric rustled against fabric. He pictured T-shirts, skirts, bras, pants, jeans, dresses flying through the air.

'So, I told my dad I was going to Gwen's because she needs a friend right now, which was kind of true – don't you dare tell him by the way, he thinks I was with her – and then I went to Theydon Bois.'

'Where the hell is Theydon Bois?'

'This village at the end of the Central Line.'

'I thought he lived in London.'

'Zone Six. Technically it's Essex. Takes *forever* to get there.'

'Essex?'

'Yeah.'

'That's like . . . another country!'

'Another *county*, Alfie! So I get there, he's a bit drunk . . . he's kissing me, getting frisky—'

'Too much detail!' cut in Alfie.

Maya went silent. Had she left the room? More rustling clothes, Maya muttering, bed springs creaking and heaving.

'So I get there, and I'm like, *Where have you been*? He's like, *Nowhere*, I'm like, *You've been drinking*! He's like, *Yeah, I have!* Then his phone goes, I swear I wasn't being nosy, both of us just, like, look at the screen, like a reflex, it's a message from his dad, says, *Here's the link. "I Wrote Your Name in the Stars" sounding good! Love the title!* Luke looks at me all guilty, like he's busted. I'm like, *What's sounding good*? He goes, *My dad decided to pay for us to record a demo. We took the last two days off college to do it.* I was like, *And you recorded the song we wrote together without me*? He's like, *Um. Yeah*?'

'Was he trying to pass it off as his?'

'I think so! That's what it felt like! He's like, *I did write most of it.* I'm like, *Jeez! Who did the melody for the chorus? Who did the lyrics for the chorus*? He's like, *You did.* I'm like, *Exactly!*'

Wham! Alife felt elated! Maybe Luke wasn't Mr Perfect! Maybe he was a ... dick! Just like Ovi!

'What did you do?' he said.

'I was really angry.'

'Did you tell him?'

'We kind of got distracted.'

'By what?'

'Horny stuff.'

'You *slept* with him?'

'I hadn't seen him for a whole week! You can open your eyes now, by the way.'

Alfie sat up straight, eyes back open. Maya had changed into a pair of black jeans and a garish purple collared T-shirt with *Café Delish* emblazoned across the front.

'You should have had a go at him. He's using you for your song. He's taking the piss. And you made him think it's OK!'

'Luke is very charming ... and very ... good-looking and ... he's very hard to argue with ...'

'Maya! It sets a precedent! You should have called him out!'

'I know! I felt really shit on the bus home, hence the knife through the heart message!'

Maya sighed. She walked over to the window and opened the curtains. Sunlight streamed in. She stood, silhouetted against the window, the air thick with dancing motes. She sat down in the middle of the room, and hugged her thighs to her chest.

'Ugh. You're so annoying!'

'Why?'

'Cos I know you're right!'

She picked up her phone. *Tap, tap, tap.*

'What are you doing?' said Alfie.

'Shhh!' said Maya.

She frowned. It became so quiet, Alfie could hear the ringtone. It went to voicemail, and a male voice told the caller to leave a message. Maya inhaled deeply.

'Hey. It's me. You tell me that I'm all special and talented and then you take my work and steal it and pass it off as your own? Record it without me being there? And then try and ... *booty call* me? From now on I forbid you to sing that song without me singing it with you, and I will sue your ass if you do!'

Maya paused. Her mind was clearly racing.

'Actually no, I forbid you to *ever* sing that song at a gig. Ever. You blew it, Luke. You had your chance! No one does that to me. Fuck you and your stupid piece-of-shit band. It's over. Find some other gullible idiot to write stupid romantic songs with. Have a nice life! Bye!'

She hung up. They sat there in silence.

'I didn't realise I was gonna get that angry,' said Maya, standing. 'I *am* too intense.'

Alfie tingled all over. She had just dumped Luke!

'No! Not at all. He deserved it!'

He held up his palm.

Maya half-heartedly high-fived it. 'Are you sure I'm not a psycho?'

'No. No way!'

Maya smiled. 'Thanks for helping me stand up for myself.'

She sat on the bed. Then she sniffed. Then she cried. Alfie got up from the carpet and sat next to her, gently rubbing her back. She was crying! She was crying because it was over!

After a while Maya walked across the room, grabbed some

tissues, and wiped her face. She picked up her phone, and played Alfie's voicenote, and now Alfie heard himself, checking if Maya was OK.

Maya stared at him. She dropped the phone and put her hands on her heart.

'I've just realised something,' she said.

'What?'

'You *were* really worried about me! I can hear it in your voice. You really, really care for me, don't you?'

Alfie nodded. His head spun. He had the same tingling, shaking feeling he had on the sofa on the green. Maya blinked. She looked dazed. Like she'd woken up after being knocked out and didn't know where she was. Her eyes were the coolest, lightest grey. They lingered on Alfie's face.

'I was worried about where it was going, you know. I'd only seen him a few times. Maybe this confirms it. I haven't even been to a rehearsal yet. Why doesn't he want to see me more? And then he booty calls me when he's drunk?'

She reached out and took his hand. She ran her index finger round the centre of his palm. The tingles – pricking, stinging bolts of electricity, shot down his legs.

'Maya! You're late!' yelled Maya's dad.

Maya stomped to the door and opened it, 'I'm ready, OK!'

Alfie, dazed, joined her in the doorway.

'Hey, Alfie?' said Maya's dad brightly. 'They subbed him off at half-time. Humiliation! We're playing the old Arsenal, pinging it around.'

'I need some breakfast,' said Maya.

'I'm trying to talk to Alfie,' said her dad.

'Do you want me to faint on the job?'

'There's food there. It wouldn't be a very good café if there wasn't, would it?'

Maya sighed and grabbed Alfie's hand. 'Come and find me later, yeah?'

Alfie nodded.

'And Alfie ...?'

'Yeah?'

She squeezed his hand, then kissed him on the cheek, her lips lingering on his skin for a second too long. 'Just ... Come and find me later.'

Alfie felt amazing. For God's sake! She *did* like him! She did feel the same! She'd dropped Luke, like a piece of trash, just like he'd dreamed!

7

Maya's finger-touch stayed on Alfie's palm all afternoon.

Back in his flat, he Googled Café Delish to double check their closing time – five-thirty p.m. He had a few hours. He showered, put on a clean T-shirt and tracksuit bottoms, spot-cleaned his Jōnetsu hoodie with a cloth, and over-sprayed himself with Lynx. Then he made a fish finger sandwich, followed the rest of the Arsenal game on a dodgy illegal stream (they won, one-nil), then watched Man U lose, barely concentrating. It ended at four-forty-five p.m., leaving him just enough time to walk – which he needed to calm his nerves.

He closed his front door and stepped into the cramped lift. As always, the metal walls seemed shiny with sweat and the gap between the doors closing and the lift moving seemed a bit too long, as if he was about to get trapped. Please, not today! But the lift lurched and sped him down, and soon he was out the exit, past his school, walking beside the six lanes of the busy North Circular; cars rumbling, motorbikes vrooming, and trucks clattering. He hurried across the winding footbridge, past the fairground, past the boxy weather-worn shopping centre, across a slip road and up a shadowy overpass. Up above was the busy Hendon Way, held aloft by hulking, graffiti-covered pillars, while down below the rumbling North Circular continued on. Somehow, flowing through this tangled mess of winding walkways and overgrown grass, was a river – the River Brent – temporarily turned into a canal, its narrow banks covered with empty food cartons. Alfie paused to catch his breath, gripping the top of the railing, watching the water (barely a trickle).

It had to be his moment. Didn't it? Would that make him a dick? Would he really just talk her into splitting up with her new boyfriend, only to make a move six hours later? That was some grade-A *Game of Thrones* shit, right there! Maybe he should wait. Take it slowly. This was Maya, though. She never stayed single for more than twenty seconds. *Don't make the same mistake as before!*

He speed-walked away, through Hendon Park, the Northern Line trains flashing through the gaps in the trees, their wheels squealing, past neatly mown grass and still-blooming flower beds, out onto the busy roundabout at Hendon Underground station, through the leaky underpass, then up by the Tesco Metro, where, across the road, was Café Delish. He was just in time.

Maya stood behind the glass display counter, with puffy eyes and a pissed-off pout, wrapping a metal dish of tuna fish and sweetcorn with cling film. She'd somehow managed, in the last few hours, to heavily kohl her eyes and apply black lipstick. The chef, a middle-aged woman in soiled whites and a hairnet, bustled around the kitchen. Other than that, the café was empty and some bulging black rubbish bags sat outside the door.

Alfie waved as Maya looked up. She disappeared into the kitchen, reappearing moments later, coat on, carrying a big Sainsbury's bag. She pulled the door open, stepped over the rubbish, knocked into Alfie with her shoulder, and clomped off up the road. Alfie followed her to the junction, where she collapsed onto a bench.

'Never work hospitality with a hangover, OK?'

Alfie sat down next to her. She rested her head on his shoulder, took out her phone and swiped it open.

'Maya.'

'Yeah?'

'I think we should talk.'

Tap, tap, tap.

'Uh-huh?'

Tap, tap, tap.

'Yeah. I do.'

'About?'

'There's something I need to tell you.'

'Uh-huh?'

Alfie hesitated. His legs shook. He felt dizzy. Her phone rang. 'Shit. Sorry, I have to take this.'

Maya stood up. Alfie punched his hand onto his forehead in frustration, but she didn't notice, circling the flower beds, deep in conversation. Alfie wandered over to a boarded-up bank and read the *To Let* sign over and over until his brain felt numb. He turned to see Maya, back on the bench, phone on her lap, her hands on her chest.

'Are you OK?' he said.

'No!' She turned to him. 'Actually, I am. I'm very OK!'

She held out her hand. It was trembling, her black nail polish cracked and flaking. She looked up at the sky, taking deep gulps of air.

'What happened?'

'You did it, Alfie.'

'What?'

'Saved my life! That was Luke, he's like, *I'm so sorry. I'm so, so sorry. I should have invited you to the recording. I was nervous about*

59

bringing it up with the others cos I didn't know what they would say. My dad just booked the studio and sprung it on me at short notice. I messed up. We're having a gig to test out the new material! In my garage. You need to come sing. Then we'll book the studio again, and you can come, we'll rerecord it, I promise. I swear, on my heart. Come to rehearsals, come and sing in our gig, let's do a trial and if it works out, I think you should join the band. You'll meet all my friends, it'll be amazing.'

Maya stood up, bouncing on her heels.

'He's was like *desperate*: *You are so beautiful, I don't want to lose you. You're not a booty call. You're amazing, Maya! You're beautiful and hot and an amazing singer! Please forgive me, please!* He was begging me not to dump him. How do you do it, Alfie? How did you get the exact reaction I wanted? I am so, so lucky to have a friend like you.'

'Unbelievable,' said Alfie.

'I know! And now I have to go because I'm going back to Theydon Bois, woo-hoo.'

'You told me to come and find you.'

'Oh.' Maya grimaced. 'I'll tell him I'll be late.'

'It's OK.'

'He can wait ..'

'It's fine ..'

'Do you want me to spend some time with you or not? Because I will! Just say the word. What did you want to tell me?'

'Nothing.'

'You wanted to tell me something ..'

'Doesn't matter ..'

'Alfie … what's wrong?' Maya's grey eyes bored into him. Impulsively, she grabbed Alfie and hugged him tightly.

'You really had my back today. Even if you did overreact in a hilarious way. I want you to know that I am here for you as well, OK?'

'I know.'

'I *so* am.'

Alfie nodded.

'You can speak to me anytime. Anytime. About anything. I'm here. I'm all ears.'

'It's fine,' he sighed. 'I did wanna hang. But now this has happened. It takes priority.'

'Alfie. You look really sad.'

'I'm not.'

'Is everything OK?'

It wasn't. But how could he say it? She was mad about Luke! The humiliation! Again! Maya reached into her bag and produced two large Tupperware boxes and handed them to Alfie. 'Half a moussaka. Three brownies. Six croissants.'

'Did you . . . steal these?'

'No! They were gonna chuck them! Moussaka is a-ma-zing! Oh my God . . .'

'Thanks, Maya.'

She kissed him on the cheek.

'Are you sure you're OK with me going?'

Alfie touched her forehead. 'I give you my blessing, my child.'

Maya laughed. Her hair swung round and brushed his face as she turned and hurried away.

8

'I don't wanna go.'

'Why?'

'It's gonna take ages ...'

'Dude, it's less than an hour ...'

'I'm skint!'

'You got Oyster?'

'I'm out of credit!'

Jack rolled his eyes. 'Give it to me!'

'No.'

Alfie was clutching his Oyster card in his right hand. Jack tried to grab it.

'Give it!'

'I forgot my passport!'

'You don't need your passport!'

'You have to take your passport, otherwise they won't let you in. It's a war zone. The zombies. They're killing everyone.'

'What you talking about?!'

'The zombie apocalypse. It's here. It's real. It's happening in Essex ...'

'Alfie—'

'Did you bring a flamethrower?'

'Of course not!'

'We need flamethrowers—'

'What are you on about?'

'No one I know has ever been to Essex and survived.'

Jack laughed. 'Maya goes!'

'Bruv. Luke's house! It's been infected! She's gone all weird and she's started talking non-stop shite about bands and singing and demos – she's a zombie, I'm telling you!'

Jack laughed. Alfie hung back, on the pavement, outside the newsagent. 'All I'm saying is, do I really wanna trek that far?'

Alfie *wanted* to say, 'Do I really wanna watch Luke-the-greatest-singer-in-the-history-of-bands reminding me that he stole the girl I care about when I could be watching *Strictly Come Dancing* with Nan?' Watching *Strictly* with Nan was his favourite thing. His guilty pleasure that he never, ever spoke about.

'Can't we go back to yours and play *Football Manager*?'

'Dude!'

'*They* can get eaten by the zombies. Me and you, stay here, in the warm, buying Mbappé for Barnet.'

'Alfie, this is nuts!' Jack gripped Alfie's arm, leaned forward and spoke in his ear in a low voice. 'Is this about Maya?'

'No.'

'Really?'

'No!'

'You sure?'

'Yes!'

Jack gestured to Maya, Gwen and Lily, who stood, huddled and chatting on the middle of the black-and-white chequered floor of the Brent Cross station ticket hall. On cue, Lily smiled, waved, bounded over, and gave Jack a big kiss on the cheek.

'I know exactly what's gonna happen tonight,' said Alfie.

'You two will just lock yourself in the bathroom like you always do and get up to Jack-Lily things, like you always do.'

'We are so not.'

'You so are!'

'Is Alfie not coming?' said Lily.

'I'd feel so much better if you were there ...' said Jack. He looked at Lily. 'If you both were there ... The two most important people in the world to me.'

'Awww ...' said Lily. She kissed him on the cheek again. 'C'mon, Alfie! Jack needs his bro!'

His bro? So it was OK for Jack to ignore him for weeks, but when he needed a bro to get rid of his social anxiety, Alfie had to be there? Of course it was about Maya! But how could he update him when he never saw him? When they never got a chance to speak without Lily butting in? And, even if he did open up, Jack would just patronise him with lame advice.

Jack and Lily looked at Alfie pleadingly.

'Everyone's waiting ...' said Lily.

'Fine!' said Alfie. He held out his Oyster, Jack snatched it, topped it up at the machine and handed it back.

'Tenner?'

'Thank you. I think.'

'Oi! Hurry up!' shouted Maya.

She was on the other side of the barriers, stupidly overdressed, wearing glistening black lipstick, a strapless red dress with a billowing skirt. She carried a black parasol even though it was dark and chilly. Lily and Gwen joined her, Alfie reluctantly following, slapping his Oyster on the reader, dawdling through the station, running his hand along the cool white-and-green tiles that lined the walls, up onto the open-air platform. They all stood, lit by the dim orange lamps, the cold evening wind rustling the bushes on either side of the tracks.

Maya was buzzed. For the long ten-minute wait she yakked about Luke: his house, his double garage which his dad had converted into a rehearsal space-slash-venue because he was so supportive of his son's dreams of the music industry. He even stuck up for him when the neighbours complained about the noise. Luke had sent her a link to the songs, and now she was sharing her AirPods with Gwen and Lily, who were nodding appreciatively.

'They're really talented,' she said. 'They're really tight. I've been to two rehearsals now. It feels so amazing to sing with a proper, proper band. I'm gonna be on the next demo. I actually think they – we – could be big! If tonight goes well they might let me join. Oh, by the way, Gwen. Mikey saw your photo and he totally fancies you. So ... er ... watch out!'

Maya snorted. Gwen blushed. Great! Now even Gwen was gonna have a band-member boyfriend too!

The Kennington train finally arrived and they bundled on. Gwen and Lily sat either side of Maya, Jack next to Lily, holding her hand, while Lily stroked the top of his head. Alfie stood, pretending he didn't know them, amongst a large African family, the men in suits, the women in colourful shawls and wrap skirts, possibly returning from a wedding, or on the way to a party. Alfie watched the two young boys swing around the poles by the doors. He still had time to bail. He could jump out at Golders Green. Get on the first train home. Boom! Gone! When the doors were beeping. They wouldn't know what hit them.

'Stop being so anti-social!' said Maya. He hadn't noticed her stand up and join him. She was looming over him, holding the rail, swaying to-and-fro.

'I'm not,' said Alfie.

'You are. What's your problem?'

'Nothing.'

'You've been moody since we all met up.'

'I'm fine.'

'Lily said you were trying to bail!'

Lily! Again! Damn her!

Alfie caught Gwen's eye. She sat on the seat, her hair tied up high, a couple of strands hanging over her face. She gave him a sympathetic smile.

'I'm just nervous. Meeting new people. You know me. I don't drink and everyone else does. It's harder.'

'Aww. Alfie!' Maya rubbed his arm. 'I'm nervous too, you know. I'm bricking it, actually. It really helps me you being there. Just your presence. We can be nervous together.'

Her pale grey eyes, her face close to his, the bare skin on her shoulders ... As the train lurched her hair flung forward, brushing his face. Her perfume smelled sweet, like vanilla and praline. Ugh. Why did he like her so much! He could feel himself melting.

'Plus, you have to look on the bright side,' Maya continued. 'Luke's got loads of single friends ... Tonight could change everything!'

Is this what he needed? Another girl? To take his mind off her? Maybe she was right. Something had to change.

The brakes screeched, as the train pulled into Golders Green station.

'Sorry. Thanks. You're right. I'm down. I'm coming. Sorry for being moody.'

The doors opened. Maya hugged him. Alfie stayed on the train.

'Tonight is gonna be legendary . . .' she whispered. 'I can feel it in my bones.'

9

Maya, Gwen and Lily led the way out of Theydon Bois station, through the small car park and onto the pavement, arms interlinked, like a stomping six-footed animal. Alfie and Jack drifted behind, following them past an Indian restaurant, an old-school country pub, and along the village green. Finally, they turned down a pitch-black gravel drive. No loud music, no shouting voices, no special decorations. Was this really a party? A light slammed on, hurting Alfie's eyes, revealing a large mock-Tudor house. A boy, squat and muscular, stood outside the front door. He spent a moment sizing them up before holding his hand out to Gwen.

'Mikey,' he said.

Gwen held out her hand. Mikey bent down and kissed it.

'Stop flirting and show us where to go,' said Maya.

'How very dare you,' said Mikey as Gwen's cheeks turned purple. 'Welcome to Luke's,' he continued. 'Very simple. Party this way. Epping Forest that way. Make your choice!'

'Party!' whooped Lily, Mikey bowed and they followed him through the front door, into the hall, past a kitchen and through a side door into a double garage, which, just as Maya had said, was converted into a venue. Two huge speakers sat on either end of a small stage bathed in purple, red and green light. On it was a drum kit, two guitars resting on stands, and, at the front, a lone microphone lit by a single spot. A loud hiss came from the corner, as a dry ice machine spewed out smoke. It was empty – they were the first ones there.

'This. Is. Incredible,' said Maya. By the side of the wall were some tubs of ice and water, full up of cans of beer and cider. 'Hey, Alfie! They even have non-alcoholic!' She handed him one. 'Just for you ..' she said, clinking their bottles.

'And Lily,' said Alfie, feeling irritated and pedantic.

A tall boy in a beanie walked in, his long hair framing his face. He held his arm up in celebration, clutching a beer.

'Drunk already!' he cried, and Lily, Maya and Gwen spontaneously cheered.

Olly. The guy who'd almost started a fight with Maya's dad.

'You're about to play a gig, you muppet,' said Maya.

'I've played a hundred gigs much more drunk than this ..' he said. The others laughed and then, for a painful couple of minutes, they loitered in silence, before Luke walked in, talking on his phone.

He was even better-looking than the photo. Big green eyes, lined with mascara, a slender nose, the swooping blond fringe, full heart-shaped lips, the lower one pierced in the middle. He was stupidly hot. Maya ran up to him and kissed him on the lips.

'Alfie?' said Luke. He shook his hand. 'So good to meet you, man. I've heard so much about you.'

Alfie smiled. All eyes were on him. Like he just met a celebrity.

'All positive,' Luke added. 'Don't worry!' He squeezed Alfie's shoulder. 'Help yourself to anything. Anything you want.'

'Thanks,' said Alfie.

'I'm buzzing already! It's gonna be a good night!' said Luke, and Alfie felt it too, a rush of happiness like he'd won a special prize. Dammit! He was supposed to hate Luke, and he was making him feel good. How could he compete with this much charm?

Alfie found a random dining chair at the back of the garage, took off his hoodie, hung it on the back and sipped his non-alcoholic beer. People arrived, two girls in hoodies and fishnet tights, a group of boys clutching skateboards. Lily handed out beers. Mikey cornered Gwen, making her laugh, his arm around her shoulder. Even Jack was joking with a skinny guy wearing glasses. Suddenly they piled in: so many teens, squealing and laughing, some of them drunk, some with dumb grins and bloodshot eyes, who'd clearly been smoking.

Luke was surrounded by girls, milking it, loving it, but just when Alfie thought he was disrespecting Maya by flirting with someone else, he turned, kissed her on the lips, stared into her eyes, beaming his beautiful smile. Maya stayed glued to him, making herself pretty, pouting, fluttering her eyelashes, swinging her hair. They did look good together. Like a couple of models. Like they were already famous. Maya caught Alfie looking and beckoned him to join her. Alfie shook his head. Instead he got into a stupid argument with a boy who was convinced that penguins could fly, then a long discussion about bands with two girls who'd started a YouTube channel reviewing music. Argh! Even Luke's friends were fun! Now, an old man was there, pushing himself around in a wheelchair, cracking jokes with Mikey, who was holding hands with Gwen on the sofa. It took Alfie a moment to work out that he was Luke's dad. Jeez! Even he was fun!

Alfie spotted a girl sitting on the edge of the stage. She wore navy blue jeans, and a slinky camisole that revealed a bright purple belly button piercing. She looked straight at him, then did an up-and-to-the-side look, smiled from the corner of her mouth, and walked off. Had she just . . . smiled at him?

She joined three boys in the corner, said something and laughed. Alfie felt jealous. One of them was gonna hit on her. Surely! But then she flicked her hair and looked over her shoulder, glancing around. No, she was bored! Their eyes locked. She smiled. Boom! Yes! She was stunning!

Maybe Maya was right. Meet someone new. Stop obsessing. Distract himself. Move on.

Alfie darted forward, aiming to tap the girl on the shoulder but accidently bumping into her back.

'Sorry,' he said.

She laughed awkwardly. She was clutching a beer can.

'I'm clumsy,' he said.

'It's OK.'

'Alfie,' he said, extending his hand. So embarrassing. A handshake? What was he, a politician? She reached out and squeezed it, firmly.

'Lyra,' she said. 'How do you know Luke?'

'My friend goes out with him.'

'Ooooooooh.'

'You know her?'

'Nope! I don't know *Ma-ya*.' She said her name slowly, hanging onto each syllable. 'My feet are hurting, I need to sit down.'

'There's not enough chairs.'

'I know.'

71

Alfie followed her out of the garage, along the drive to the front of the house where they both sat down on the porch. Somewhere inside a toilet flushed, and someone was stacking plates in the kitchen. Lyra took a swig from her beer can.

'It's always nice and quiet here,' she said.

'You been here before?'

'Yep.'

'I guess Luke has a lot of parties. With a garage like that,' said Alfie.

'Yup.'

'This is the first time I've been to Essex, you know.'

Lyra turned and frowned.

'Where do you live?'

'Brent Cross.'

'Oh.'

'Zone Three.'

'Oh.'

'I thought everyone in Essex was a zombie, so . . .'

'Whaaat?'

'In my mind Essex is a post-apocalyptic wasteland. The edge of the world. The end of civilisation.'

'This is Zone Six!'

'I know! It's just my lame joke.'

'You're weird.'

'I don't get out much.'

Lyra laughed. 'Do I look like a zombie?'

'No.'

Their eyes met.

'Definitely not,' said Alfie.

Lyra smiled. She swigged her can until it was vertical, looked through the ring like it was a telescope, and then scrunched it and chucked it across the gravel.

'You want a drink?' she said.

'Sure.'

Lyra stood up.

'Non-alcoholic.'

'What?'

'Non-alcoholic, please.'

'You drink non-alcoholic?'

'You got a problem with that?'

'Bo-ring! Have a proper drink!'

'No, thank you.'

'C'mon!'

'I don't drink.'

'Bo-oring!'

Alfie shook his head.

'C'mon! Just one!'

'I don't want to!'

'Whhhyy!'

Alfie sighed. 'You really wanna know?'

'There is no reason! It doesn't exist!'

'My mum is a drug addict! I'm teetotal. I just don't . . . I just don't wanna go there. OK? It's a choice.'

Lyra put her hand to her mouth. She took a step backwards. 'Oh my God. I'm so sorry!'

'It's OK.'

'I'm so, so sorry!'

She sat back down and leaned forward and spoke into his ear: 'I was really out of order.'

'It's OK. Really, it is. I get this a lot.'

Lyra put her head in her hands. 'I'm so embarrassed,' she said, muffled.

'You're not the first person to say it. Really, it's OK.'

Lyra didn't reply.

'Looking forward to the band tonight?' said Alfie, in an attempt to change the subject.

Lyra looked up at him. An icy mist descended over her eyes. 'And why would I be looking forward to the band?'

'I heard they're good?' said Alfie. 'I heard they're gonna be big!'

'*Yeah* . . .' she said.

The drive-light slammed on as another group of chattering people arrived.

'Twisted Dreamland will do well until Luke gets offered something bigger and better,' she went on, 'then he will dump them for the next thing. Because that's what he always does.'

'You think?'

'I think? I know. He's amazing when he decides he likes you, but when he gets bored . . .' She picked up a stone from the gravel, held it up, and dropped it.

Alfie frowned. 'Did you used to go out with him?'

She looked him in the eye. 'Does that bother you?'

Alfie realised something. One, she was drunk. Really, really drunk. She must have got drunk before she came. How did he only just notice? Two, she was Luke's ex? Of every girl in this Godforsaken place, he chose Luke's ex? Who was clearly not over him?

'Did you two split up recently?'

'Oh, you know . . . summertime.'

'Summertime?'

'Ancient history. The distant past.'

Alfie's mind was racing. Did Luke dump Lyra for Maya?

'Sorry. I shouldn't have mentioned the band,' he said.

'It's fine,' she said. 'You're right. They are amazing. Genuinely.'

Lyra hiccupped loudly. All the good vibes, all the optimism, all the excitement disappeared. They were just two sad lonely desperate idiots flirting because they were hung up on someone else. They had no connection. They didn't get on. He wasn't even sure he fancied her any more. He felt lonelier than he'd ever felt in his life.

'What's wrong?' she said.

'Ah, man!' said Alfie.

'What?'

'Why are we here? Why? Are. We. Here?'

She leaned forward, breathing beery breath over him. 'This isn't the time for philosophy . . .' she said. 'We're at a party. We're supposed to be having fun.' Alfie watched her lips. Despite it all, he thought about kissing them. What the hell was he doing?

'Hold on,' he said. 'I'm busting for a piss!'

He ran inside and into the garage. Everyone was facing the stage. Mikey was sitting behind the drum kit doing random little drum rolls. Olly stood twanging his bass guitar aimlessly. Something knocked into Alfie's shin. A white Nike trainer . . . belonging to Jack . . . sitting on a chair, Lily straddling him, snogging him . . . Alfie's Jōnetsu hoodie which he'd so carefully hung on the back of it had been knocked onto the floor, the right arm trampled.

'Jeez, guys, you promised!' said Alfie, rehanging his hoodie on the chair.

'We promised not to go in the toilet!' said Jack, turning towards him.

'I would have preferred it if you did! Get a room!'

There was a loud disharmonious clang as Luke tested his guitar. He stood, centre stage, casually basking in everyone's attention. Laid back, beautiful. It was all about him.

Maya caught Alfie's eye and smiled. Alfie pulled a face. Maya mouthed, *What?* She pointed next to her, as if to say, *Come here!* Alfie shook his head. Alfie mouthed, *You come here!* Maya shook her head. She looked so beautiful, in the smoky, misty, multi-coloured gloom. His heart was trying to burst out of his chest, smash through the audience and land in her hands.

Alfie pushed his way through the crowd. 'We need to talk,' he said.

Luke walked up to the microphone. 'One-two, one-two,' he repeated over and over, his lips too close to the mesh, the sound hurting Alfie's ears.

'I can't hear you,' said Maya, cupping her hand over her ear and leaning towards Alfie.

'I think I love you!' shouted Alfie, just as Luke stopped speaking and the room went silent. Everyone turned to look at them.

'What did you say?' Maya's voice tailed off as she realised that everyone was listening.

'I mean it,' said Alfie.

What was the point of hiding? What was the point of pretending?

'I said, *I think I love you.*'

Luke was eyeing Alfie carefully, like he wanted to say something but was hyper-self-conscious that everyone was staring.

'What are you lot looking at?' said Maya, turning to the room. 'Haven't you got anything better to do?'

Alfie pointed at Luke. 'He doesn't like you. I mean, he doesn't like you like I do. Like you deserve to be liked!'

'*What* did he say?' said Olly.

Alfie stared at Luke. 'He's ... just a *player*, Maya! A *user*. You're just this temporary ... thing. He doesn't see you like *I* do.'

Alfie thumped his chest. He watched Maya, searching for a response, a reaction, anything.

'What did you say about my friend?' said Olly.

'This is nothing to do with you,' said Alfie.

Olly took off his bass guitar and placed it down on the stage. 'What did you say about my friend?'

'This is nothing to do with you, you drunk idiot!' said Alfie.

'Olly, don't!' said Luke, as Olly launched himself at Alfie, rugby-tackling him to the floor. Maya screamed. Luke shouted at him to stop. Two big punches into Alfie's ribs. Some fingers pressed into Alfie's chest and then he was up, up, up over Jack's shoulder, the hall carpet looming, past Lyra's surprised face, down the driveway, along the road, and *whoomph*, onto his back, on the grass, looking up at the starry sky.

10

'My Jōnetsu hoodie!' said Alfie.

Jack's ADIDAS trainer was close to Alfie's face, covered in flecks of mud, half visible in the dim light. 'What the hell just happened, dude?'

'My Jōnetsu hoodie!'

Alfie stretched out his arms, as if expecting Jack to hand it to him. 'On the chair. Where you and Lily were eating each other. I need it! I can't live without it!'

Jack sighed. 'Don't move. OK?'

The squelch of Jack's trainers became fainter and fainter and Alfie was left alone. The cold night air was refreshing. No people. No banter. No Maya. No Luke. Just him, the sky, and its vast, twinkling pattern of stars, some bundled in clusters, some scattered, some bright, some dim. Maya was right. The starry sky *was* beautiful. Something about it took the edge off. Maybe she was onto something.

Two boots appeared in Alfie's peripheral vision and a dress brushed against the top of his head. 'I literally spend all my time telling Luke how amazing you are, and then I tell you how much I was worried about tonight and how much I need the support, and this is what you do?'

'Hi, Maya.'

'The band were about to start. Everyone was listening. You get in a fight with the bassist? Are you drunk?'

'I meant it. I've been trying to say it for ages. It just came out at the wrong moment—'

'The wrong *moment*? You just humiliated me in front of my new boyfriend, right before the biggest opportunity of my performing life. Are you trying to destroy me?'

'Of course not!' Alfie hauled himself up. His ribs were hurting. 'I just . . . couldn't hold it in any longer.'

Maya's fists were clenched.

'I should have kissed you!' continued Alfie. 'On the sofa. Before you went to Greece. It's the biggest regret of my life. None of this would have happened.'

Maya's mouth hung open in shock.

'We could have got together! It could have all been different!'

'Oh my *God*!' said Maya.

'You know it's true!'

'You totally friendzoned me! I was beating myself up on the plane! Double rejection in twenty-four hours! I was like, *Forget all about it, you're being oversensitive, he's your best friend, what the hell were you thinking, pretend it never happened.* I thought it was one of those embarrassing moments that we never ever mention ever again.'

'It was the most stupid thing I ever did in my life! I froze *because* I like you!'

Maya tried to respond but she couldn't. She just screamed, at the top of her voice, wild, frustrated, the noise swallowed up by the vast night sky. She walked away from Alfie, facing the darkness of Epping Forest.

'I discovered something,' said Alfie. 'Luke *is* a player. He dumped Lyra for you. He'll dump *you* for someone else. The whole taking-the-credit-for-the-song thing. Big red flag. He's a user. He'll tell you sweet words but he's not what you think he is.'

'You've been talking to Lyra?'

'Yeah!'

'She's bitter and twisted. She's not over him. You don't know anything about her. You shouldn't take her seriously.'

'Oh yeah, is that what Luke said?'

'Yes, actually . . . She's the least of my worries.'

'What's the most of your worries?'

'Take a wild guess!'

Alfie went up to her, put his hand on her shoulder and turned her towards him.

'Why do you keep rubbing my hand?' he said.

'What?'

'When you're upset and I say something nice, you rub my hand.'

'Cos I'm grateful! I'm an affectionate person!'

'Why did you ask me if I was weird about Luke?' said Alfie.

'You *were* weird. That day in the lunch hall.'

'I was weird for a reason!'

'I didn't know that, did I? You friendzoned me, Alfie! I cut my losses and moved on.'

'You always spend more time with me than you do with your actual boyfriends.'

'I spend more time with you cos we're really good friends. My best friend.'

Maya folded her arms, shivering.

'You spend more time with me cos there's something going on. Something more than friendship.'

'This is crazy, Alfie!'

'Are you really telling me you don't feel anything?'

Maya stared at him. She tried to speak but nothing came out.

'I dare you to tell me you don't feel anything,' said Alfie.

Her face was shadowy and grey, almost ghostly, translucent, beautiful . . .

'Don't,' she said.

'What?'

'Your eyes.'

'What about my eyes?'

'Don't look at me like that!'

'You're feeling it, aren't you. You *do* like me!'

Alfie leaned forwards, moving into kiss her . . .

'Alfie! No!' Maya took a step back. 'I am in a relationship with Luke. I'm really into him. I believe him when he says he's into me. It's creative, it's exciting! I think this could actually be a really special thing!'

Alfie shook his head slowly.

'Did you really think that I would say, *Of course, Alfie. I'll just dump my boyfriend and run into your arms!* How self-centred can you get? If there *was* a moment for us, it's gone! And even if it hadn't, we probably wouldn't have lasted, cos Luke is everything I ever dreamed of in a boyfriend! And you are not! You come up way fucking short! Sorry, but it's true!'

'Are you talking about my height?' said Alfie.

'I'm talking about everything!'

Alfie felt winded, like she'd punched him in the stomach. He searched for a reply, something to counter her, something to assert himself. Nothing came. Maya put her palm over her mouth, her eyes stricken, as if she was realising the severity of what she'd said. They faced each other for what seemed like an age.

'Alfie, sorry.'

'It's fine.'

'That was really harsh.'

'It's fine.'

'I didn't mean to—'

'If that's really how you feel, then we can't be friends any more,' croaked Alfie. 'I can't see you. At all. It's too painful. Just pretend that we're two people in the same friendship group who don't get on but are just polite to each other. OK?'

Maya nodded, then let out a sob. Alfie cried too, breathing deeply, desperately trying to be quiet, hoping that the darkness would hide his heaving chest and wobbling shoulders.

Something whistled through the air and Alfie's hoodie landed on his head, covering his face. In spite of it all, they laughed.

'It's all calmed down. The gig's started,' said Jack.

'Argh!' said Maya. 'Gotta go.'

Alfie looked up at Maya pleadingly.

'I've got to go!' she said. 'Bye, Alfie.'

She hurried off across the field, lifting her dress so it didn't get muddy. Alfie put on his hoodie.

'Bye, Maya,' he said, miserable and quiet.

'Dude!' said Jack. 'It *was* about her. Why didn't you tell me?'

Alfie just walked.

'Where are you going?' said Jack.

'Home.'

'You're walking into Epping Forest!'

'I don't care!'

'We need to talk about this!'

'No, we don't!'

'Yes, we do! Stay here!'

'If I'm not at school on Monday ... tell everyone ... I got eaten by zombies!' said Alfie, disappearing into the gloom.

Gwen

11

'How much?' said Nan.

'I dunno. Twenty?'

'Twenty!'

'Yeah.'

'For *lunch*?'

'It's at Lit Chick!'

'What's Lit Chick?'

'The free-range chicken place.'

'Twenty quid for a piece of free-range chicken! What's so special about free-range chicken?'

'It has a happy life.'

'A happy life? Does it live in a palace? With servants? A live-in chef to feed it grain? Does it sleep on silk sheets?' Nan shook her head.

'Twenty will cover me. With a drink. Maybe dessert. So I don't have to scrounge, like I always do, which I hate. Plus, the chicken is amazing.'

'You can buy a full English breakfast with tea in Café Delish for nine pounds fifty.'

'We're not going to Café Delish.'

'Do you know how much a chicken breast is in Sainsbury's?'

Alfie shrugged.

'You could buy twelve chicken breasts, frozen chips and feed all your mates for under twenty quid!'

'Do you really think I want to cook chicken for all my mates?'

'No! I'd end up doing it! Muggins, here! Slaving over the cooker! While you lot lounge on the sofa!'

'No one is asking you to cook chicken, Nan!'

Nan was sprawled on the sofa, her hair poking out from underneath a Nike baseball cap, pink hoodie, pink slippers, her reading glasses perched on the end of her nose. She was watching the World Snooker championship on TV.

'Everyone is going to be there. I was only invited just now. You're the one who's been having a go at me for staying in.'

Nan's attention drifted back to the snooker. A black ball rolled slowly across the baize and just when it looked like it was going to stop, it somehow inched forward and plopped into a pocket. The player, a baby-faced bald man, punched the air and Nan murmured in approval. Any sport that was on the TV, she could get into it. Even the weird, obscure Olympic ones.

'Fine, I won't go!' said Alfie.

'Great. You can clean your room. It's starting to smell.'

Alfie went into his room. She was right. He couldn't remember the last time he had changed his sheets and the floor was covered with dirty clothes. He should tidy, open the window, put on a wash. Instead, he picked up his phone and reread the conversation.

Hey. Some of us are going Lit Chick!
Wanna come?

ALFIE:

Who's this?

88

GWEN:

Gwen

ALFIE:

I thought I had your number

GWEN:

Changed my phone a year ago

ALFIE:

Has it been that long?

GWEN:

ALFIE:

I'm skint

GWEN:

You always say that

ALFIE:

It's true

GWEN:

Everyone's gonna be there

ALFIE:

When was this decided?

GWEN:

Ten minutes ago

ALFIE:

Why hasn't Jack told me?

GWEN:

Probably cos Maya's gonna be there.

Does that bother you?

ALFIE:

I guess . . . if we're in a
group . . . it's OK

GWEN:

Good. You need to stop being a recluse.

We all wanna see you

ALFIE:

Thanks

GWEN:

So?

Alfie?

Fine

Up to you

Whatever

But I think you should come x

It was weird, Gwen messaging him. She never messaged him, ever. *Someone* had to invite him. She was probably just being polite. But Gwen was pretty shy. Sending that message was probably a big thing for her. And Alfie liked the *I think you should come*-plus-kiss. It felt kind, made him feel fuzzy, like she wanted him to be there. And she was right, he had been a recluse. He hadn't been out for almost three weeks. It was nearly half term. Should he go with no cash and annoy everyone by scrounging?

'Alfie?' Nan was standing in his doorway. 'There is *one* way for you to get money.' She sniffed the air, wrinkled her nose.

'What?'

'She sent me another email. She said you hadn't replied.'

Alfie sat up. His pulse quickened. 'Serious?'

'Yes.'

'When was this?'

'A few days ago! I wish you would.'

'What?'

'Reply.'

'I tried to, but I got too angry, so I didn't.'

He got up from his bed and opened the window. He picked up boxers, T-shirts, tracksuit bottoms, socks, until his arms were full.

'She's offering me money,' said Nan.

'You what?'

'A contribution. For childcare.'

Alfie pushed past Nan and shoved his clothes into the washing machine. 'Does she think that's gonna make everything OK?'

'I don't think so.'

'What's she trying to achieve, then?'

'This is why I didn't tell you, because I knew you'd be like this.'

Nan turned around and walked back into the living room. Alfie followed.

'I'm damned if I do, damned if I don't. Saying nothing does my head in. Tell you, and you bite my head off.'

'So what, is she rich now?'

'I'll show you the email—'

'No!'

Alfie closed the washing machine and set it to do a forty-degree wash. He poured powder into the dispenser.

'The money would be for you,' continued Nan.

'So you two been chatting behind my back?'

'She *is* my daughter!' Nan stood up. 'It's easy to reject your parents. Not so easy your kid!'

Alfie pressed *start* on the machine. Water poured into the drum, roaring and gurgling.

'Me and you have been through a lot together. And believe it or not, I respect what you want.'

'She doesn't deserve us,' said Alfie. 'Promise me from now on you won't reply to her, meet her, or give her the time of day?'

'Alfie—'

'Promise me!' He went into Nan's room and picked up the lead. 'If I can't hang out with my human friends, then I'll hang out with my animal friend.'

Bailey scampered over, wagging her tail.

'Why don't *you* get a job, then?' said Nan.

Bailey barked three times, enthusiastically.

'Nothing wrong with having one at your age.'

Alfie sat on the sofa. 'How?'

'Apply.'

'Where?'

'What about Maya?'

'No. Not Café Delish. *No.*'

'What about a paper round? At Super Save?'

'Child slavery. Jack worked for them when we were twelve. It would take me a whole month to pay for one Lit Chick! Plus no one buys papers any more.'

'What about Brent Cross?'

Alfie felt his cheeks heat up. He pictured the shiny marble floors, neon-lit promenade and endless glass shopfronts.

'Ah, man,' he said, rubbing his face.

'What?'

'I don't know how to work in a shop.'

'They'd train you.'

'They'd laugh at me.'

'They'd be lucky to have you.'

'What about my school? You're always telling me I have to do well in school, now you're telling me that I have to get a job, which means I won't be able to do my homework?'

Nan raised her eyebrows. 'No one said that life was supposed to be easy.'

Bailey barked again. Nan stood up, walked in to her room and came out with her handbag. Alfie watched as she opened her wallet and took out a crisp twenty-pound note.

'I'll do you a deal . . . I'll give you this today . . . if you promise to get a job. At the weekends.'

'Yes! Promise!' said Alfie.

She pulled the note back, out of Alfie's reach.

'I promise!' wailed Alfie.

Bailey whined urgently.

'You've got her in a tizz!' said Nan. 'I'm gonna have to walk her and miss the rest of this match!'

'Sorry,' said Alfie.

She handed him the note. 'Bugger off and eat your expensive chicken!'

'Thank you. And sorry. Again.'

Nan kicked off her slippers, walked into the hall and picked up her trainers. She paused, looking at Alfie, her eyes becoming sad.

'She is insistent,' she said. 'She'll keep emailing until she gets a response. I know she will.'

'I'm insistent too,' said Alfie. 'Insistent that she can piss off.'

12

No restaurant came close to Lit Chick. So much chicken, it barely fitted on their table! Crispy wings and legs piled high in cartons. Big double chicken burgers with hash browns and onion rings. Chicken breasts covered in criss-cross marks from the grill, drenched in luminous dipping sauces with names like Ching Ching!, Badaam! and KaBoom! No one knew what was in them, only that they tasted good (apart from KaBoom!, which was the crazy hot one that you never ordered). They didn't even bother to serve it on plates, they used wooden boards with rolls of paper towels, because they knew it was gonna get messy.

And the fries. Cooked with a secret spicy recipe. They piled them high, more generous than Nando's or McDonald's or anywhere else. They had nine large cups of them, nine mountains of curly, crispy, orange potato. Nan would never understand!

They all sat, stuffing their faces, Lily on Jack's lap, feeding chips to him like she was a mama bird and he was her needy chick. Next to them sat two friends from Lily's swimming club, and opposite, Ovi and Yaniv, both in the year above.

Ovi was handsome in a different way to Luke: high cheekbones and hollow cheeks, thick eyebrows, a moody frown. He looked serious and sober – until you actually talked to him and realised he was a clown – a womanising clown. He wore a white T-shirt with a plunging V-neck, his curly black hair spilling onto his shoulders. Maya was sitting at the opposite end of the table, overdressed and beautiful in a bustling black dress, her lips glossy. It was the first time she'd seen Ovi since they'd split; Ovi kept staring and Alfie could feel the tension. Samira sat next to her, in a grey Nike tracksuit, long coiled hair flowing around her face, and Gwen next to her, in a baggy Hello Kitty hoodie, rosy-cheeked, with scraggly shag hair. Alfie squeezed in and she gave him a flicker of a smile.

Alfie had arrived, sick with nerves, expecting them to laugh at him. But no one mentioned Luke's gig. People treated him like a normal person, and even Maya said hello, briefly, before launching into her famous story about Café Delish getting robbed by two teenagers in balaclavas, her dad chasing them down the street with a frying pan. She acted it out, holding court, doing the voices – *I'll shank you, bruv!* – making it sound like a scene from *Top Boy*. Lily's friends made everyone laugh with stories about their sadistic swimming teacher. Alfie got inspired and poured some Kaboom! into a saucer, soaked some chips in the orangey-red liquid and dared everyone to see how many they could eat. Gwen and Samira managed one before giggling and turning bright red. Jack and Yaniv managed two before going silent, Ovi did three and kept slapping the table. Alfie won, eating five whole chips, keeping a straight face and getting a round of applause. Now, post-meal, everyone was satiated, phones had come out and the table was quiet. Alfie'd been enjoying himself. He even felt . . . happy.

'So . . .' said Ovi, rubbing his hands together. 'I'm taking things to the next level.' He made sure everyone was looking at him. 'Halloween party. Fancy dress.'

'Ooooh!' said Lily.

Ovi stretched his arms across the backs of the adjacent chairs, his legs splayed open, always acting the playboy.

'But you better make an effort. No costume? No entry.'

Lily smiled to herself. 'Is Alfie invited?' she said.

'Of course. You all are.'

Lily held Alfie's gaze. 'You have to be careful,' she said. 'He might do something crazy and inappropriate.'

Ovi frowned. Jack squeezed Lily's arm.

'What? It's public knowledge? We were all there!' She circled her shoulder, breaking his grip, pushing Jack away. Lily was so annoying! She had zero sensitivity about anything. And Jack just sat there and let her do it.

'All where?' said Ovi.

'The last party we went to, Alfie declared his love for Maya and started a fight with her boyfriend—'

'Leave it, Lily,' said Alfie.

'And then she rejected him, so he stormed off into Epping Forest.'

'I'm so confused,' said Ovi.

'He turned his phone off! Maya thought he was gonna get murdered! And Alfie's like, I'm just walking into this deep dark wood all by myself, see you later, bye, guys!'

Jack poked Lily in the ribs.

'Declared love for Maya?' said Ovi. 'Got in a fight with *who?*' He raised one eyebrow quizzically.

'Alfie told Maya he *lurrrrved* her in front of her boyfriend. Then he slagged off her boyfriend to his face, in front of the whole audience, who were there to see his band play – if you're gonna do a really big romantic gesture, that was the dumbest possible way to do it. My mind boggles!'

'This sounds ... epic ...' said Ovi.

'Shut up, Lily,' said Gwen.

'Yeah, Lily, that's enough!' said Maya.

There was a tense silence. Jack looked down at the table. Samira glanced between Alfie and Maya, enjoying the drama.

'Technically it was her boyfriend's mate who started a fight,' said Alfie.

'Yup!' said Lily. 'We all need a drunk best mate who'll start fights on our behalf ...'

One of Lily's friends giggled. Gwen gave Alfie a sympathetic look.

'You seem OK about things,' said Ovi to Alfie.

Alfie glanced at Maya, who nodded at him. 'It's all good,' he said, as if to say *end of story*.

'All good, eh?' said Ovi.

'I'm also dead. The zombies got me. I no longer have emotions. Braaiiiinnns!'

The others laughed.

Alfie folded his arms. 'I definitely didn't just walk to the nearest road and take the first night bus that came along.'

'Who's this *Maya's boyfriend* person?' said Ovi, clearly trying to sound like it was just a fun piece of gossip that he didn't really care about.

'He's in a band. Twisted Dreamland. He's beautiful and talented and they're totally amazing,' said Lily. She picked up her phone. 'Maya is kind of like an unofficial member. She sung a song with him. I filmed it. Best. Gig. Ever.'

'Really?' said Ovi.

'Yup!' said Gwen.

'We can say we knew them before they were famous,' said Jack.

'Maya and Luke are gonna be on magazine covers,' said Lily.

'Guys!' said Maya. 'You're embarrassing me! Chill out!'

Great. So Jack only piped up when it was all about Luke. Maybe they were gonna have a bromance. Jack would get a job as the Twisted Dreamland roadie.

Lily pressed play and handed Ovi the phone. They all sat and listened. The riff was catchy. The band were tight. Damn! Maybe they would be famous! Ovi was staring, his cheeks flushed.

Alfie zoned out. He'd had enough. The whole exchange had killed it. It was fun, and now it wasn't. He didn't come here to get roasted. Everyone else had moved on. Why hadn't Lily? When the song finished, Alfie got up, grabbed his coat, said his goodbyes, and left.

13

Alfie hurried down the escalator to the ground floor. He stopped, blinking up at the big glass dome as people crisscrossed around him: three muscled men with shaved heads, an Asian dad holding his young son's hand, some older women in hijabs. He drifted along the grey marble concourse, past the open-fronted shops lit with blinding white neon – an electric car showroom, a clothes shop, a jewellery store – meandering around the concessions – halva, raisins, nuts, mobile phone repairs, massage machines – and sat down on a posh grey sofa surrounded by plastic plants. He stared at the chandelier above – a glittering silver ring with dangling diamante strings – and wondered what to do.

Coffee Boss was close: the popular café chain built into the walkway. There wasn't much of a queue. He stuck his hand in his pocket – he still had a few quid left – so he got up and ordered a caramel latte from a harassed woman with pink hair and a few minutes later a broad-shouldered boy handed him his drink. All the tables were taken, so Alfie sat at the breakfast bar near the till, drinking fast, with long milky slurps. He liked it in here, the lowered parquet floor, the gleaming industrial coffee machine, big letters spelling COFFEE BOSS in lightbulbs above the bar. His stomach felt heavy, full of chicken and chips, but the caffeine and sugar kicked in, and he started to feel better.

'Hey!'

Alfie jumped.

Gwen stood there, alone, smiling, face bright pink, clutching a drink.

'Hey!' said Alfie.

'I'm sorry,' she said. She was holding a caramel latte, like him.

'About what?'

'That.'

Gwen tilted her head backwards towards Lit Chick.

'It's OK,' said Alfie.

'No, it's not.'

Alfie nodded to the stool next to him. In a rushed, awkward move, Gwen sat down, almost spilling her drink.

'Thanks for sticking up for me,' he said.

'Lily was out of order.'

'It's OK.'

'You did a great job of covering. You made everyone laugh. You didn't even look upset. I would have melted onto the floor. But then you left and I knew you must be pissed off.'

'I'm fine, honestly.'

'Then why did you leave?'

Alfie sighed. Gwen's face was bright red.

'It's my fault!' she said. 'I invited you out ... and you're like, *I come out and get this? Maya, in my face. Maya's ex, in my face. Abuse from Lily.*'

'It's fine. I mean ... Everyone *did* see it. They're gonna gossip about it in private. They might as well do it in front of me.'

'We haven't forgotten you, you know. Maya wanted to invite you, but she was like, *He's told me I can't be his friend any more plus he's doing his thing of locking himself in his flat, so ...* Are you sure it's not too raw?'

'I see her at school every day.'

'You don't really speak. You eat your lunch and shuffle off. Like a zombie. Maybe you *did* die in Epping Forest!'

Alfie laughed. The steam wand squealed and hissed, frothing up some milk.

'I'm not gonna lie. After Luke's ... I wasn't exactly Mr Happy. I mean, she did brutally reject me.' He paused as the barista banged the milk jug hard on the bar. 'But, in a way, it was kind of a good night? Cos I found out, one hundred per cent, once and for all, that nothing was gonna happen.'

Gwen nodded.

'I mean ... did she say anything to you?' he asked.

'About what?'

'Me and her ... Before she went on holiday ... we almost kissed ...'

Gwen nodded.

'She might have messaged me. On the way to the airport. She felt knocked back. And embarrassed. But then she met Luke so quickly ...'

Alfie nodded. 'I'm actually more pissed off at myself. For confusing friendship with more. I can see that now. In the cold light of day. Luke is such a good fit. Of course she's gonna choose a rock star over me. And Maya was pretty much the only person I saw this summer ... I guess I thought she was the only girl in the world. It gave me a warped perspective.'

Gwen laughed.

'Plus, I'm skint! I hate scrounging! It might look like I don't go out cause of Maya, but that's a reason too. It was a proper battle to even get the money for Lit Chick. I had to promise my nan I'd get a job.'

'Aaah.'

'I'm really glad you invited me! It was actually really easy. It's just Lily who's a dick.'

'Are you sure you're not in denial?'

'No way! Being humiliated like that was a gift. I'm really happy it happened.'

Gwen frowned.

'Ovi's the one who hasn't moved on!' continued Alfie. 'Did you see his face? He treats her like he doesn't care about her then gets really jealous when she finds someone else. His cheeks went all red. He nearly exploded watching that video.'

Gwen giggled, and took a long slurp of her drink. She wiggled her cup, sloshing the golden liquid. A toddler screamed. An old man coughed behind them. Some young teens were arguing about something.

'It's too loud,' said Alfie. 'You going Brent Estate?'

Gwen nodded.

'I'll come with you.'

They stepped out of the side exit. In front of them were rows and rows of parked cars, then six lanes of motorway, some trees, then Alfie's tower block rising behind them. Gwen led them along the narrow pavement that lined the shopping centre, past the fairground and up the winding footbridge, the North Circular traffic zooming and rumbling below them.

She stopped, put both her hands on the rail, and turned to him with a lurch. 'I just wanna say ... none of us think the worst of you. Maya still performed her song. It was great. No need to feel embarrassed or ashamed.'

'OK. Thanks. I don't.'

They walked on, to the end of the bridge and down the

spiral path to the ground. They jogged along a patch of road which had no pavement, wing mirrors whizzing by, and into a quiet lane, past his old primary school, a collection of temporary portacabin classrooms, before stopping outside Alfie's block.

'Sorry!' said Gwen. 'I'm not trying to open old wounds, I just wanna say . . . Don't take Lily seriously, OK? Don't let it get you down. Or knock your confidence. You're a *gorgeous, gorgeous* person. You're *fun* and *funny* and you're a catch!'

She said the last two sentences so emphatically, that Alfie's stomach tingled.

'I just wanted to tell you that,' said Gwen, her cheeks reddening.

Alfie shifted from foot to foot. 'Thank you. And thank you for sticking your neck out to be nice to me.'

'It's OK.'

'I really, really, appreciate it.'

'Sometimes things just need to be said.' Gwen smiled. She held up her cup.

Alfie chinked his against hers. 'Snap.'

'Caramel latte twins!' She slurped the remains of her drink.

'Maya is a big personality . . . she takes over *everything* . . . it's actually nice to talk to *you* for once,' said Alfie.

Gwen's face was still red. 'It's nice to talk to you, too.'

'See you soon, yeah?' said Alfie.

'Hope so,' said Gwen.

She turned and walked towards her flat, stopping briefly to turn, smile and wave.

14

The week after Gwen found Alfie in Coffee Boss, he noticed her everywhere.

As usual, she and Maya were inseparable, Gwen talking energetically into Maya's ear, resting her head on her shoulder, walking so close it was like their arms were attached with Velcro. Alfie watched them run across the playing fields, singing a song, before breaking into a dance routine, arms up, legs kicking, screeching and laughing.

They'd started this weird thing of saying, 'Hi Alfie!' in a girly sing-song way, patting the seats next to them and giggling when Alfie sat down, which was kind of affectionate, but also made Alfie feel shut out. But then, one afternoon, Gwen was chatting to Samira, Samira placing her hand on her shoulder, watching a video on Gwen's phone. Gwen looked up at him, smiled, blushed, then looked back to the screen. She was shy with *him* ... but if you were her friend, if she felt safe, she was tactile, louder, she opened up. Alfie felt jealous. He wanted Gwen to open up with him.

One day at lunch, Alfie did an impersonation of Nan. Gwen laughed loudly and abruptly. Everyone looked at her and she slammed her palm across her mouth. Another time, he was sitting on a bench by the Astroturf, watching some Year Sevens play football. Alfie found himself pacing up and down, shouting, *'Man on! Into him! Time!'* and *'Shoot!'* like he was their manager. He looked up to see Gwen on the other side of the pitch, head cocked, looking at him, smiling. Then Maya called her name and she turned and scampered off.

On the Friday before half term, Gwen arrived at lunch with Samira, and Alfie found himself butting in, sitting next to Gwen. They both stared at their fish fingers and chips, too nervous to eat, until Alfie poked a chip with his fork, dipped it in ketchup, put it to his mouth, then dropped it down his shirt, which made Gwen laugh, which made him laugh, which made him say it's half term, which meant it was nearly November when the Jōnetsu gig was, and Gwen said they should get to Brighton early, maybe do some sightseeing, go on the Pier, it was gonna be this amazing day, the best day ever, talking in her low, shy voice as if the school leadership team had bugged their table and was listening in.

He *liked* spending time with her, he realised. He *wanted* to spend time with her. And she wanted to spend time with him. He could feel it. Even that day on the tube when he was feeling uncomfortable about going to Luke's ... she'd smiled at him. As if to say, *I see you, Alfie!* She stuck up for him in Lit Chick and praised him after Coffee Boss. No girl had ever said he was gorgeous before. No girl had ever said he was a catch before. She said it like she meant it. No girl praised him like that, ever. Apart from Nan. And she didn't count.

It was like she'd been covered by this dense grey fog and the conversation in Coffee Boss blew it all away. Now he could *see* – her fierce green eyes, her brown shag hair scrunched back into a tiny ponytail. Her full lips. She was beautiful! She was! She had no idea!

It struck him, in the hall, as they ate their fish fingers. What if he'd been into the wrong girl? What if the right one was under his nose, all along? Damn! He felt something! For Gwen!

106

Maya arrived late, interrupting, taking over, telling everyone that she'd been added to two other Twisted Dreamland songs, that Luke had given her a last-minute invite to guest-play a gig with him in Clacton, but her dad said she couldn't go because she had to work and they'd had such a big argument about it. Why did he think everything artistic was lame and stupid, when it was all she wanted to do with her life? If this went well, Luke might let her join the band! Officially! Contracts, everything! By the end of it she had gone out of the lunch hall, locked herself in the toilet, and booked her train ticket on her phone.

But Alfie didn't care. He was blissfully detached. He stayed buzzing until the end of the day. That night, before he went to sleep, he pictured himself and Gwen at the Jōnetsu gig, their fingers gripping the top of the metal barriers, within spittle-distance of Joey Silveira, the heaving crowd behind them. Gwen's fingers inched along the railing, she turned her head towards him, her lips rising to meet his . . .

When he woke up he knew he had to do something. It was the first day of half term. No way was he making the same mistake again. Dreaming. Hoping. Holding off. Sitting on his arse.

After lunch, he took Bailey for a walk. It was a misty cold day, a flat blanket of cloud covering the sky, and players were arriving at the Brent playing fields pitches. He skirted round the edges, Bailey straining at the lead, stopping when he reached the new-build flats on the far side. He took out his phone, his legs trembling, and messaged Gwen.

ALFIE:

Hey what u up to?

He stood there for two, long, painful minutes, then jumped when she pinged a reply.

GWEN:

Watching my brother
scream at my mum

ALFIE:

Why?

GWEN:

Because he's a dick

ALFIE:

OK

GWEN:

He's 4 but he's still a dick

ALFIE:

I'm taking Bailey out for a
walk
Wanna come?

GWEN:

Why?

ALFIE:

Because I thought you liked
dogs?

GWEN:

OMG I thought Bailey was your ill
great grandfather in a wheelchair or
something

ALFIE:

No.

GWEN:

OK

ALFIE:

Do you wanna come?

GWEN:

Is it just you?

ALFIE:

Yeah

GWEN:

I can't

ALFIE:

Why?

GWEN:

Um . . .

Alfie's guts twisted.

ALFIE:

I think we'll have fun

GWEN:

Do you?

ALFIE:

I really want to get to know
you better

GWEN:

😮

ALFIE:

What?

GWEN:

I shouldn't

ALFIE:

Why?

GWEN:

I can't

Sorry

ALFIE:

Really?

GWEN:

Yeah

ALFIE:

What if I told you I'm
outside your flat?

GWEN:

OMG
Serious?

ALFIE:

Yeah
And I won't leave until you
come out and play

15

'What the hell are you doing?' said Gwen.

It took a moment to spot her. She was hunched over a first floor balcony, her hands clasping the bright pink towel that was hung over the rail to dry. Stacked garden chairs blocked her to her right, a black mesh satellite dish to her left, its stick-like feed-horn practically poking her in the ear. Her balcony was almost as cluttered as Alfie's.

'Come and walk Bailey.'

'Look at me.'

She was wearing a black ADIDAS tracksuit.

'You look hot!'

Embarrassed at his boldness, Alfie bent down and stroked Bailey. When she didn't reply, he lifted up the dog, taking care to keep her stomach parallel with the ground – as Nan had taught him, as you had to do with all sausage dogs to avoid hurting them – and waggled her paw, making her wave at Gwen.

'I really want to hang out with you,' said Alfie in a stupid voice.

Gwen laughed.

'It's her fault,' said Alfie. 'She made me invite you.'

On cue, Bailey barked, making her laugh again.

'You're such a weirdo!' she said.

Two young children joined her on the balcony, a girl clutching a teddy bear and a taller boy holding a giant water pistol, a big smile on his pudgy face, casting around for his next victim.

'Go away!' Gwen shouted.

The boy squirted her.

'Oi!' she cried.

Both kids ran inside, Gwen chasing after them. Alfie waited. Her flat was only a few years old, the bright yellow bricks clean and unweathered, the window frames still shiny, in contrast to Alfie's shabby, scaffold-covered, uncompleted tower. He messaged her.

ALFIE:

I'm still here

No reply. He watched the players warm up. There seemed to be one from every corner of the world, European, Asian, African, Latin Americans, Middle Eastern, he even heard a North American accent. They were a mixture of muscled gym boys, athletic twenty-somethings, and lanky teenagers. They gathered round the edges of the pitches, changing into their kits, some of them talking and gossiping, some of them stretching and jumping. He thought he saw Raheem in the distance. Of course! He'd dumped the school team. The standard wasn't high enough. He'd had trials for Watford and AFC Wimbledon. He didn't want to be a big fish in a small pond. He could play with the grown-ups. A bit of Alfie felt excited for him. And jealous. Soon the air would be full of their urgent bellowing, the thump of boot meeting ball, the decisive peeps of the referee's whistle. He messaged again.

ALFIE:

Hello?

No reply. A branch cracked, a squirrel leaped and Bailey sprinted. Alfie yanked the lead, pulling the dog back.

'Hey.'

Alfie yelped. Gwen was behind him.

'Why do you always sneak up on me?' he said.

'You literally screamed like a girl.'

Bailey stopped, turned, and trotted up to Gwen, tail wagging. She took a step back.

'She's really nice,' said Alfie.

Bailey barked. Gwen took another step back.

'She's the shape of a sausage. The least dangerous dog ever.'

Gwen turned red. 'We're out of milk,' she said. She held up a Visa debit card. 'Come with?'

'You want me to come with you to buy milk?'

'Yeah.'

Alfie eyed the card. 'That yours?'

'Mum's.'

Alfie's eyes widened. 'Shall we go to Lit Chick?'

'No!'

'Shall we buy plane tickets and run away to America?'

'Shut up!'

'So that's how we're gonna hang out: a trip to the shops to get milk?'

Gwen shrugged.

'I guess beggars can't be choosers,' said Alfie.

Gwen nodded to the opposite end of the fields, where the Super Save was. They set off, Bailey perking up, leading the way, Gwen and Alfie side by side. They skirted round the pitches, past one man stripped to his boxers, changing into his kit. Alfie tried to catch Gwen's eye, to see if she'd seen him, to make her laugh, but she stuck her hands in her pockets and looked at the grass. It was muddy and churned-up, full of stud-holes. All the crows, normally spread across the whole green expanse, had been forced to gather underneath the one small tree, hopping up and down, stretching their wings and cawing, looking resentful, as if they were holding a sinister meeting.

'The footballers stole their field. I think they're plotting revenge,' said Alfie, as they crossed the road.

But Gwen didn't smile at his joke. She hurried on to Super Save, disappearing inside while Alfie waited by some dilapidated shelves that once held newspapers but now housed some cheap-looking dustpans and brushes. The windows were covered with peeling signage, enormous posters of freshly baked sourdough (as if they sold that), carrots with luscious green tops (they didn't even stock fresh veg), the English words all misspelled, and badly translated: *Off Lisence, News agent* (two separate words, like a James Bond of news), *Health Lottery*. What was a *Health Lottery*? Drinking their milk and seeing if you would survive? Seriously, what was the point of this shop? What was Nan on about, getting a job here? He had so many jokes, but it was so tense with Gwen that he couldn't say any of them.

'Why did you come out if you didn't want to see me?' he said, when she exited holding a carton of milk.

'I did want to see you.'

'I'm so confused. You said you couldn't come out. Then you came. You invited me to buy milk. But now you're acting like you don't want me to be here.'

'I'm sorry!'

'I thought it would be fun!'

'It is fun!'

'It's the opposite of fun! Go home and drink your milk!'

Gwen crossed the road. She stopped, swivelled, and walked back to Alfie. She folded her arms and rocked on her feet, staring at her trainers, white scuffed ADIDAS, just like her tracksuit.

'Do you know the Exploratory?' she said.

'What's that?'

She led them to the end of the road, through a large metal gate and into a wide open space full of asphalt paths and neatly trimmed turf. In the middle stood a yellow helter-skelter, surrounded by a see-saw, a sandpit, climbing frame, a roundabout and some swings. The orange Holiday Inn tower loomed over the far side.

'I didn't know this was here,' said Alfie.

'It's practically your back garden,' said Gwen.

Despite it being Sunday there was hardly anyone there, just some grandparents with toddlers and a young mum playing chase with her twins, their shouts lost in the North Circular's ever-present roar.

'I don't think anyone else knows about it either,' said Alfie.

'It's only been here for a couple of years. When they finish the redevelopment they're going to knock it down.'

Gwen ran off, suddenly full of energy, scampering up the helter-skelter and sliding down the twisting yellow tunnel.

'Come play!' she cried.

Alfie took Bailey off the leash and followed her up the ladder, sliding down behind her. Up and down they went, Alfie chasing Gwen, both of them giggling, before Gwen jumped onto the roundabout, Alfie spinning her as fast as he could, Gwen screaming and begging him to stop. Alfie yanked the handles and when Gwen stepped off, she was so dizzy she fell onto the ground, smashing the milk carton on the asphalt. Now she was in hysterics, and Bailey was too, running rings around her, yapping.

Alfie held out his hands, she took them, he lifted her up, falling into him, holding herself there for a second too long, before running across to the see-saw. Alfie joined her and they had a competition: who could launch the other highest in the air, until Alfie banged his groin, and had to get off, clutching his crotch, groaning in pain.

Gwen stood there, watching him, her hand over her mouth, until Bailey licked Alfie's hands, which put her back in hysterics. He hauled himself to his feet, and hobbled to the swing.

'You castrated me!' he shouted as she sat down next to him.

'Who can go the highest!' she cried, giggling, swinging, legs out and in, out and in, and soon she was practically horizontal to the ground. Alfie followed, but no matter how hard he tried, he couldn't get as high, until Gwen leaped off, flying through the air, landing with a couple of steps and neatly bent legs. Alfie did the same, his trainers slapping down, steadying himself by placing his hands on Gwen's shoulders. She smiled at him.

'I'm tired,' she said.

She took his hand and led him up the ladder to the top of the helter-skelter, where they sat, backs the against sides, in their own private treehouse.

'I'm sorry I'm being weird,' said Gwen. Her fierce green eyes became lost in thought. 'I'm just going through a really tough time.'

'Wanna talk about it?' said Alfie.

'No thanks.'

'I'm a good listener.'

'Doesn't matter.'

Alfie touched her shoulder. 'Of course it matters.'

She pursed her lips and folded her arms.

'Is it awkward? Telling your parents you're hanging out with a boy? Is that why you needed an excuse?'

'Kind of.' She hugged her knees tight towards her chest. 'I'm just ... a bit of a stranger ... in my own family ... or something?'

Alfie frowned.

'My mum met this guy ... and then they got married ... and had my brother and sister, and now they're like, sickeningly happy ...'

'Isn't that a good thing?'

'Not for me! I'm the odd one out!'

Alfie folded his arms around his knees, mirroring her. 'Who did she marry?'

'This *guy*. He's a mechanic. He's really traditional ... he works and Mum does the childcare ... He's obsessed with his kids and acts like I don't exist.'

'Where's your actual dad?'

'Thailand.'

'Wow.'

'I hate him.'

Alfie nodded. Where the hell was his dad? London? Some other country? Dead? He didn't even know the slightest thing about him. Mum had just acted like he didn't exist. Hell, maybe *she* didn't know.

'My dad is a terrible person,' continued Gwen. 'He went to prison. I remind my mum of him or something. Like I'm a burden who gets in the way of her new happy family. Like I'm a stranger in my own flat.'

A tear ran down her cheek. Gwen wiped the tear with her wrist. 'Why are you making me talk about this?'

'I'm not making you talk about anything!'

'I know! It just comes out! How do you do that?'

Alfie blinked. People *did* seem to open up to him. He hadn't really noticed that before.

'I'm embarrassed! I've overshared!' said Gwen.

Gwen stretched out her legs, and Alfie did too, their thighs touching.

'If it's any consolation, I hate my mum too.'

'I know.'

Alfie scoffed. 'You know?'

Gwen nodded.

'How much has Maya told you about me?'

'Um. A lot.'

'That's not fair! She won't tell me *your* secrets!'

'What secrets?'

Gwen looked worried.

'You know . . . if you're stressed and you send her a message, she won't tell me what it is.'

'OK. Good!'

'And anyway,' continued Alfie, 'what's all this got to do with hanging out with me?'

'I dunno! I've never really been on a date before! I'm crap with the whole flirting thing!'

Alfie frowned, his head whirring. 'You seemed OK when Mikey was hitting on you at Luke's. Oh my God. Are you being funny cos you're actually going out with Mikey?'

Gwen looked at him incredulously. 'I do have *some* standards.'

'You looked pretty into him—'

'I might have kissed him, OK! I only did it to make him go away!'

'How does kissing him make him go away?'

'Listen! I'm not going out with him. *Eugh!* He's like a horny rhinoceros. It was a one-off! That I regret! Deeply. You're not the only person who did something embarrassing at Luke's.'

Alfie laughed. He could tell she meant it.

'I feel the same, you know,' he said.

'What? That Mikey's a rhino?'

'No! Feeling like a stranger.'

'But . . . your nan is really nice!'

'I don't mean at home. I mean . . . generally . . . in life.'

Alfie pulled his hood up. Now they'd stopped running around, he was chilly. Somewhere behind them a little girl shrieked and a truck horn blared.

'What you said in Coffee Boss . . . I didn't feel like a stranger then. You looked out for me. You had my back. I saw this whole new side of you . . .'

Gwen's cheeks went bright red.

'Maya isn't the only person you can talk to. Maybe there's other people . . . Maybe you can talk to me, too.'

Gwen put her hands in her lap and stared at her feet. 'Thanks,' she murmured.

'You are not some terrible person. You are beautiful! Inside and out!'

'Alfie!'

'You are!'

She rubbed her face with her hands.

'You have to believe it. You're so much more special than you realise. And if your mum can't see it, then she's dumb.'

'This is a bit intense,' said Gwen, staring into the distance. She let Alfie take her hand and their eyes met. 'Sorry! I appreciate it. I do.'

She smiled. Alfie smiled.

'I mean it,' he said. 'A beautiful person.'

Gwen looked at him shyly. She held his gaze. Impulsively, he leaned forward and kissed her. She let him, his tongue wiggling.

'You haven't done this much, have you?' said Gwen.

'Yes,' Alfie lied. 'Not really.'

Gwen raised her eyebrows.

'Just a few drunk things. Them, not me. God, that sounds so sad.'

'Slow down, OK?'

This time Gwen led, more gentle, and Alfie copied, wondering if anyone could see them, wondering when they were supposed to stop, but they didn't, it went on and on and on. Eventually Gwen pulled away.

'You're a fast learner,' she said, looking at him in the same way she'd done at the Astroturf. 'And you have beautiful eyes.'

'Excuse me,' said a squeaky voice, making both of them jump. A little girl, her frizzy blonde hair in braids, stood at the stop of the ladder. They separated, allowing her to squeeze past and go down the slide.

'Come on,' said Gwen, sliding down after her.

They walked in silence back to the shop, where Gwen bought more milk, then back across the playing fields, the football matches now in full swing. Alfie spotted Raheem and waved to him. Raheem waved back, staring at Gwen. Finally, when he reached her front door, Alfie could feel his heart thumping.

'First I got you to leave your flat. Now you got me to leave mine!' said Gwen.

'I guess that makes us even ... or something ..'

'Thanks for being persistent.'

Gwen took out her keys and opened the door.

'Aren't you forgetting something?' said Alfie.

Gwen sighed. She looked to the left, then to the right, then up to her balcony. Satisfied that no one was watching, she kissed him on the lips.

'That was fun,' said Alfie.

'Yeah,' she said. 'It was.'

When Alfie got home he lay on his bed, his head spinning, deliriously happy.

16

That night, Alfie watched TV with Nan.

'Stupid man,' she muttered as the Prime Minister made a speech, her whole body tensing, tightly gripping her tea. It was something about housing and the green belt and new flats, and millions of pounds, and whatever it was, it wasn't happening in London, but it would be bad for the environment, and the new houses were too expensive for people to afford.

'If he was standing there, I would kill him!' she said.

Alfie chuckled. 'Crazy grandma breaks into Downing Street and murders Prime Minister with tea mug.'

Nan laughed and changed the channel. 'I wouldn't use a tea mug. I'd strangle him with my own bare hands.'

'Are you actually a paid master assassin and you just never told me?'

'There's lots you don't know about me, Alfie. I was alive for a long time before you came along.'

'She seemed like such a nice woman. All she did was sit in Delish and drink cheap tea. I was shocked to learn she'd killed fifty politicians in the eighties.'

'Ha!'

Alfie put his arm around her and she rested her head on his shoulder.

'You're a good boy really,' she said.

They watched *Strictly Come Dancing*, arguing over who danced better, who was annoying, which judge talked sense and who talked rubbish. Nan kept disappearing to the kitchen and coming back with snacks: Jaffa cakes, small neatly-cut squares of home-made fruitcake, chocolate ice cream; it never stopped.

'Nan. Guess what? I think I've got a girlfriend,' said Alfie, as he stood up to go to bed.

'I knew it!' said Nan.

'Excuse me?'

'You've got a twinkle in your eye. Go on, then! Who is she?'

Alfie scratched his head. *Was* Gwen his girlfriend? At what point were they official? 'It's kind of early days ... It's going well, though.'

'Does she have a name?'

'Of course she does!'

Alfie hesitated. What if they weren't official? Was it a one-off? What if he said her name and it turned out to be nothing?

'She's not one of these virtual reality artificial intelligence girlfriends, is she?' said Nan.

'She's real! We've kissed!'

Nan held up her hands. 'I'm staying out of this.'

Sunday morning, when Nan was at Café Delish, he put on Jōnetsu, and his new favourite song, 'Twisted'.

Whenever I talk it comes out TWISTED
Whatever I do it comes out TWISTED
Me and you, it's always TWISTED!

He bounced around the living room in an imaginary mosh pit, surrounded by an imaginary crowd, then onstage, singing the song, he was the lead – but he couldn't concentrate, Gwen's face kept interrupting, dragging him back to the top of the helter-skelter, her eyelids slowly closing as her lips touched his. Afterwards, he collapsed onto his bed, grabbed his phone, opened his message app. Nothing. He sent Gwen a message.

ALFIE:

Hey

I really enjoyed yesterday

We should do it again

No use staring at his phone waiting for her to reply. Maybe he would reply to his mum instead. Maybe it would be easier if he wrote by hand. He took out his notebook and found a pencil. But his fingers were so tense he could barely write. What did she say? Whatever he felt, it was her responsibility? Why didn't he just write what he actually felt then? The lead touched the paper, words came, a kind of stream-of-consciousness poem:

Why you writing now?
When you weren't there to read me a story.
Why do you want to hang out?
When you couldn't even walk me to school.
Why do you want to see me?
When you couldn't give me a hug when I fell and grazed my
                                                                        knee.

Now I can go to school by myself.
And holding your hand would be embarrassing.
And I can make my own breakfast.
And I fall over and don't cry.
And do my own homework.

Why do you want to love me now?
When your job is basically over.

Jesus! A poem? When was the last time he'd done that? Year Six? Pathetic! He wasn't a poet! He flung the notebook across the room. The balcony door was open, and it flew into the air, ten storeys up, and seconds later he heard a *thunk*. He looked over the railing. The book was on the tarmac and a car alarm was blaring. He ran out of the door, into the lift, and out of the fire exit and grabbed it – the cover was off, the glue on the spine was loose, it was wet from a puddle, but it was still intact, just about, and he clutched it to his chest in relief.

He tapped his pockets. He'd forgotten his keys. He was locked out. He'd have to wait for Nan. He sent her a message. She replied straight away. She'd be back in an hour.

He was only wearing a T-shirt and tracksuit bottoms. He had to stay warm, he had to move, so he walked across the playing fields, the turf churned up from yesterday's matches, the crows back on their territory, hopping around proprietorially. He circled Gwen's flat a few times, but her balcony door was closed and the lights inside were off. He pictured her, lying on her back, laughing uncontrollably. The first time with him she'd really been herself. He checked his phone. No reply. Just an invitation from Jack to go shopping in Camden. When was the last time they'd done that? At least that was something. He couldn't sit outside Gwen's flat. That was stalkery. What was wrong with him? It was half term! Would he really have to wait seven whole days to see her again? Why hadn't she replied? ARGH!

*

Two days later, at Tuesday lunchtime, Alfie and Jack sat on the low stone wall by Camden Lock, underneath a large weeping willow, looking out across the canal to a sea of temporary canvas roofs, all housing multiple food concessions, humming and buzzing with activity. Jack was on a video call to Lily, removing a shoebox from a plastic shopping bag, opening it and pointing his camera at the shiny black boots inside. This was the fifth time they'd spoken – he'd called in every shop, getting her opinion on every single pair he'd tried. She was like the meanest *Strictly* judge, hating them all, apart from these, and now she was squealing with delight and telling Jack they would make him sexy.

'I'm starving!' said Jack when they hung up.

'Can't we get a sandwich at home?' said Alfie.

'Dude. We're in food heaven! Look! Chicken shawarma!'

Alfie shook his head.

'Pizza!'

'I don't have any money.'

'I'll pay.'

'No!'

'Dude, I don't care—'

'I'm sick of you paying for me.'

'Are you hungry?'

'No!'

'Don't lie!'

'I'm not!'

'Steak sandwich!'

Alfie shook his head.

'You know you want one,' said Jack, rising up to his full six-foot-three, and walking over the cast-iron bridge that crossed the canal. Alfie followed him into the crowded warren of stalls, full of young people, groups of two, three, four teens, clutching cardboard cartons of noodles, fish and chips, chicken curry and rice, the smell of warm salty food making Jack groan. He ordered two steak sandwiches from an Argentinian stall, the white-aproned chef slapping meat on the grill while salsa music played from a tinny Bluetooth speaker behind him.

'I'm gonna get a job,' said Alfie. 'Then I'll buy you lunch.'

'Where?'

'I dunno. Anywhere you want.'

'I meant, where you gonna get a job?'

'Somewhere.'

Then it hit him. Alfie knew exactly where he'd apply. He'd do it this week. He had to. But he didn't want to say unless he got rejected. And they probably wouldn't take him anyway. And it was stressful even thinking about it.

The baguettes looked delicious, thick steak slices, browned onions, mustard, mayonnaise. Alfie held his while Jack ate as he walked, dropping crumbs and sauce splodges onto the pavement. They reached the main road, where an old-school punk with an enormous Mohican and studded leather jacket was taking selfies with tourists for money.

'Dude! Eat!' said Jack, chewing.

'I will.'

'You've been moody all day.'

'No, I haven't.'

'You have! What's up?'

A maroon barge inched down the canal, its engine loud and chugging.

'I kissed Gwen.'

'What?'

'And I think I really like her.'

'What?'

Jack's mouth hung open in an *O*. A piece of chewed bread fell out and onto the pavement.

'Gwen?'

'Yeah.'

'As in our friend, Gwen?'

'Yeah!'

Jack's mouth opened wider. Alfie could see some unchewed steak on his tongue.

'When?'

'Saturday.'

'Gwen?'

'Why's this such a big surprise? I really like her!'

'Dude!'

'I know!

'Dude!'

'Yeah!'

'Finally!

'No. Not finally. She's ghosted me.'

'Has she?'

'We haven't spoken since. She won't reply to my messages.'

'Hold on a second. Back up.'

Alfie told the whole story, the weird date, the playground, the snogging up the helter-skelter.

'Has she read it?' said Jack.

'Read receipt says so.'

'Maybe she thought it was a one-off?'

'It didn't feel like a one-off!'

'Have you told her how you feel?'

'Not this again.'

'Dude—'

'I sent her that message.'

'How you *really* feel?'

Alfie groaned. Jack thought for a moment. 'Dude.'

'What?'

'Dude!'

'What?'

'I think I know why she hasn't replied!'

'Why?'

'Maya's her best friend. You're not allowed to date your best friend's ex. It's the rules!'

'But she said she was going through a difficult time at home.'

'Yes, but it also might be cover for the girly code of friendship.'

'That makes no sense! I'm not even Maya's ex!'

'You liked her once. That's enough. You're a marked man. My sisters go on about it.'

'Seriously?'

Jack stroked his beard. 'It's the way of the world, my friend.'

Alfie went pale. 'But what if we're meant to be? That would be too messed-up! That two people who are meant to be together can't get together because of some stupid random rule?'

Jack thought for a moment. 'OK. OK.' He puffed his cheeks and blew out. 'If you really think that you're meant to be together . . . you have to tell her, simple as that.'

'I'm sick of you and your *you have to tell her* nonsense.'

Jack's phone rang. It was Lily. Again. He had a low, whispered conversation, and hung up. 'Lily wants to see my boots.'

Every single time. Why couldn't he just say, *No, Lily, leave me alone. Just for two hours!* Was that too much to ask?

'No need to be like that,' said Jack.

'Like what?'

'Rolling your eyes! You never hang out when Lily's there … It annoys me.'

'*We* never hang out. That annoys me!'

'We are hanging out! Now!' Jack wiped his hand with a tissue. 'Alfie … Do you … like Lily?'

'Of course!'

'Sometimes I think … she might not be … your favourite person.'

'Dude! Of course I like her! She's amazing!'

'Really?'

'Hundred per cent. Apart from when she roasts me. Relentlessly. In front of everyone.'

'You're being over-sensitive. She doesn't mean anything bad.'

'Seriously? Cos anyone else would think she has a problem with me!'

'What? She likes you, dude!'

'Does she?'

'She does!' Jack's voice squeaked. He held out his arms. 'C'mon, man. This is silly. We shouldn't be fighting.' He hugged Alfie, slapping his back, then bent down and looked into Alfie's eyes. 'I just … really hope … No, I don't hope, I *pray*, I pray to *God!* That you will get to experience … just a little bit … of what I've experienced with Lily.'

'Please just fuck off now,' said Alfie.

Jack pursed his lips, nodded at Alfie, solemnly turned on his heels, and walked towards the station.

Alfie called Gwen. No answer. He called twice more. No answer. He walked along the main road, past a Ray-Ban shop, a KFC, a shop selling *I* ❤ *London* T-shirts, stopping by a pub. He decided to message her.

ALFIE:

What you up to?

Wanna hang out?

The message delivered and two blue ticks showed she'd read it. He walked and walked and walked, away from Camden, past the Roundhouse music venue, past Chalk Farm station, left up a steep hill to Swiss Cottage, and sat on a bench outside the library.

ALFIE:

I meant what I said

I wish you knew how great

you are

You're kind and loving and

beautiful and sexy

You're special, Gwen. I

mean it

The other day, you can't

deny it

Me and you go well

together. I think it could be

the start of something and

we need to give it a chance

It would be tragic if we
didn't
Please, Gwen, give 'us' a
chance?

Two blue ticks showed she'd read it. But she didn't reply.
That day or the next. Or the next. On Friday morning, she sent
two words.

GWEN:

I'm sorry

That's when Alfie knew it was over.

17

Then it was Halloween, and Ovi's Halloween party. Everyone was getting ready at Maya's. Alfie stood on his balcony, the leaning arch of Wembley Stadium rising above the horizon, lit brilliant white for the World Cup qualifier that evening. It would be so easy just to stay home. He could watch the match on an illegal stream. Avoid the two best friends who'd smashed up his heart. No girls equalled no stress. His anger rose, so strong that he wanted to punch the window. It wasn't fair! Why *shouldn't* he enjoy the party? Why shouldn't he enjoy his life? Why did girls have to decide his mood? So he grabbed his coat and left.

It was the first time he'd been to Maya's since the morning he thought she was dead. A lit pumpkin sat in her window and on the doorstep was a stupid tatty witch doll. He felt a twinge of nostalgia that he stamped straight down. No way. Not going there. He rang the doorbell, glimpsing Maya's face in the upstairs window. Maya's dad opened it, wearing a scary *Scream* mask, stomach bulging under his T-shirt. He presented Alfie with a bucket of sweets.

'Trick or Treat!'

'I'm the one who's supposed to say that,' said Alfie, grabbing a packet of fried eggs.

Maya's dad ripped off the mask. 'Alfie!' he cried, squeezing his hand, slapping his back like a long-lost brother. He ushered him inside, where the England match was on the TV. 'I love Halloween!'

'Me too,' said Alfie.

'Better than Christmas!'

'Serious?'

'Deadly!'

Maya's dad shoved the mask back on and picked up a bread knife from the table. He lunged at Alfie. Alfie sprang back in alarm.

'The look on your face!' said Maya's dad.

Violence with bread knives runs in the family, thought Alfie.

'Look at that line-up!' said Maya's dad, nodding at the football on TV.

'Why's the manager so defensive?' said Alfie.

'Hundred quid! For one ticket! To watch us park the bus!' said Maya's dad.

Alfie found himself lingering, staring at the screen.

'Alfieeeeee!' came Maya's voice from upstairs.

'I'd better go,' he said.

The air in Maya's room was thick with hairspray and the smell of cheap white wine. A whole beauty counter's worth of make-up covered Maya's desk; curlers, face paint, hair dye, brushes, highlighter, concealer, foundation, primer, contour palettes, and other mysterious tubes, potions and bottles. *The Dark Knight* was playing on her laptop, Heath Ledger as the Joker flashing up on the screen. Maya was bent over, doing Gwen's lipstick, wearing a black pleated mini-dress so short he could see her blood red underwear and the edge of her arse cheeks.

'Jeez, Maya, please!' said Alfie, covering his eyes. Maya stuck two fingers up at him and Gwen laughed. Her dress was modest, with long sleeves and a white collar. She wore a black wig which extended her hair into long pigtails, and shiny black lipstick. Alfie's heart fluttered. She looked so different. The cute-girl-dark-heart look suited her.

'Wednesday Addams!' he said.

She nodded and looked down. A really awkward response. Alfie's body tensed. *Just ignore her! Get on with the evening.*

'Gwen looks so good!' said Lily, clapping her hands together, irritating Alfie. She wore a bright yellow wig, a red-and-white baseball jacket, and a T-shirt with *Daddy's Little Monster* emblazoned across the front.

'Harley Quinn!' said Alfie.

Lily hugged Jack, his hair slicked back and wavy, a silver chain with dog-tags around his neck. Three long, plastic-looking prongs appeared to extend from his knuckles.

'Wolverine!' said Alfie.

Jack tried to pick his nose with one of the prongs, making Alfie laugh.

'What are *you* wearing?' said Maya.

'Yeah, what *are* you wearing?' said Lily.

'Err . . . Nothing?'

'Oh my God! Typical!' said Lily.

'What?'

'If anyone was gonna forget . . .'

The room fell silent, apart from the screech of the Batmobile's wheels.

'Did you not listen to a single word Ovi said?' said Lily.

Alfie shrugged.

'No costume. No entry!'

135

'I don't have a costume, get over it!' said Alfie. 'I've been distracted!'

He looked at Gwen. She caught his eye then turned her head away.

'You're always distracted!' said Maya. 'Head in the clouds!'

'Actually, you don't need a costume,' said Lily. 'You can go as yourself.'

'Ha, ha,' said Alfie.

'He did this at primary school,' said Maya. 'He was the only one in uniform on non-uniform day and everyone took the piss.'

'What about you?' said Alfie. 'Wolverine, Wednesday Addams, Harley Quinn, everyone here is a character from a movie – you're just a—' Alfie held himself back.

'I'm just a *what?*' said Maya.

'You're basically wearing your underwear!' said Alfie.

'What are you? My dad? I'm not taking fashion advice from someone who dresses like a twelve-year-old gamer!' spat Maya.

Lily burst out laughing. 'Oh my God, that's exactly what he is!'

'Can we open a window, my lungs are being poisoned?' said Alfie, changing the subject.

Maya reached past Alfie, across the desk to the window, fumbling the latch, making the window pop open with a screech. When she stood back up she glanced at him, then clapped her hand over her mouth.

'Oh. My. God.'

'What?' said Alfie.

'Oh. My. God. Oh. My. God. Oh. My. God!'

She charged out of the room. Minutes later she returned,

holding a purple suit on a hanger, covered with dry cleaner's plastic. She held up the suit to Alfie's body.

'I'm not being funny, but my dad used to wear this in the nineties,' said Maya.

Everyone laughed.

'Your dad was stylish!' said Lily.

'No way am I wearing your dad's old suit,' said Alfie. 'Which has literally nothing to do with Halloween.'

Maya pointed to her laptop screen. Heath Ledger, with straggly green hair, white face, red smile, laughing hysterically. He was wearing a purple suit.

'Oh, shit,' said Alfie.

'Do it!' said Lily.

'Do it!' said Gwen.

Maya fussed over him, slapping on bright white face paint, and thickening his eyelashes with a mascara wand. She straightened Alfie's curls, which led to a lot of laughing and shrieking. She combed bright green hair dye into his hair and they made him put on Maya's dad's suit right there, stripping down to his boxers while the girls covered their eyes.

'You look so, so good,' said Maya, pushing Alfie towards the mirror.

A bright red smile. Pale white skin. Green hair, straggly and slicked back. He looked like the Joker!

'Everyone say cheese!' said Maya's dad, taking picture after picture downstairs, making them pose in character.

'Bye, Dad!' said Maya, flinging open the front door.

'Hey Alfie! Nice suit!' said her dad.

'I, er ...'

'Looks a bit like—'

'Go, go, go!' said Maya.

She ushered them outside.

'Maya, did you—?!'

'Alfie! C'mon!'

Alfie ran out, giggling.

'Maaayaaa—'

'Ruuuuuun!' said Maya, slamming the door behind her.

They all crammed onto the top deck of the bus, the windows steaming up, car headlights glowing with an eerie neon, the chassis juddering and vibrating every time they stopped. Alfie Googled the Joker's catchphrases and memorised them while Maya played Jōnetsu on her phone speaker, and everyone except Alfie and Lily drank from a bottle of sour wine.

Alfie loved it, the feeling of eyes-on-them, Jack flashing his stupid plastic prongs and scaring a little kid, an older man slack-jawed at Maya because she was practically naked, and Alfie sitting next to Gwen, who was suddenly chatting now she'd had more wine. Everyone laughed. Everyone was happy. Everything was normal. Thank God.

Ovi lived in a detached house in Colindale and Alfie knew it was going to be a good night when they saw Yaniv on the porch, talking to three girls dressed as M&Ms. He was in a tuxedo – he was the bouncer – and he wasn't even checking anyone, he was too busy flirting. A central staircase dominated the hallway, the light fittings were old-school chandelier-style, a black-and-white chequered floor covered the hall and the kitchen. It was perfect, like he lived in a haunted house. This was why they'd stayed friends with him!

Ovi had one of the most extravagant costumes: a goth Mad

Hatter, quilted coat, polka dot bow tie, thick black rings around his eyes, a giant top hat. He was meeting and greeting at the bottom of the stairs – hugging Maya for too long, squeezing her a bit too tight – leading them into the kitchen where two huge buckets sat on the floor, bigger than the ones at Luke's, filled with mountains of ice, bottles of Budweiser poking out the top while the counter was full of bottles of wine. Five guys with green zombie faces and ripped white shirts stood in a row, drinking beer. One boy had dressed as a YouTube video, a giant cardboard rectangle strapped to his front, video title: *Ovi's Halloween Party Gets Twisted*, with five million subscribers and thirty million views.

'You win, dude. You win the whole party!' said Alfie, before heading upstairs to Ovi's attic room where he played PlayStation with a random boy. Maya and Gwen kept walking in, scoffing with disapproval, Maya barking, 'Twelve-year-old gamer!' like a playground cuss.

Later, he chatted to the M&Ms, who went to a school in Hendon, and they had a long conversation about who they knew in common. He saw Gwen watching him, staring, standing in the doorway, holding a glass of wine, but when he was done she'd gone. Alfie went up to random strangers and barked his Joker catchphrases. People squealed, gave him a thumb's up, shook his hand. He looked amazing, they loved his costume! Was this what being drunk felt like?

He found himself in the living room as 'Twisted' came on.

'I love this song!' shouted Alfie. 'Who put this on?' But no one knew, there were so many speakers in every single room. One of the M&Ms knew the words, and they were singing together.

Whenever I talk it comes out TWISTED
Whatever I do it comes out TWISTED
Me and you, it's always TWISTED!

There was Gwen: head round the door, but once he'd finished singing, she'd disappeared. Everyone was shouting and screeching, the air thick with weed smoke. There was some rumour flying about that Lily and Jack had locked themselves in Ovi's parents' bedroom, so Alfie squeezed himself upstairs to find Ovi shouting into the door, 'You better use a condom! You better put it in the bin! And not my mum's bin!' Then Ovi turned to Maya and said: 'Are you feeling nostalgic?'

Maya rolled her eyes.

'We were good together . . . weren't we?'

'I've got a boyfriend!'

'He's not here though, is he?'

Maya squared up to him. 'If you hit on me one more time, I will slice off your Mad Hatter head and stuff it down a rabbit hole.'

Ovi laughed. 'Now I remember why we split up.'

'Hi,' said a voice.

Alfie yelped. Gwen laughed.

'Come,' she said, taking his hand. She turned and tripped, falling onto the carpet, her shoulders heaving with laughter.

'Are you OK?' said Alfie.

She hauled herself to her feet. 'I'm drunk.'

She yanked Alfie forward, leading him down to the hallway and into the bathroom under the stairs. She locked the door.

'Errr . . . what are you doing?' said Alfie.

'You know what?'

Gwen kissed him, her mouth acidic with wine.

Alfie pulled away. 'No!'

'Yes!'

'No!'

'Why?'

'I'm so confused,' said Alfie.

She pushed him onto the toilet – the seat wasn't even down – straddling him, her hands reaching underneath his T-shirt and roaming around his chest, drunkenly kissing his neck, his bum dipping down towards the toilet water.

'Gwen—'

'Shhhhh.' She kissed him again and finally Alfie relented, ignoring the pain around his thighs where the toilet seat pressed so hard it might cut his skin. She'd pounced on him, that had to be a good thing, right? Even if he had to amputate his legs and spend the rest of his life in a wheelchair?

'You have the most beautiful eyes,' she said.

She stood up, beaming at him, then suddenly slipped, sprawling onto the floor, banging her head against the bottom of the sink.

'Oh my God,' said Alfie.

But Gwen just laughed and extended her arms. He hauled her up, but she fell onto her knees, and now she was retching, puking in the toilet, filling it with greeny-winey sick.

'Sorry,' said Gwen. 'Sorry, sorry, sorry.'

When the retching finally stopped, her hands rested on the toilet seat, her hair hanging down, staring into the bowl.

'I don't feel so good.'

Someone banged on the door.

'Out the way,' said Alfie, flushing the toilet, placing her arm around his shoulder, hauling her up.

'Sorry,' said Gwen.

'You just proved the Ovi Party Rule. Something crazy always happens.'

'I said I'm sorry!'

'Hey! Do I sound like I'm complaining?'

Gwen smiled.

'Come on. I think we should go,' said Alfie.

It was weird being at the bus stop after the chaos of the party, the pavements empty, everything quiet and still. They sat at the back of the bus, Gwen's head on his shoulder, clutching her stomach, her face blotchy, the wig in her lap. The window reflection made them look undead, their skin pallid, Alfie's Joker smile smeared and smudged. She held his hand as they walked across the edge of the Brent playing fields, everything eerie and shadowy, the goal posts fuzzy.

'I've worked it out,' said Alfie.

'What?'

'You're actually a ghost.'

'What do you mean?'

'Tonight! One second you were there. Then – poof! Disappeared! Then you reappeared behind me and made me jump.'

Gwen laughed. She grabbed his hand, pulled him towards her, and kissed him.

'Gwen?'

'Yes?'

'What's going on?'

'What?'

'With us?'

Gwen shrugged her shoulders.

'I think I know.'

'What?'

'The reason.'

She looked up, startled. 'You do?'

'I do!'

'What's the reason?' Gwen's chest heaved in and out.

'Maya!' said Alfie.

'What?'

'We have to tell her!'

'What do you mean?'

'I'm not gonna see you in secret. Her being your best friend – it shouldn't matter!'

'Oh. Right. Yeah. No. It shouldn't!' said Gwen.

'Why is there some stupid rule about seeing boys that your friend had a thing with? It's dumb. If something's meant to be, it's meant to be, right?'

'I know! It's ridiculous!'

They walked on to the entrance to her flats.

'I'm sorry I'm so messed up,' she said.

'I'm messed up too.'

'No, you're not. You're lovely.'

He grabbed her hands. 'So are you! You're ... Amazeballs! And you make a really hot Wednesday Addams.'

Gwen laughed. She opened her door. 'Amazeballs!' She laughed again.

'Gwen?'

'What?'

'Please don't go silent. Please don't ghost me. I can't take it.'

Gwen shook her head. 'I won't.'

'When am I gonna see you, then?'

Gwen shrugged. 'My parents are out tomorrow. Wanna come round?'

'Sure.'

Gwen smiled. The door slammed.

Alfie punched the air. 'Yes!' he shouted, his voice shooting across the wide open fields.

18

Gwen stood in her doorway, her eyes glistening, her hair damp from the shower, her lips turned down. Alfie held out his arms. She hugged him, pressed her head to his chest, and sniffed. Alfie leaned down to kiss her and she moved her head away.

'What?'

'Feel sick.'

'Still?'

'Says the boy who's never had a hangover.'

She turned and slunk inside, leaving the door open, and Alfie on the doorstep.

'Can I come in?'

'Of course!' she snapped.

The place was a mess. Toys strewn everywhere: a doll, a giant fire truck, diggers, Nintendo Switch controllers, half-finished cups of juice and a cheese-and-ham sandwich with little bite marks in. A clothes horse dominated the living room, full of boxers, bras, towels, rows and rows of kids' T-shirts, giving off a musty stench. Gwen sat down on the sofa, a bowl of Rice Krispies on the coffee table in front of her, an iPad propped up against a bright yellow digger.

'Where is everyone?'

'Clown Town.'

'What's that?'

'The most depressing place in the world.'

Alfie let his rucksack drop to the floor, slipped off his

trainers and sat down next to her. The door to her room was open. It was even smaller and messier than his; her duvet scrunched up, a rainbow tote bag in the middle of the floor.

'It's a soft play,' she said. 'They go there a lot.'

He felt for her, living here, the five of them. She had zero space. It must be suffocating. He only lived with Nan and even she went out a lot.

'Will you help me get a job?' he said.

Gwen's eyes widened.

'I was in Camden the other day and I realised what I wanted . . . and I should at least apply so I can say to Nan I've done it . . .'

'Where?'

Somewhere he felt at home. Somewhere that had chilled him out after Lily had a go at him. Somewhere where Gwen came and found him, in order to cheer him up.

'Coffee Boss!' said Alfie.

'Great,' said Gwen, unenthusiastically.

'You think I shouldn't apply?'

'I didn't say that . . .'

Alfie took his laptop from his rucksack and went to the Coffee Boss website. *Hi! What's your name?* was written in massive letters, an empty text box below, inviting him to answer.

'I'm a bit nervous . . . I wanted to do it with someone else there . . .'

'I'm probably not going to be much help. My brain is broken,' said Gwen.

'You don't have to write it for me . . . I just wanted . . . moral support . . . or something . . .' said Alfie.

He kissed her quickly on the lips. For a split second, Gwen smiled. Alfie typed in his name. A large Coffee Boss takeaway cup appeared on the screen, A-L-F-I-E appearing on the side in handwritten scrawl.

'Cool', he said. He showed the screen to Gwen. She grunted. He typed in Gwen's name. Then some stupid ones.

Dickhead. Twat.

Gwen rolled her eyes.

'What?'

'Apply for your damn job!' she said.

Alfie searched for Brent Cross Shopping Centre. *Barista – Store #12186*, popped up on the screen.

'Oh my God! They actually have a vacancy!'

Alfie typed in his details while Gwen sat there, holding her head.

'Oh no!'

'What?'

'I haven't even offered you a drink.' She rubbed her face like she'd seriously messed up.

'Doesn't matter!'

'It does! What do you want?'

'Coffee?'

'Coffee is good.'

Gwen got up and bustled around in the kitchen while Alfie read the job description.

'*Delivers world class customer service to all customers by putting the customer's needs first and connecting with the customer.* Shit!'

'What?'

'This is scary!'

'Alfie, you could do it in your sleep. You're really good with people', she said, presenting him with a mug. Alfie sipped it. It was watery and weak.

'I am?'

'Yes!'

Alfie clicked to apply, read the privacy statement, clicked *agree*. He didn't have a CV so he filled it out manually, slowly, because he was checking for mistakes, while Gwen lay back on the sofa and closed her eyes.

'Weekends or evenings?'

She shrugged her shoulders.

'Overnight. There's an overnight? Who works in Coffee Boss overnight?'

'Zombies?' said Gwen.

Alfie laughed. 'My name is Zombie Alfie and my availability is night times. I'm very good at connecting with vampires.'

Gwen laughed, then clutched her stomach in pain.

'I'm a zombie and I'm going out with a ghost.'

Alfie watched Gwen's face for a reaction. He thought she might puke. He ticked the options for all day Saturday, Sunday and weekday evenings. He wanted to look enthusiastic.

'*Please tell us why you want to work at Coffee Boss*. I'm desperate.'

Gwen laughed, then groaned. Alfie typed:

> This will be my first job. I'm really good with people, I love coffee, I smile a lot. I want to develop independence, and I work really hard.

No one was gonna buy this! There must be thousands of people more qualified than him! Alfie read and reread his words, frozen, unable to edit.

'Maybe this is a bad idea.'

'Why?'

'They're just gonna say no.'

'Alfie . . .' Gwen grabbed his arm. 'Just do it.'

Alfie took a deep breath, pressed send, then slapped the screen shut, making Gwen jump.

'Now for the real reason I'm here.'

He leaned over and kissed her. Finally she woke up, kissing him back, stroking his hair, swinging her leg over his so she could sit on his lap. Would this be a good moment to ask if she'd heard the *going out with a ghost* comment? Could she please confirm that they were official? Could he go home and tell Nan her name? Did he actually really, honestly, finally, have a girlfriend?

'I can't do it!' said Gwen.

'Do what?'

'*This.*'

'What do you mean?'

'Us!'

She swung back onto the sofa and folded her arms.

'I'm sorry!'

'I don't get it!'

'I'm sorry!'

'I'm gonna call her,' said Alfie, standing up. 'She can't control our lives!'

'It's not Maya!' exclaimed Gwen. Her mouth curled down and her eyes became moist. 'It's nothing to do with her . . .'

'What is it, then?' Alfie sat back on the sofa.

Gwen held her chin to her chest. 'I wanted to try . . .' she said.

'Try what?'

'I wanted to try a boy!'

Alfie frowned.

'I wanted to *see* ... Life would be so much *simpler* ...' Her whole body was rigid, arms crossed, legs crossed, she was probably crossing her toes too.

'You're saying ... you don't like boys?'

'No! Yes, I am! I'm saying I don't like boys!'

'Then why did you call me gorgeous? Why did you call me a catch!'

'I meant it!'

'Why did you lock me in the toilet and kiss me?'

'I was drunk!'

'So if I start drinking alcohol, am I gonna pin Jack to the wall and kiss him?'

Gwen laughed. 'No! Maybe! I wanted ... to see if I liked it ... with someone who wasn't a ... rhinoceros ... with someone I actually like!' Gwen stood up and kicked the fire truck across the floor.

'Easy now,' said Alfie. He stood up and placed a hand on her shoulder.

Gwen continued in a small voice, staring at the floor: 'I had a thing with Samira, didn't I? My mum walked in on us.'

'You had a thing with Samira?'

'My mum's in denial. She thinks it's a phase. I thought, maybe she's right.'

'You had a thing with *Samira*?'

Alfie thought back, Samira and Gwen talking in the lunch hall, on the first day of term ... Gwen missing Ovi's summer party because she was at Samira's ... watching the video on Gwen's phone, Samira's hand on her shoulder.

'I really like her ...'

'So, what, you're just using me as an experiment? To try and forget her?'

'I meant what I said! I wanted to cheer you up. When Lily was rude in Lit Chick. You got the wrong end of the stick. You thought I was coming onto you ..'

'Oh my God ..'

'I'm sorry!'

'I thought we had a connection!'

'We do have a connection!'

'Why didn't you say—'

'*Because* ..' She sniffed. 'You're a *boy*. Boys are so *insistent*! You wouldn't stop *hitting* on me! It's just so much easier to say yes. I thought that maybe if I could make you happy, and then I could make Mum happy ... You know ... If I came home with a boyfriend ... A nice one ... like you!'

'Oh my God!'

'So I got drunk and went for it! I'm so *dumb*!'

'Oh my God!'

'I'm so sorry!' Now Gwen was crying. 'It's not you, Alfie, it's me! I'm messed up! I've just got a really intolerant family—'

'Does Maya know?'

'Yes.'

'Why didn't—'

'I told her not to tell! If I was gonna come out, then I wanted it to be on *my* terms.'

'Well, you've done it with me.'

'Don't! Tell! Anyone!' Gwen sat back on the sofa, pulled her knees to her chest, like she'd done on the helter-skelter. 'Everything's a mess ..'

Alfie sat back down next to her. 'What about Jack?'

Gwen winced.

'What if I swear him to secrecy?'

'No!'

'So you get to tell your best friend about all your problems, but I can't tell my best friend about mine?'

'Just . . . do what you want . . . doesn't matter.'

'I'm not gonna be like Lily and roast you in public.'

'Whatever! Do what you want.'

Alfie sighed. 'I'm just . . . I'm gutted, Gwen!' He put his head in his hands. 'I thought I was gonna get the greatest moment of my life, kissing you in the front row at Jōnetsu!'

'Alfie!' Gwen was laughing and crying at the same time.

'I thought we were gonna have this long-term thing! I had it all planned out!'

Gwen laughed again, more tears rolling down her face.

'I *did* see a rainbow tote bag in your room, so I guess it's on me as well. Dammit!' Alfie bashed his forehead with his palm.

'It takes more than a rainbow bag, Alfie . .'

Two fat tears rolled down Alfie's cheeks. 'I just . . . Ah, man. This sucks!'

She put her hand on his cheek and rubbed away the tears.

'Someone's chopping onions,' said Alfie.

Gwen laughed.

'I'm stupid, Gwen. I'm crying because I'm stupid. What the hell's wrong with me?'

'There's nothing wrong with you, Alfie. You're amazing! I *do* care for you . . . If I was that way inclined . . . I'd be all over you . . . I mean it!'

'Thanks . .' said Alfie. 'I *think* . .'

They both laughed, then sat quietly, sniffling.

'Forget your mum! You like who you like, and that's that!' said Alfie suddenly. 'And who knows, if you're like, honest with her, if you're like, *This is me, nothing's gonna change,* maybe *she'll* change . . .'

'Thanks, Alfie.'

'You could have any girl you want!'

'I can't believe you're being so positive.'

'I'm just glad that I could be the one special person who proved beyond all doubt that you're gay.'

They laughed.

Gwen rested her head on Alfie's shoulder. 'We can still be friends?'

Alfie sniffed. More tears were coming.

'Please?' said Gwen.

'Ah, man.'

'*Please?*'

'It's hard!' Alfie's eyes welled back up. 'Every time I think I've found someone . . . something like this happens!' Two more tears rolled down his face. 'It's driving me nuts!' He stood up and packed up his laptop. 'Just give me some time, OK?'

'How much time?' asked Gwen.

'I dunno. A lot, maybe?'

'Can I give you a cuddle?'

'You can. You can give me a cuddle.'

They hugged, tight and long, and then he left, ran down the stairs, bursting onto the street, found Jack's name on his phone, and called him.

Lily

19

'How much?'

'A hundred?'

'A *hundred*?!'

'I'm going to Brighton!'

Nan's face reddened. She shoved two slices of bread into the toaster and yanked down the handle. She whisked the eggs as fast as she could, twisted the cooker knob and pressed the ignition. The gas flame burst into life.

'We bought the tickets months ago. It's not exactly a surprise.'

'You mean, *I* bought the tickets months ago.'

Nan opened the fridge, took out the butter and sliced some into the pan. 'I can't even remember.'

'It was April. Before GCSEs.'

'Was I drunk?'

'No!' Alfie laughed.

'Why are you going all the way to Brighton?'

'Cos London sold out fast. This was an extra date they added later.'

'Who's going?'

'We all are! We're meeting at Lily's, then we're getting the train.'

Nan scoffed.

'I've been looking forward to this for months!'

A flickering bright blue flame shot up the side of the pan,

reaching the rim. Nan poured the egg mixture over the melting butter and stirred it with a wooden spoon.

'Why a hundred?'

'Train tickets. Food. Drinks. Brighton Pier.'

'Do you *have* to go?'

'Do I have to go?' Alfie panicked. 'This band . . . you don't understand . . . they keep me alive . . . Literally.'

The toaster popped and Nan buttered the slices quickly. She stirred the egg mixture rhythmically, and they watched the gloopy liquid slowly solidify.

'I'm sorry, Alfie,' said Nan. 'It's too much money.'

Alfie left the kitchen and collapsed onto the sofa. Nan bustled in, placing two plates of scrambled eggs on the table, followed by the toast, butter and some ancient green lime marmalade. Bailey trotted in, paws skidding across the laminate floor, looking hungry and hopeful. Outside, the sky was slate grey.

'I'll pay you back,' said Alfie.

'How?'

'I did what you wanted. I applied for a job.'

'Where?'

'Coffee Boss.'

'Coffee Boss?'

'What's wrong with Coffee Boss?'

'Everything! They don't pay tax! It was on the news. They're tax dodgers!'

'You told me to get a job in Brent Cross!'

'I didn't mean Coffee Boss! Maya's dad pays his taxes. Every year, since nineteen-ninety-seven. And don't get me started on their prices! Four pounds for a coffee! It's daylight robbery!'

'I *like* Coffee Boss coffee!'

158

'Dishwater! Overpriced dishwater!' said Nan. She sat at the table, and picked up her knife and fork. 'So you've actually got this "job".'

'Not yet ...'

'So this is fantasy money you're promising me.'

'*If* I get the job, I'll pay you back.'

'And what if you don't? What then?'

Alfie stood up abruptly, Bailey's tail wagged, and she barked. 'Doesn't matter,' he said.

'What?'

'Doesn't matter. I won't go. I'll just stay here and contemplate jumping off the balcony.'

'Now, now,' said Nan.

Alfie put his head in his hands. 'Do you really have that little faith in me? Do you really think I'm that much of a loser? That I can't get a job at Coffee Boss?'

'Have your breakfast,' said Nan, mouth full.

'I'm not hungry.'

Bailey barked.

'You'll feel better after some food!'

'No!'

Alfie sniffed. He pushed back the tears.

'Why are you only asking me now?' she said. 'If you've known about this for six months?'

'Because I hate asking you for money, that's why!' Alfie ruffled his curls, scratching his head in frustration.

'That makes two of us. It does my head in, Alfie.'

'Why?'

'Every time you come, hands out, begging for cash. Where does it end? I'm scared you'll put us out on the street.'

'I don't exactly ask for much.'

'My mum used to make us hide under the table and turn off the lights because the bailiffs were knocking on the door. I'm very aware of how it can happen.'

Alfie sighed. He walked over to Nan, put his arms around her shoulders and kissed her on the cheek.

'If I don't get the Coffee Boss job, I'll get a different one. I will pay you back. This is the last time I'm gonna ask you for anything. I swear on my life.'

Nan grunted.

'I cannot express how much this concert means to me. I would literally stay in, for a whole year, just to go out today.'

Nan made a point of slowly chewing her mouthful and swallowing before she spoke.

'We'll have to walk to the cash machine,' she said in a small voice.

'Yesss!' said Alfie, punching the air.

Twenty minutes later they stood on Cricklewood Broadway in front of the cash machine, as Nan withdrew a hundred pounds.

'There's something you should know,' she said.

'What?'

'Think of this as a present from your mum.'

Alfie's heart beat faster. 'You're kidding me.'

'No.'

'I told you not to take her money!'

'I know.'

'When?'

'A couple of weeks ago.'

'Why?'

Alfie felt dizzy.

'It's almost Christmas!' said Nan.

'I don't want it!'

'Come on, Alfie!

Nan held the money out, waiting for Alfie to take it.

'Are things really that bad . . . ?' he said.

'Well . . . the service charge has gone up . . . energy has gone up . . .'

'It's tainted! I don't want it!'

'She is the only reason you *can* go . . . you understand?'

Alfie folded his arms. 'You promised me . . .'

'No, you *asked* me to promise. She is my daughter.'

Alfie kicked at the pavement. 'I don't want it.'

'Think of it this way. She owes us. She owes *you*.'

Alfie rubbed his face. He glared at the money, then reached out and snatched it. 'She owes me a million Jōnetsu concerts.'

'I still want it back,' said Nan.

Alfie nodded.

'Next time I buy coffee, you better be serving it to me,' she said.

'Even though you hate the place?'

'Only if you give me a discount!'

Alfie stuffed the money into his pocket. 'I can't avoid her, can I?' he said. 'She was like a god to me. And she just fucked off. How could anyone do that to their own kid?'

Nan pursed her lips sympathetically.

'I feel like I'm gonna come home and she's gonna be in the living room.'

'I wouldn't go that far . . . Not unless you wanted it . . .'

Alfie sighed.

'Go and have fun in Brighton. When you're ready to decide, you can decide.'

Alfie nodded.

'I haven't needed her for the last ten years. Why would I need her now?'

20

'Alfie!'

Lily blinked rapidly in surprise.

'Hi.'

'Hi!' She held the door half-open, hesitant. 'Didn't anyone tell you?'

'Tell me what?'

'I told Jack to tell you!'

'What?'

Lily smiled brightly. 'Everyone's bailed!'

'What?'

'Yeah!'

'How did everyone bail? That makes no sense!'

The tips of her jet-black hair were newly dyed neon green. She wore baggy black combats and a camisole which revealed her strong and powerful torso, arms and shoulders toned from swimming. Her feet were bare, just her left toenails painted. She didn't look like she was bailing.

'It might make no sense . . . but it definitely happened!'

Alfie hurriedly took out his phone and swiped through his messages. Nothing.

'I don't get it.'

'I can't believe Jack didn't tell you!'

A gust of icy wind made them both break out in goose bumps. He looked up at her, pleading, shivering, his chin juddering.

'Oh, for God's sake.'

She swung the door open. Alfie stepped forward.

'Wait! Shoes off . . .'

Alfie took off his trainers, left them in the hallway, and followed her up the stairs to her room, hanging back in the doorway while Lily sat down on the fluffy beige carpet and resumed painting her right-foot toenails. Her room was massive, bigger than Alfie's living room and bedroom combined. A wide bay window with a balcony; an out-of-service fireplace framed by fairy lights; prints on the wall, each one with a motivational phrase: *Live, Love, Laugh*; *Believe in yourself*; *Push your limits*. Two photos of Lily on the mantlepiece: one in swimming costume and cap, beaming smile, holding a trophy triumphantly. One blown-up photo of her and Jack's heads pressed together in four, cringey, sickening, happy-couple photo-booth poses: beaming smiles, raucous laughter, gurning stupidity and snogging.

'Alfie! Come in!'

Alfie skirted around Lily and sat down tentatively on the edge of her bed. He stared at her belly button, and was reminded of the time when she wanted to get it pierced but she couldn't because it wasn't safe to have a new piercing in the pool. Lily noticed, and covered it with her non-painting arm.

'Where is everyone?' he said.

'My mum and dad are away until Sunday.'

'Everyone else.'

'I told you. They bailed.'

'How? Why? And why didn't anyone tell me?'

'It's all a bit last-minute . . . Luke's playing some battle of the bands thing and there's gonna be music industry people there, so Maya's going to that. This is a really big day for her.'

'*What?*'

'Luke told her she's an official member or something, so it's all about Twisted Dreamland now. Even more than it already was,' said Lily with unexpected bitterness.

'Maya's not coming?'

Lily shook her head.

'But she loves Jōnetsu, almost as much as me!'

Lily shrugged, flicked her hair, before resuming on her middle toenail. Her nail polish was ruby red, matching her bedspread. Its sweet acrid smell burned Alfie's nose.

'Gwen is going with Maya. She wants to support her. It's the biggest moment of her performing life, or something.'

'Seriously?'

'It was supposed to be you, me and Jack . . . Then his granny in Bexhill swept him away!'

'Eh?'

'It's her birthday, or something. Really inconsiderate of her. He totally forgot about it.'

'And why didn't he tell me?'

'I told him to message you. I promise I did!'

Alfie guessed Gwen was probably avoiding him. Maya's gig made sense. But Jack? The whole thing felt like a lame excuse. And why was he so disappointed? He'd reached out after Gwen told him she was gay – and what did Jack say? Same as he did when Maya rejected him. *Chin up. Plenty more fish in the sea.* Again. As if heartache and pain could be magically healed by lifting up his chin. Jack was rubbish. Consistently.

'Damn you, Jack!' exclaimed Alfie. Lily frowned.

'Maybe he knew you'd react like this—'

'So he chickened out of telling me. Lame, lame, lame, lame, lame!'

Alfie checked his phone – still nothing. He fired off a message.

ALFIE:

Dude!

'We were supposed to go as a group.'

'I know!'

Alfie's shoulders tensed horribly. He rubbed his left one but it didn't make any difference.

'And now it's me and you . . .' said Lily witheringly. 'Kind of feels doomed . . .'

Without thinking, Alfie lay back on the bed. 'What do you mean?'

'We aren't exactly the sort of people who spend time together?'

'You think we shouldn't go? After it's been this massive thing? For months? After we've paid all this money for the tickets?'

'I dunno. Maybe?'

'Do you not care about seeing the greatest band in the history of bands?'

Lily raised her eyebrows.

Was he gonna have to go on his own? A whole day in Brighton? Ditched by his friends! Like a sad, pathetic idiot loser with no life?

'I guess we've never had the *opportunity* to spend time together,' said Alfie.

'And why is that?'

'I dunno! It's weird!'

'Yeah! Really weird! Can you sit up, please?'

Alfie sat up.

'I think I know,' said Lily casually. 'I mean ...' She frowned and concentrated hard on her little toe, dabbing the nail with the brush, before replacing it in the bottle and screwing it shut. She stood up, splaying her toes and replaced the polish in a zip-bag by the fireplace. 'You obviously don't like me ...'

'Excuse me?'

'You kind of ... *hate* me.'

'What? No! You hate *me*!'

'No, I don't!'

'Why are you always roasting me, then?'

'You deserve it. You do dumb stuff.'

'Lily!'

Lily sighed. 'You got through Ovi's party, well done, gold star.'

Alfie folded his arms. At least he and Gwen had gone under the radar. Jack hadn't told Lily. If she knew Alfie had a thing for a gay girl, she'd be roasting him by now. He'd sworn him to secrecy. Jack had managed to do one thing right.

'I don't hate you. I just don't like being roasted. And normally I just ... suck it up. So maybe if you're picking up on something, that's what it is.'

Lily screwed up her face in confusion. 'But you've never liked me, from the beginning! Jack was like, *Good news, we're together!* You gave me this *look*. You just *frowned*!' She frowned, squaring up her shoulders, pursing her lips. 'Every time I'm *near* you, I get these *vibes* ... like I'm a *bad, bad person* ... like I'm ... *toxic*!'

'*Really?*'

Lily looked at him, her eyes hard, forehead creased into a frown.

'Maybe I roast you because you pretend everything is OK and you don't have the balls to say how you really feel about me.' Her bottom lip wobbled. 'Maybe I roast you ... to *protect myself*.'

'What you saying? I started it?'

'I don't know who started it, all I know is you hate me and I hate that.' Lily wiped her eyes. 'Maybe I should go to Maya's gig.'

'Listen, Lily! No! I think I can explain. Me and Jack. Neither of us had had a girlfriend before ... We were both kind of miserable and single ... Nothing was gonna change ... Then you and him get together ... It's like he won the lottery. One of the hottest girls in the year. A perfect relationship. All I get is non-stop disasters. So, yeah ... That has been a bit ... *annoying*. Maybe I've been a teensy bit *jealous*. I'm sorry, OK?'

Lily nodded. Alfie stood up and circled around her. In the corner of the room was a backpack, navy blue, with the Nike swoosh. Jack's. The zip was open and a pair of Jack's boxer shorts stuck out of the top. Soon Jack would be moving in. Soon there'd be an invitation to Jack and Lily's wedding. Soon Jack would be driving the people carrier out the front, with little Jack-Lilys screaming in the back.

'We have to accept Jack is a fact of our lives!' he blurted.

'What's that supposed to mean?'

'You're his girlfriend. I'm his best friend. We have one thing in common. We both love Jack.'

Lily folded her arms.

'Jack *knows*. Jack *knows* me and you ... are an issue ... This whole ... *thing* ... I think it stresses him out.'

168

Lily nodded.

'And it isn't gonna go away, is it? At least we finally talked about it.'

Lily nodded again.

'Maybe this could be our chance to ... sort out our differences. We've never actually hung out. Properly. Me and you. We can put it all behind us. Do it for Jack.'

'Jack's always saying, *You've got the wrong end of the stick, Alfie's my brother, I love him, he's amazing. You just have to get to know him.*'

'Exactly! Maybe we just need to spend some proper time with each other. Maybe we need to ... bury the hatchet!'

Lily very slowly dried her eyes with the outside of her hand. 'It would make Jack happy ...' she said in a faint voice.

'Brighton is an amazing day out. The gig will be incredible. It's the others' loss ...'

'Yes. You're right.' She sounded like a robot. She stood up, flung back her hair, bunched it into a ponytail and tied it up with a hairband. She stared at the photos of her and Jack. She lifted a finger and placed it on Jack's face. She rubbed her finger over Jack's nose.

'You're right. Yes. Let's go to Brighton.'

She turned to him.

'For Jack.'

'For Jack.'

Alfie held up his palm. Lily high-fived it. Lily flashed him her bright white smile, so fake that Alfie felt sick.

21

They didn't talk much, wedging themselves into a double seat, sitting a bit too close, both of them glued to their phones, only speaking to work out which platform the train was on and which carriage the toilet was in. Alfie could smell Lily's shampoo, his bare arm kept threatening to bump into hers, and he could see down her top – which he hated, forcing himself to not look, terrified that she would think he was staring.

Alfie listened to Jōnetsu, and felt a strong urge to play her some songs. Maybe that could break the ice – but he felt so awkward, he held himself back. Instead he Googled *Jōnetsu gig*, reading about other people's experience on Reddit, and felt a surge of anxiety when he realised just how early people queued to get to the front row. He really wanted to be close to the stage! He was relieved when they finally arrived at a packed Brighton station.

They shuffled down the platform, automated announcements booming out of the tannoy, bouncing off the glass and iron roof, passengers bottlenecking at the barriers, the gates clattering open and shut, and when the machine finally sucked up Alfie's ticket he followed the neon ends of Lily's hair across the concourse, emerging into a small, cold piazza. The crowds streamed forwards, heading down a steep hill, and Alfie felt a thrill as he glimpsed the grey-green sea.

'We're actually here,' he said, feeling himself relax.

'Duuuh,' said Lily, before squealing and running across the road.

Outside a Budgens stood a slight girl with bright pink hair wearing a large pair of clear-framed glasses. She disappeared from view as Lily crashed into her, squeezing her with a massive bear hug, and for a second Alfie thought that she had swallowed her up completely. He approached them as they spoke animatedly in Cantonese.

'Alfie, this is my sister Amy,' said Lily.

'I didn't know you had a sister.'

'Guilty as charged!' said Amy, laughing.

'You live in Brighton?'

'I do! I'm at university here. Didn't you tell him about me?'

'I guess I forgot!' said Lily, flashing her smile.

'Does he know where we're going?' said Amy.

'Um . . .' said Lily.

'Do you like Chinese food?' said Amy.

Alfie frowned.

'You didn't tell him anything?' said Amy. She giggled.

Lily shrugged. Why hadn't she told him? But Alfie didn't want to complain. *Remember Jack. Better just run with it.* He was hungry. They still had time to queue.

'Yes, I like it,' he said.

'Great,' said Amy. 'Let's get out of here.'

Alfie followed the sisters down the hill, the pavement so congested it was like a crowd heading to a sporting event, until they reached a large junction at an old clocktower. Amy led them away from the throng, past the Churchill Square shopping centre, and down a narrow street of restaurants – Turkish, Persian, Japanese, Italian – into a small Chinese restaurant, the kitchen by the door on the left hot and steamy with sizzling pans, white-coated chefs barking at each other and a smiley woman at the till, who greeted them loudly, shoving laminated menus into their hands.

'This is where all the international students come,' said Amy. 'It's how you know it's good.'

They sat down, their table so small their knees touched underneath.

'How much do you know about this kind of food?' said Amy.

Alfie shrugged.

'You happy for us to order?'

Alfie nodded.

'Don't worry, you won't regret it.'

Amy beamed – she and Lily had the same toothy smile – and soon the table was packed with dishes: grilled pork dumplings, rice with egg and mushrooms, chicken in black bean sauce, braised roast pork with bean curd, squid with chilli-salt. Alfie tucked in, enjoying the warm stodgy buns, the big hunks of meat, the texture of the squid. The girls spoke intensely, always in Cantonese, Lily leaning forward and touching Amy's arm, squeezing her shoulder, holding her hand. At one point Amy produced a tissue from her pocket which Lily snatched, wiping away a tear before looking at Alfie self-consciously.

'Are you OK?' said Alfie to Lily.

'I've got an issue with my girlfriend,' said Amy.

'It's a really sad story,' said Lily.

'You have a girlfriend?' blurted Alfie.

'Don't look so shocked,' said Amy.

'I'm not,' said Alfie.

'You saying I look like a lesbian?' she said.

The sisters cracked up with laughter. Amy said something in a shrill voice to Lily, all the while holding Alfie's eyes. Alfie's ears burned and his cheeks became hot.

'We're bad. We're talking about him when he's in front of us,' said Amy.

'It's fine,' said Alfie.

'Sorry,' said Amy.

'Doesn't matter,' said Alfie. 'You gave me food. Food makes me happy.'

Just get through the day. A weird meal with Lily. The price to make Jack happy. The price to see Jōnetsu. They ate quickly and it felt good to slap a twenty-pound note on top of the bill. They said goodbye to Amy, Lily hugging her like she was never going to see her again.

'What do you want to do now?' said Lily impatiently.

'Er . . . Queue up? I miscalculated the time we should get there. We might have to sacrifice sightseeing if we want to stand at the front.'

'You have to be joking me. We're in Brighton. I want to see stuff.'

'Listen, Lily. People will have been queuing since nine a.m.'

'They're weirdos, Alfie.'

Alfie sighed.

'We haven't even seen the sea yet.'

'I saw it from the station.'

'That doesn't count. Come on, we have to see the sea!'

Fine. Screw it. He could wait longer. It would be OK.

At the bottom of the hill the seafront opened up before them, the wind slammed into their faces, the smell of salt filled

Alfie's nostrils, foamy waves pounded onto the shore, the red lifeguard flag was flying, warning people not to swim, and charcoal-grey clouds skidded across the sky. They crossed the road and went down to the stony beach, pebbles sliding into his trainers, cutting into his heel.

'Can you skim?' he asked, picking up the thinnest stone he could find and whipping it forward, where it bounced once before disappearing into a wave.

'That was terrible,' said Lily.

Alfie gave her a look. She picked up a stone and hurled it forward, mis-throwing badly, it didn't even make the water.

'What was that?'

'Wait!' said Lily.

She tried again, throwing hard, but the stone slipped out of her hand and landed on the beach behind her.

'That was the worst girl-throw I've ever seen,' said Alfie.

'Oi!' said Lily, pushing his shoulder playfully.

They both chucked more, Alfie teaching Lily about skimming, that you needed a flat stone, you had to hold it between your index finger and thumb and throw it with a flick of the wrist. They both practised, falling into a skimming-trance, drizzle wetting their faces, the seagulls soaring above them, gliding, screeching, until a large wave broke, soaking Alfie's feet. He yelled and ran, trudging across the stony beach back onto the promenade, where he sat on a breeze block and took off his trainers.

'If you don't want to have wet feet then don't stand by the sea!' said Lily. 'You're such a—'

Alfie shot her a look.

'OK!' said Lily. 'I'm not gonna say anything.'

The drizzle stopped as they walked along the front, Alfie's socks squelching, up a ramp and onto the wooden planks of the pier itself, to the entrance of a large hall, two towers on the left and right, *Brighton Palace Pier* in bright blinking rainbow lightbulbs across the façade. Inside it was rammed with arcade games – racing games, shooting games, fighting games, classic games – a cacophony of jingles, bleeps and explosions, lit by garish red and yellow neon.

'Are you a gamer?' Alfie asked.

Lily shook her head.

'You are now.'

He stuffed a twenty-pound note into the change machine. It spewed out pound coins like a machine gun spewing out bullets, clattering into the dispenser. They sat inside a dark booth, shooting zombies with big yellow laser guns, then raced each other on two life-size motorbikes. They sat in red leather chairs and played a retro version of *Space Invaders*, Lily shouting, 'My gun's not working!' for the whole thing.

'My choice now!' she said at the end.

She led him to a bright blue air hockey table, handed Alfie the bat, paid a pound, and the red puck glided onto the table. Lily immediately smacked it, it shot off an edge, then another, and into Alfie's goal. Lily crowed in delight, pissing Alfie off. He smashed the puck, Lily parried, it cascaded around the table, Alfie blocked it, and it flew into Lily's goal. Alfie pumped his fist, and Lily frowned, getting serious. She scored twice more, then Alfie came back level, and Lily finally won with a dead straight smack down the table, punching the air, screaming with triumph.

'Now I know why you're a champion swimmer,' said Alfie, as they left the pier.

Lily flashed her beaming smile.

'And now I know, you're actually fun to hang out with,' she said, bumping into him with her shoulder.

Alfie checked the time on his phone.

'The queue is gonna be really, really long now.'

'Will you shut up about that stupid queue!'

'I've been obsessed with that queue for six whole months.'

Lily's brown eyes lingered on Alfie's face.

'Alfie. There's something I have to tell you.'

'What?'

'I've decided. I'm not gonna go to the gig.'

22

The drizzle had returned, somewhere behind the clouds the sun began to set and things became murky and dank. They stood at the edge of the pier by the roundabout, and in the twilight the car headlights hurt Alfie's eyes.

'Amy . . . she invited me out . . .' said Lily.

'Where?'

'Her house. Tonight. I don't get to see her any more. She even stayed here for the summer. She's like, my best friend.'

'You saw her at lunchtime. You had a whole conversation with her in another language and pretended I wasn't there . . . !'

'I was gonna come, I really was, but I'm worried about her. She's really emotionally vulnerable and she needs some comfort . . .'

'She looked pretty happy to me!'

Lily took a step back onto the bike lane and Alfie had to put his hand on her shoulder to stop her from being hit by a cyclist. Lily swore and gathered herself.

'We're supposed to be doing this for Jack, remember?' said Alfie. 'Plus you made me sacrifice the queue!'

'I'm sorry!'

'You only just decided this?'

'I've been conflicted!'

'Since when?'

'For ages, actually. Jōnetsu – they're not really my style of music.'

'What?'

'I'm not really into music . . . Not like you guys are . . .'

'Really? Listen, Lily. This will be a whole other level!'

'You guys, are like, metal-heads . . . I'm more of a . . . K-pop girl.'

'K-pop?'

'Yeah! I just happened to go out with a guy who's into sweaty man music.'

Alfie ran his hand through his hair.

'Is this really about Amy? Or are you scared of going to the gig?'

'It's gonna be full of hairy blokes moshing.'

'That's the best bit!'

'Jack described it. Sounds rough. I don't think I'm gonna enjoy it! I think it could be traumatic . . .'

'Oh my God. This is you when we booked: *Yay Jack, I'm so excited, let me fondle and kiss you!*'

'That was different! That was when it was all of us. I didn't want to be left out!'

'Why didn't you tell me this morning?'

'I'm sorry!'

'You're chickening out? Where's your sense of adventure? Where's your . . . bravery?'

Alfie felt the same urge he felt on the train. He should have done it! She wouldn't be saying this if he had!

'Have you actually even heard them? Has Jack played you any of their songs?'

Lily shrugged. 'Not really. He's normally round mine . . . we normally play my stuff.'

'Jack listens to K-pop? And he doesn't complain?'

'I think he likes it!'

'Jesus Christ! OK. Let me play you a song! One song! Let me show you how good they are.'

'But—'

'Two songs. Three songs! How can you call yourself Jack's girlfriend if you've never listened to his favourite band? Seriously, Lily, going tonight could change the course of your very existence!'

A gust of wind drove the drizzle against their bodies.

'Alfie! You're so annoying!'

'What?'

'Just . . . play me the goddamn songs.'

They traipsed up through the Lanes, through the Pavilion Gardens, and then into the North Laine, before settling on a place called Bubblicious, a tiny takeaway with a bright orange sign and a bar with stools. It sold one drink – bubble tea. Alfie sat down by the window, gave Lily some change for his drink while Lily queued and paid. Five minutes later she placed two drinks on the bar, both in large plastic cups: ice white, with a thick top layer of golden caramel oozing downwards. Both had a pile of small round tapioca balls sitting on the surface like a clutch of fish eggs. The rain became heavy, pummelling the pavement, and clusters of shoppers hurried past, pulling up their hoods and huddling under umbrellas. Alfie took out his phone and a battered pair of earphones. Lily took the earbuds, looked at each as if examining it for diseases, and then put them in her ears. Alfie opened his web browser and Googled Jōnetsu. He tapped on a picture of Joey Silveira in a black dress shirt, with long matted hair and a goatee.

'OK, so Joey, Joey Silveira,' Alfie tapped on the phone.

'He's had this really messed-up life. You won't believe it. His parents were part of a cult. A suicide cult? Like they all lived on this farm in Arizona and there was this guy who ran it who had ten wives and stuff and Joey was made to farm on it when he was seven, and his mum was one of the wives, and the guy who ran it used to hit her, and it was pretty messed up. There were lots of guns, they basically grew marijuana to keep the whole thing going. Then the Feds caught them, and then there was this siege and loads of them got shot and they burned the place down cos they all had a suicide pact and everyone died but Joey got rescued, and he was only thirteen, and got put into care. And that was a whole other thing, like going from home to home and—'

'Is this supposed to make me like them?'

'Just listen! Anyway, he had this passion for Japanese culture – he used to read manga, *Ghost in the Shell*, Guyver – it was the only thing that kept him going!'

Two thick lines deepened across Lily's forehead.

'So Jōnetsu means "passion" in Japanese, like lust for life, like fervour; it's like, even though things are dark, even though things are really bleak, there's still passion. It's like, passion to beat your demons, passion to pursue your dreams . . . I dunno, I'm not explaining it very well . . .'

Lily's eyes were distant, like she was looking through Alfie, into another dimension.

'OK, so this song is called . . . "Puppet".'

Alfie opened his music app, found the song and pressed play. Lily grimaced, covering her ears with her hands while the blender whirred, tinny pop played from a Bluetooth speaker in the back, the door clanked as it opened and closed. 'I think it's finished?' she said after a few minutes.

'So, it's basically about being under the spell of someone you like, so that anything they do, it's like they control you and how hard it is to break out of that.'

'It's kind of *heavy*,' said Lily.

'OK, listen to this. This one is more melodic.'

Alfie selected 'Twisted' and pressed play, and finished his bubble tea, making loud slurpy noises with his straw, avoiding Lily's face, watching the song timer tick down, a wave of nerves flooding his thighs.

'Yeah, that was more melodic.'

'Don't you ever feel like – no matter how good a relationship seems at first, things always end up twisted?'

'Err . . . can't say that I do . . .'

Alfie faltered, his brain freezing, scrolling up and down the playlist.

'OK. This one. This is the poppy one. This is the one that people who don't like them really like.'

He put on 'Surplus to Requirements.' Lily nodded her head in time to the beat. Alfie sung the lyrics in his head.

At first I was a good idea,
I gave you what you needed,
And now it's done, I'm surplus to requirements . . .

The room was uncomfortably stuffy and hot, and Alfie felt sweaty and claustrophobic.

'You see what I mean? You think someone wants you, then

they change their mind and reject you? When they see the real you?'

Lily shook her head.

'I shouldn't be explaining. I should let you make up your own mind.'

'That's OK! There *is* a lot of feeling.'

'Exactly!'

'Mostly anger. And pain.'

Alfie winced.

'It definitely wasn't as bad as I thought ... It was actually pretty good.'

'You think?'

'Yeah!'

'They just get it, you know? Joey! He gets it more than anyone!'

'Alfie, I think the music is awesome!' Lily slapped her hand down on the bar. 'Hear me? Awesome!'

Alfie look at her hopefully. 'You mean it?'

'But I'm still not going to the gig.'

Alfie rubbed his face.

'Come on. You look like I told you someone died!' said Lily.

'Why did you listen to those songs?'

'Because you asked me to.'

'You ... you were never gonna change your mind, were you? You just let me humiliate myself!'

'I find it hard to say no to people.'

'I feel like an idiot! Like I've just stripped naked and you laughed at me.'

'That's crazy. This is about Amy. Companionship.'

'What about me? Where's *my* companionship!' Alfie

snatched his earphones, stuffed them into his pocket and slapped his phone on the table. 'I thought we were having fun together. Why are you chickening out?'

'Why are you so scared of going by yourself? You're the chicken. Stop being such a wuss.'

Alfie blinked, stunned. He hated that she was right. He was terrified of going alone. It was like his stomach was full of poison.

'Fuck you, Lily.'

'What?'

'This whole day, it's all about you. What *you* want. Where *you* want to go. Who *you* want to see. Then when it comes to doing the one thing I want? The queue? You mock me. You don't let me do it. You make out like I'm an idiot for even wanting to do it.'

Alfie shook his head, grasping for words.

'You were always planning on seeing your sister, weren't you? So why didn't you tell me this straight after lunch? You "making up your mind" and "feeling conflicted" has messed up my day. This morning: you wanted to go by yourself to see Amy. All day you've been thinking about the best way to ditch me.'

'You made a convincing argument about doing it for Jack,' said Lily meekly.

'You lie about liking music just to fit in. You just treat me like some annoying thing you have to put up with. You treat Jack like a pet dog. You're probably just using him to show off. So people don't think you're a *virgin*. You guilt trip me for my "vibes" or whatever, but it's fine to just abuse me whenever you feel like it. Is there anyone you're not just using? You don't care about *me*, Alfie the person, you just care about my opinion of you and not thinking you're a bitch and using me to get your own way!'

Lily stood up abruptly.

'Yeah! I am scared of going on my own! So what?' said Alfie. 'At least I'm not empty. At least I'm not some heartless selfish psychopath!'

Lily's face crumpled. She put on her coat and hurried out of the door. Outside she stopped and stared at Alfie through the glass, squinting as the rain blew onto her face, before turning and stomping through the puddles, shoulders hunched, away into the rainy gloom.

23

Alfie sat there until the rain finally eased. He drank Lily's bubble tea until the sugar rush made his body shake. He took out his phone, and called Jack. No answer. He let the voicemail record but nothing came out of his mouth. His phone sat in his palm, recording the blenders whirring, the door banging, the till slamming open.

Abandoned! By all of his so-called friends! Was that the lesson of today? The only person in life you can trust is yourself? He'd actually thought she was OK. That some lame stone skimming and an epic game of air hockey had changed things. Screw her! He was gonna prove her wrong. He was gonna go by himself. He had to conquer his fear.

And maybe Lily leaving was a good thing. He could enjoy Jōnetsu without feeling awkward and weird and trying to make sure she enjoyed it.

Alfie opened his maps app. The venue was fifteen minutes away. The doors were opening soon. He was hungry. Fifteen per cent battery. He walked to the Churchill Square shopping centre, bought himself a McDonald's, ate it quickly, then followed the map to the venue.

Maybe Lily going had set him free . . . to meet someone new. Someone amazing. Someone special. Maybe, tonight, he would fall in love!

The female bouncer patted him down, searched his bag, and he went on into the cavernous space, the stage at the far side, lit with purple, green and amber beams of light, the crowd extending out from the barrier, filling most of the room. There were so many girls. Thick fake eyelashes. Heavily kohled eyes. Bare legs. Corsets. Cleavage. The front row was rammed with them. Smoking hot superfans. If only he'd had the guts to leave Lily, and queued up early, his fingers would be wrapped around that rail, within touching distance of Joey Silveira, and making conversation would be easy!

Instead he went to the bar, where brightly backlit upside-down spirit bottles lined the wall. He wanted alcohol more than ever, to stop the ten thousand mice which were scrambling around his thighs, their little claws digging into his muscles. He wanted to feel like Gwen did at Ovi's, to have the confidence to kiss whoever he wanted. That was the point of drinking, right?

Some whoops and shouts. Alfie turned to see a three-man band led by a small guy with thick glasses. A distraction! They were poppy and punky, a twanging rhythmic bass, pounding military drums, the singer's voice scratchy and rough, heads and bodies bouncing up and down. Actually, they were good, he Googled their name on his phone – battery seven per cent – then closed his eyes and danced. Some of the crowd knew the chorus. Actually, this was OK, forget the girls, enjoy the music.

Then, just as they finished, he glimpsed her – or did she glimpse him? Fake mascara tears from her eyes to her chin, fishnet sleeves and big baggy jeans. She was beautiful! *Zing!* An electric cattle prod stabbed into his ribs! She led her mate across the room, both of them stifling giggles, hurrying away on some mission.

He stood there, scanning the crowd. Where had they gone? The roadies were setting up the stage for Jōnetsu. He checked his phone – battery five per cent – they were back, to his left now, giggling, animated, absorbed in each other. Did she even notice him? Then Mascara Tears turned, caught his eye. Alfie smiled, she smiled back. This was his opportunity. He should to talk to her. He had to say something. She turned to her friend, her hair swung round, brushing Alfie's face. She felt it, turned back to Alfie, leaned towards his ear.

'Sorry,' she said.

Her hand brushed his. *Zing!* went the cattle prod!

'That's OK,' he said. 'This the first time you're seeing them?'

'Who?'

'Jōnetsu.'

The girl shook her head.

'You seen them before?'

She nodded.

'Where you from?'

She leaned towards Alfie, put her lips towards his ear. They actually brushed his skin. Did she mean to do that?

'Chichester,' she said.

Alfie nodded.

'Nice,' he said.

'You been there?'

'No,' said Alfie. She laughed. Her friend yanked her away.

'Sorry,' she said.

'Come back soon?'

She pressed her palm down onto Alfie's curly hair, enjoying its springiness and bounciness, then looked into his eyes and smiled while running her hand down his cheek.

'OK,' she said.

Alfie was elated. He felt dizzy and ecstatic. She was insanely fit! She was coming back! It was definitely on! The game was afoot!

'What do you think you're doing?'

A boy stood before him. Tall and wiry, his hair shaved so close you could see patches of skin. He had a tattoo on his neck, and his sleeveless top revealed taut, wiry arms.

'Excuse me?'

'What you doing?'

'Nothing.'

'Why you talking to my girlfriend?'

'What? I didn't know . . . We were just talking.'

'Prick!'

He shoved Alfie hard. Alfie stumbled backwards and bashed his butt on the floor. No one seemed to notice. Alfie scrambled to his feet. The boy didn't move, his shoulders tense, his breathing short.

'What?' said Alfie, holding out his hands. 'I didn't know!'

The boy's fists curled up. His arms sprang back.

'Hey!' said a voice. 'He's telling the truth!'

Someone yanked Alfie's forearm – he turned, and two lips pressed hard onto his mouth, for five seconds, ten seconds. Someone was kissing him!

'He's gone,' said the voice and Alfie opened his eyes to see a bright, beaming smile.

24

Alfie blinked. The same camisole, the same baggy combats she'd been wearing earlier – which seemed a very long time ago. She yanked him backwards, away from the boy.

'You're developing a really bad habit of getting into fights at gigs!' Lily said.

Alfie pointed to Lily, then to the door, then back to Lily.

'What the hell?' he shouted.

Lily shrugged. 'I'm here!' she said, brightly. 'And not a moment too soon!'

Lily pointed over Alfie's shoulder. There she was, Mascara Tears, the wiry guy's hand resting proprietarily on the small of her back.

'She's cute!'

'She was hitting on me!'

'You just keep telling yourself that.' Lily laughed at her own joke. 'I came in here and put my coat in the cloakroom, the first thing I hear is that guy ranting, *That bloke's taking the piss.*' Lily clenched her fists and flexed her muscles. '*I'm going to kill that prick! I'm not joking!* I'm like, *Who's he talking about? Oh, of course, it's Alfie, I should have known! Hitting on some boy's girlfriend.*'

Now Mascara Tears was full-on snogging him.

'Looks like she got what she wanted!'

'She was hitting on *me*!' said Alfie.

'The first stage of rejection is denial,' said Lily, laughing. 'To be fair, she is stunning . . . I would.'

Alfie's head wouldn't stop shaking, like one of those bobble-headed toys.

'Girls are terrible,' Lily said. 'You should totally turn gay.'

'What the hell are you doing here?'

'I'm like a white knight charging in to rescue you!'

'You said you weren't coming!'

'I changed my mind!'

'I called you a psychopath!'

'Yeah, well ...' Lily flicked her hair and flashed him her smile. 'Maybe you don't know me as well as you think you do.'

The lights went down before Alfie could reply. Static radio blared out of the speakers. An old American voice spoke, sounding like dialogue taken from a movie. Alfie glimpsed the silhouettes of three hulking men. One turned sharply, his dreadlocks swinging, a fuzzy, furry beard jutting out. He knew that profile. From publicity shots online, on the wall in his room, from Instagram and YouTube. It was actually him!

Everyone hushed. Then came the opening riff to 'Puppet,' the same four notes he'd heard a million times, in his room, in his headphones, walking round the estate, sitting on his own in the library at school – recorded, polished, perfect, sounding rough, raw, fresh, alive! The whole room erupted with a deafening roar, the crowd surged. Alfie tingled, he knew what was coming, so did everyone else, and *BOOM!* The snare drum cracked, then there was the ugly, percussive, crunching riff. The bass pounded, and there in the middle, holding the mic, was Joey Silveira.

'Why don't you cut me loose?
Please will you cut me loose?

You have to cut me loose!' he shouted, over and over and over, until his voice became a wild cathartic scream.

There it was: the rousing, uplifting, yearning, exhilarating chorus. Alfie held his hands up in reverence: *'Somebody cut me free!'* Joey stopped, held out the mic, and a thousand people sang, 'Noooooooooooow!'

Alfie stood on tiptoes, straining, hopping from foot to foot, there was the head of the bassist's guitar, Joey striding to the left, a drumstick popping high above someone's head then disappearing with a resounding pound. He looked for Lily. Damn! Where was she? No, right here, grabbing his forearm.

'You wanna go to the front?' she shouted.

'Impossible,' said Alfie, gesturing to the wall of bodies.

Joey sang acapella, voice cracked, flat, out of tune, but messing up made it better, even more angry-fragile, even more tormented. The drummer pummelled a rat-a-tat marching band-rhythm and Lily danced, gyrating her hips. Alfie was embarrassed, she did look out of place, no one here danced like that. Then, abruptly, he felt full of affection. Fair play to her, she didn't want to come and now she was going for it. She grabbed his hand, a small space temporarily opened up and she led them into it. She cocked her head towards the stage and Alfie got it: now it was a game – could they move forward – could they do the impossible? The crowd swayed and lurched and surged, and every time the smallest patch of floor opened up, Lily would step into it, squeezing ahead, sliding between bodies, taking Alfie with her. Alfie knew this song, he knew all the words, but he only half-listened, half-followed Lily's neck, and soon they were by the mosh pit where bodies were flying and things were getting rough.

191

Alfie wanted to explain they weren't actually fighting, it was personal choice, she didn't have to be scared, but to his total surprise she leaped into the fray, pogoing, jumping, slamming her back into two tall men, having the time of her life. Dammit, she was the one facing her fears! Alfie joined her, hundreds of bodies jostling, shoving, jumping-fighting-dancing. Delirious and exhausted, Alfie tried to whistle with both his fingers, as Joey Silveira rasped the opening to 'Twisted'.

'I love this song!' screamed Alfie, but she didn't hear him, craning her neck to see the stage. 'Lily! Remember this? Remember?' shouted Alfie, but still she didn't hear. Then – *smash* – a foot kicked Alfie's ear – *bang* – a thigh crashed into Lily's forehead. It was a boy, high above their heads. Alfie and Lily stuck up their hands, cushioning his fall, keeping him aloft, everyone doing the same, the boy bobbing around like a buoy on a choppy sea, screaming in pleasure. They sent him on his way, watching him until he landed by the barriers in front of the stage.

Alfie felt a surge of adrenaline. He wanted to crowd surf too! He tapped the shoulder of a bloke with a backwards cap, pointed to the sky, the man bent down and held out his hands for Alfie's foot. Alfie placed his trainer in the centre of the man's palms and – *whoosh* – he was up, and then – *wompf* – he was falling. Hands came out of nowhere, holding him, flexing with his weight, a ring of red, green and yellow spotlights, a projector, the green and white arches – *wheee!* – he was thrust forward, surfing a wave, right onto the stage.

Alfie stood up. The big beard, the baggy combats: Joey Silveira was small! Pretty much the same size as Alfie! *I have to remember that*, he thought—

'Whenever I talk it comes out TWISTED
Whatever I do it comes out TWISTED
Me and you, it's always . . .'

Joey held out the microphone towards Alfie, and he shouted 'Twisted!' into it. Two security guards made for him, one from each side, and in a split-second Alfie ran forward and launched himself up, up, up, hanging in the air as ten, twenty hands reached towards him, arms almost buckling as they caught him, helping him down to the floor.

'They're just having fun,' said Joey Silveira, after the song had finished.

The guards slunk back into the dim, dark wings.

'I don't make the rules,' said Joey.

Everyone booed the guards, they were the villains now.

'I didn't fly all the way here from America so we couldn't all have some fucking fun!' shouted Joey.

The outcry was ear-shattering, a random woman winked at Alfie, some hands patted him on the back, people gave him the thumbs up. He felt delirious, buzzing, overwhelmed, like a celebrity, like he'd died and gone to heaven.

'Ever get the feeling you're . . . surplus to requirements?' said Joey, and it was haywire again, backs and shoulders slamming into Alfie, and Lily was gone, disappeared, she had to be here somewhere – a scream – he knew that voice! Lily, ahead of him, crowd surfing!

'Liillllllyyyyyyyy!' he shouted, but she didn't hear, she was held aloft by strong, purposeful arms, pushing her towards the band.

'Now you've got what you want, I'm surplus to requirements,' rapped Joey, looking down at Lily, who stood on the stage,

smiling a big terrified frozen smile as the security guards hurried towards her—

'Jump!' screamed the crowd.

Two strong arms wrapped around her chest. Joey signalled for the band to stop playing. The place erupted into a chorus of boos as Lily was dragged into the darkness of the wings.

25

Joey Silveira was on a rant. It wasn't fair! Health and Safety was bullshit! Bring back stage diving! The crowd booed, the atmosphere soured as Alfie pushed his way to the bar at the back of the venue.

'That was my friend!' he said. 'What will they do to her?'

The barmaid shrugged. Alfie peered into the darkness at the side of the stage. What the hell was back there? He imagined a tiny room, windows with bars – no, no windows at all – Lily tied to a chair, interrogated by the bouncers, bright spotlights shining in her face. No, Lily was a girl! Locked in a room with big, scary older men! They were either gonna beat her up, steal her money, or, ugh, something worse, something much, much worse, her body washed up on Brighton beach, the police interviewing Alfie! Why had he encouraged her to crowd surf? Did he realise he was breaking the law? And now she was dead! And Alfie was accessory to murder!

Joey Silveira sensed where things were going, he reined himself in, telling people to *Relax, calm down, enjoy yourselves, that's what you're here for, right?* They restarted 'Surplus to Requirements'. Alfie checked his phone – one per cent battery – the gig had barely started. Surely Lily would call? Unless they'd taken her phone, smashed it on the ground, removed the sim card and chucked it out of the window!

The security guard who patted him down was standing by the exit.

'What happened to my friend?' he said. 'The girl on the stage. Where did they take her?'

'You don't wanna know,' she said, smirking.

'What will they do to her? Are they gonna beat her up?'

'They'll kick her out.'

'Can she get back in?'

The guard smiled mockingly and shook her head.

Alfie handed his ticket to the boy in the cloakroom. The boy frowned, as if to say, *What the hell are you doing leaving Jōnetsu half-way through?* But Alfie said nothing, his legs juddering as the boy ruffled through the coats, squinting at the ticket numbers – hurry up, dammit – Alfie snatched his coat, put it on, was immediately boiling, sweltering, he could still hear the band, muffled –

At first I was a good idea,
I gave you what you needed,
And now it's done, I'm surplus to requirements

It was like his soul was soldered to them! It was so, so painful, walking out, leaving that song behind, like ripping off a layer of skin. Then, out in the cold night air, a blast of wind smacked into his face. Alfie shivered, his ears ringing as the waves pounded. The boulevard was quiet and empty, the pier jutted out in the dark, lit by hundreds of bright amber bulbs; there was the dome of the arcade where they'd been only hours before; there was the moon, almost full, spilling a pool of milky light onto the sea below. Alfie walked away from the pier, the pavement becoming darker, colder, emptier, so he turned and walked the other way, towards the streetlights, towards civilisation.

But what if she hadn't been kicked out yet? What if she was still in there? Was this the only exit? Was there one round the back?

He checked his phone. Dead. Shit! Should he look for her or wait? Damned if he did, damned if he didn't!

He waited, no idea of the time, twenty minutes, forty minutes, jumping up and down to keep warm, the second half of the best gig ever happening on the other side of the wall, while his lip was wobbling and his legs were shivering.

A group of girls came out of the entrance, chatting in a kind of blissed-out calm. The gig was over, he'd definitely missed her.

Alfie trudged along the seafront, towards the pier, then across the roundabout at the Sea Life centre, past the Old Steine fountain. At once it was buzzing. Saturday night, groups of people drunkenly joking, a taxi swinging round the corner beeping, three homeless guys sitting outside a closed Greggs. Alfie spotted the clocktower – OK, so he knew where the station was – but rather than relief, he felt awful. What should have been the highlight of his life, the greatest moment ever, high-fiving Joey Silveira, on stage, was poisoned forever.

He hopped across the road and heard a snatch of a voice, a giggle – surely not?! – Lily! Talking to a tall man with a scraggly beard and a guitar on his back.

'Hi!'

'Oh, hi!' said Lily, extending her arms and hugging him. 'Alfie, this is Eddie. Eddie, Alfie.'

Eddie nodded at Alfie. 'You got Netflix?' he said to Lily. 'There was a documentary on Netflix. My mate had Netflix.'

Something wasn't quite right with Eddie. His voice was weedy and slow, and he reminded Alfie of a primary school kid, even though there were flecks of grey in his beard.

'We have to go,' said Alfie.

'Do we?' said Lily.

'Do you have Netflix?' said Eddie.

'WE HAVE TO GO,' said Alfie.

'I'm talking to my friend,' said Eddie.

'Nice to meet you!' said Lily, smiling. Alfie dragged her across the road.

'Wanker!' shouted Eddie.

'You need to stop pissing off all the guys,' said Lily.

'And you need to not talk to crazy men in the middle of the night.'

'He was nice.'

'He was not.'

Their arms were interlinked.

'I thought something had happened to you!' Alfie said.

'Oh my God, I'm fine! I called you like, six times.'

'I ran out of battery! I have to stop doing this.'

'What?'

'Freaking out about girls when they're actually OK.'

'More than OK! I had the best night ever!'

They made it to the station, onto the concourse – a train was leaving in five minutes. The carriage was empty and they sat opposite each other by the window.

Lily took out her phone while Alfie watched her reflection in the glass. She was messaging someone, probably Jack; the train moved off and he sighed with relief, the electric whine of the engine, the dim, shadowy outskirts of Brighton, they were heading home, finally, the last lap, he felt inside his pocket and took out a tenner – result! – he could spend it tomorrow on coffee, food, sweets – it had worked out OK in the end.

Lily flashed him her big smile before closing her eyes. Soon she dozed off. Her head hit the glass. She woke, her eyes startled, before dozing again and the cycle repeating.

She had kissed him! Of her own accord! OK, it was to save him from that guy. No tongues. Maybe it was just a mechanical thing to solve a problem. Like doing a job. Like an actor in a movie. But why did she have to *kiss* him? Why did she feel the need to press her lips onto his? Did she *want* to kiss him?

He was still thinking about it as they walked through the barriers at Victoria and then onto the Night Tube, where Lily fell asleep again, her head resting on Alfie's shoulder. Alfie felt paranoid that Jack would randomly get on the train and see them. They finally got out at Brent Cross station and Alfie walked Lily to her house.

'OK!' said Lily, holding out her arms. She hugged him. 'You were right. Thank you!'

'About what?'

'Jōnetsu! I am officially a fan!'

'Really?'

'Yeah! I'm sorry I nearly wussed out. I'm really glad I came.'

'I have so much respect for the way you just went for it.'

'And I have respect for you for going on your own.' She squeezed his arm. 'No respect for the fight though.'

'Yeah ... about that ..'

'It's OK. I saved your life. You owe me forever.'

'I'm talking about the kiss?'

'What?'

'You did kiss me, right?'

Lily folded her arms. 'What about it?'

'I mean, we did this for Jack, right? That was the whole idea? So if we're like, *We're friends now, but by the way, Lily kissed me*, he might not like it? If you know what I mean?'

Lily thought about it. 'It's kind of a typical hilarious Alfie story, me saving you from getting beaten up.'

'How can you tell the story without mentioning the kissing?'

'I dunno!' Lily suddenly snapped. 'If you're that worried about it, pretend it didn't happen!'

Lily took out her key, opened the door and punched in the code to the burglar alarm, its bleeps sounding loud in the quiet of the night.

'So we both pretend it didn't happen,' said Alfie.

'Whatever you want.'

'Yes or no?'

'Whatever you want!'

She stepped into her hallway.

'Do you think we succeeded? Are we gonna make Jack happy? Can we all hang out now in a weird happy family?' said Alfie.

'Yes!' Lily smiled insincerely.

'I'm gonna message him. Tell him the good news!' said Alfie.

Lily's face fell.

'What?'

Her lip wobbled.

'Lily. What's up?'

Lily shook her head. Alfie frowned.

'It's nothing! Message him!' She placed both her hands on her face. 'Do what you want!'

'Lily!'

Suddenly Lily sobbed. Alfie stuck out a hand and placed it on her shoulder.

'Lily, what is it?'

26

'He's not gone to see his granny? It's not her birthday?'

Lily nodded.

'You don't know where he went?'

'Cos we went there in the summer, it was the first excuse I could think of.'

'Why did you lie?'

'I was stressed! He stormed off in a huff. It would have been a really awkward conversation to have with you! *This* is a really awkward conversation to have with you!'

Alfie sat, exhausted, slumped against the wall in Lily's bedroom, scrunching his toes in her fluffy carpet, his still-damp trainers and socks discarded downstairs in her hallway. The silence of the early morning had revealed a stinging ringing in his ears, the heating was on high and the crystal lamp on her dressing table filled the room with a soft amber light. Lily was perched on the edge of her bed, newly changed into sweatpants and T-shirt, chewing gum, forehead creased, eyes bloodshot, wide awake and pissed off.

'I mean, why would I confide in you? You hate me! Or at least, you did this morning . . . So I tried to subtly get out of it, but you were like, *Let's go to Brighton for Jack!* And then I thought, what if it's not a big break up? What if "doing it for Jack" had the potential to save our whole relationship?'

Could it really be true? Had Lily split up with Jack? Out of nowhere? That was big, big news! He couldn't believe it!

Lily lay down on the bed, her hair spilling outwards. She covered her face with her hands, made a long, low, grunt of frustration, before sitting up with a start. 'If I tell you what happened, I'm scared we'll ruin our progress.'

'We won't.'

'Promise not to hate me? Again?'

Two more tears rolled down Lily's cheeks. She sat there, hands by her side, looking pathetic. Alfie resisted the urge to hug her.

'You have this image of me and Jack. You think everything is romantic and awesome and perfect.'

'It is!'

'It isn't!' Lily's eyes became vague and unfocused. 'OK, so maybe it was kind of perfect, for a while. Then Jack had to ruin it.'

She stood up and sat cross-legged on the carpet, ripping up bits of fluff absent-mindedly.

'Jack asked me what university I wanted to go to.'

'So? That's what we're supposed to be doing. Mr Hawton's banging on about it every assembly.'

Lily looked at Alfie fiercely. 'Jack wants us to go to the same university.'

'What's wrong with that?'

'Everything is wrong with that. It's like he wants to plan out the rest of our lives.'

'He's your boyfriend—'

'And I've got the British Swimming Championships! I've got to train. If I win then it's gonna affect everything! I might have to live in another city! Or another country!'

'Jack'd go with you.'

'That's exactly the problem! He says to me, *Wherever you go, I'll follow. Even if you tour round the world, I'll do Open University and study from my laptop in the hotel bedroom, cos I love you.*'

'Isn't that romantic?'

'Romantic? He made me feel like I was locked in a really, really small room, with only *this* much air.'

Lily made a choking sound. Alfie snorted.

'*Wherever you go, I'll follow*. I don't want to go out with my pet dog!'

Alfie laughed.

'You know the worst bit? We've slipped into this thing where he just does what I want. I clap my hands and he barks. And I say, *Good boy, Jackywacky*. Why do I do that? Why do I behave like his owner? I *am* controlling! You called me on it. In Bubblicious. You challenged me for being wrapped up in my stuff, and I liked it! Jack's never challenged me, ever! Even this morning he went mopey and pathetic. I don't want to go out with a dog! I want to go out with a *man*!'

Lily squeezed Alfie's calf as she said it. He felt a surge of adrenaline.

'I wish he'd said, *I'm going to Edinburgh and that's that!* That would be a problem but it would also be sexy! Instead, he's like, all pathetic: *I just said I love you, and you didn't say it back.* All clingy and . . . *icky*.'

'Do you love him back?'

'It's like, everything was really intense and going really fast, and I was fine with that, and then he mentions "university" and "love" and "long term" and I was like, *Woah, woah, woah, woah!* Shit just got real!'

'You guys are nymphomaniacs! I thought you'd be together forever!'

'I know! I mean, maybe we've been going *too* fast, know what I mean? I'm sixteen fucking years old! What if I become a pro swimmer? What if I have to live in the USA and train, and dedicate my life to it?'

'Is that actually gonna happen?'

'Maybe. I'm up at five a.m. five days a week! I don't think any of you get what that's like. And the thing is ... He's the *first ... my* first.' She leaned towards Alfie, touching his knee. 'Do I really want to go through my A levels and university in a committed relationship? Having only ever shagged one guy? It's like he brought up all my issues at once!'

It was like a halo of fire was around her face, her eyes raging.

'So you want to shag lots of different guys?'

'What would be the problem if I did?'

Alfie held up his hands. 'Nothing!'

Lily stared at him, frowning.

'He's been researching. He had the open day dates in his diary. He wanted to stay in London. He wanted to move in. Here. With me. And when I didn't say *I love you* back, he was like, *So you're saying you're not in this for the long haul?* I couldn't answer! I just clammed up! He freaked! Stormed out the house and ghosted me!'

'Is that what you were talking to Amy about? Is that why you didn't want to come to the gig?' said Alfie.

'Yes. I lied again. Amy doesn't have girlfriend issues! I have boyfriend issues! I told her about our fight and she was like, *You need to come and feel sorry for yourself with me, we can eat ice cream and watch bad films*. I wasn't sure and I did have fun with you, but as the day went on I felt so sad. I wanted to go to Amy's and hide! And then we had our bust-up and I stormed out and called Jack and left him, like, *another* message, saying me and you were in Brighton and can he call me, in addition to the *five billion* messages I left saying that I wanted to talk. No reply! Nothing! Like, screw him! So I went to Amy's and told her about you playing me all the tunes, and I *did* like them, Alfie, and I felt so bad about bailing, cos I'm not a total psychopath, I do actually care about your feelings, believe it or not. She was like, *Jack's throwing it away, Alfie's cute, he's a nice guy, don't stay here, I'll call you a cab, go out and have some fun with a cute boy*. I was like, *Yeah! I need to make it right with Alfie!*'

Alfie stretched his legs, brushing Lily's knees.

'And drum roll ...' Lily patted the carpet. '... now I love Jōnetsu! And maybe a whole new genre of music!'

'My work here is done,' said Alfie.

Lily laughed. He stood up and walked to the window, gazing into the empty street. A fox scurried into the centre of the road, froze, then hurried on, disappearing behind a bush. Alfie didn't feel tired any more. It was like someone had plugged him into an emergency battery pack. He was *glad* that this had happened to Jack. Maybe he'd stop acting so smug.

'I'm furious with him for making things so serious,' mused Lily. 'And I'm furious with him for walking out and ignoring me. Like both extremes. I really don't see a way back! Maybe ... maybe it's over.'

Alfie felt a righteous thrill. Was single Jack gonna beg him for friendship? After ignoring Alfie for months? Why should he take him back? He should get a taste of his own medicine.

'Sorry if I was rude,' said Alfie.

'I'm sorry too.'

He turned and smiled.

'Look at it this way,' he said. 'If you have split up – you can have sex with anyone you want!'

'I guess . . .' said Lily, doubtfully. 'Silver linings and all that.'

There was an awkward silence. Lily stared at the carpet.

'So now that you heard what happened, you're not gonna go back to hating me?'

Alfie shook his head. 'I don't even think you did anything wrong.'

She stood up and hugged him from behind. 'Thanks, Alfie. See? You're not the only one with a disastrous love life.'

'Excuse me?'

Lily laughed.

'What?'

'Something Amy said.'

'What?'

'Doesn't matter . . .'

'What?'

'Now he's found out I'm gay, is he gonna fall in love with me? Do you even have a Gaydar?'

'I could kill him, I could actually kill him! I will never tell Jack a secret, ever again!'

Lily was giggling. 'It's not rocket science. *Gwen*! I mean, like, *duh*!'

'She kissed me! She jumped on me! At Ovi's party. And Jack didn't know she was gay either, it's not that obvious!'

They faced each other by the window.

'It's like Maya rejecting me, really mullered my confidence.

Like, I can't trust my feelings. Every time I fall for a girl, every time I allow myself to dream ... life comes along and kicks me up the arse. Hard! How do I know ... if something is real?'

Lily nodded, her eyes became distant.

'I guess I just ... really, really, really, really, really, really, really, really, really want a girlfriend,' said Alfie.

'You don't have to be so desperate!' said Lily, snapping back. She grabbed Alfie's hand. 'Seriously, you don't! And I'm sorry for roasting you. I have been cruel. You really touched a nerve! I'm not gonna do it any more.'

'Thanks, Lily.'

'You wanna know the real reason I roast you? It's like, I'm so bloody conscious of how I just stormed into your life and stole your best mate. And how you felt about that was really bloody obvious. So, yeah, maybe I was just ... overcompensating and being defensive.'

'Thanks, Lily.'

'And I got really annoyed with you at Luke's gig! You were such a romantic klutz! I was like, *Alfie's attractive, why is he wasting his time with all this ... stupidity! Chasing after a girl with a boyfriend!*'

'You think I'm attractive?'

'It's not exactly the done thing to be flirting with your boyfriend's best mate, is it? Much easier to roast you.' She inhaled deeply and exhaled loudly. 'So, really, honestly, Alfie, no need, OK?'

'Thank you.'

'Pleasure.'

Alfie yawned, a wave of tiredness sweeping through his body.

'Are you OK?' said Lily.

'Very,' said Alfie. 'It's just ... deep and meaningful chats are exhausting.'

'I know! It's been a long day. We should get some sleep.'

They both stood there, neither of them moving.

'I'll go,' said Alfie.

'Don't be silly! You can crash!'

'I only live round the corner.'

'You look like you're gonna collapse.'

'Which is why I should go.'

'Just crash here!'

'Where?'

'Amy's room.'

But Lily and Alfie were frozen. Her eyes were brown with flecks of gold. They were beautiful, Alfie realised.

'You know what I liked about tonight?' he said. 'How you're the only one apart from me who doesn't drink.'

'No way! My body is a temple!'

'It's good to know someone else who doesn't do it ..'

'We don't need drink to have a good time.'

'Exactly!'

Lily's fingers interlinked with his. Alfie's body tingled.

'Can I ask you a question?' she said quietly.

'Sure.'

'Do you really think I'm hot?'

'What?'

'Did you mean what you said? This morning?'

'What did I say?'

'I'm so *not* one of the most hottest girls in the year!'

'Oh. Yeah. You are.'

'I'm a swimmer! I have massive shoulders! My boobs are tiny! Literally, since I was thirteen, people have been taking the piss!'

'Well . . . I disagree with those people. Strongly.'

Lily smiled brightly, holding Alfie's gaze.

'God dammit, your eyes,' she said. 'They're like . . . an icy blue lake. Really, Alfie . . . you have nothing to worry about.'

Alfie shuddered. She liked his eyes too.

'What?' said Lily. 'It's like maybe I kissed you in the venue because . . . it was a good excuse to . . . or something . . .'

He wasn't sure who did it first. His head dipped forwards, but so did hers. Lily's hands touched Alfie's cheeks. Her tongue pressed into his mouth, filling it with sweet strawberry.

'Woah,' said Alfie.

'Woah, indeed.'

Lily put her lips to his ear.

'I've always thought you were . .'

'What?'

'Shaggable,' Lily whispered.

She took a step back, grabbing onto his fingers, beaming, tugging him towards her.

'Yes, Alfie. That's what I said.'

Maya

27

'Why do I have to keep saying it?' said Nan.

She sat on the sofa in her pink onesie, pasty-faced, hair unkempt. It was eleven a.m.

'I stayed at my friend's . . .'

'And how was I supposed to know that? Am I psychic?'

Alfie shrugged.

'One tiny message. Five small seconds of your busy important life.'

'I'll make you some breakfast.'

'Don't change the subject!'

Alfie was blissfully detached. Bra-less Lily flashed across his mind. Pant-less Lily. Naked Lily. Wow! He felt high!

He went into the kitchen, stuffed two slices of bread into the toaster, and ate a handful of cornflakes. They tasted delicious. Even Radio 2 sounded good.

'I'm still angry with you,' said Nan as he handed her the plate of buttered toast.

He collapsed onto the sofa. 'My phone ran out of battery.'

Nan plonked herself down next to him. 'Did no one have a charger?'

'I was distracted.'

'With what?'

'Stuff.'

He closed his eyes and saw Lily again. Her strong bare shoulders, reaching into her drawer, taking out a condom . . .

The heat of her body ... her beautiful belly-button ... The flashbacks wouldn't stop. If they carried on like this he'd walk into a lamppost or get run over.

'I trust you spent it all,' said Nan.

'Every penny. Actually, no, I saved a tenner!'

'A tenner! How frugal!'

'Soon I'll be eighteen and you officially won't have to care any more!'

'Ha! You have no idea.'

'Plus, I got an email. From Coffee Boss. I have an interview! Tomorrow after school.'

Nan folded her arms.

'And soon I'll be the CEO and you won't have to work any more and I'll be able to pay a personal driver to take you to Café Delish, every day, whenever you want.'

He'd lost his goddamn virginity to Lily! Life comes at you fast! First, the Maya Disaster. Then, the Gwen Debacle. And now ... the Lily Romance? Was that why there'd been so much beef? There was something deeper ... some connection ... It was like they were magnets that repelled and someone had flipped them, and now they went *click*!

Alfie imagined watching Lily in the Olympics, in her navy Team GB costume, strong, powerful arms and shoulders wheeling around, butterfly stroke, swimming cap glued to her skull, mouth open, gulping air. Lily touching the edge, winning by a split second, turning, glancing up at the time, realising she'd broken the world record, then screaming at the top of her voice, and then meeting Alfie in the hotel room, kissing him, ripping off his T-shirt.

Stop! Wind it in. Dreams of the future was what had got

Jack into trouble. Jack! What would they do about Jack? Last night, she'd placed the picture of them face down on the carpet. So they didn't have to see him when they were ... That said everything. Bye, bye Jack. They would have to find a way of breaking it to him. It would be hard. Crazy hard. *But if it's meant to be, it's meant to be, right?*

He felt so happy, that literally nothing could hurt him. He picked up his phone, and opened his email and drafted a message, concentrating hard on every word. He typed in his mum's email address and wrote *Meeting Up* in the subject line.

> I didn't reply to you because I get too angry.
> I tried to write a poem about it.

He opened his notebook and carefully copied in the angry poem he'd written the day he'd flung it out of the window.

> So ... yeah ... this is what I feel.

He hit send. Better to tell the truth, right?

'Nan,' said Alfie.

'Yes?'

'You know what you said about being unlucky in love?'

'What?'

'Mum being unlucky in love ... you being unlucky in love and then maybe *me* being unlucky in love ..?'

'Yes ..?'

'It's not true!'

Nan frowned. 'Oh. Now I know where you were last night. Does this one have a name?'

'Yes!'

'What is it?'

Alfie hesitated. 'We need to keep it under wraps. For now. We've got a couple of things to sort out.'

Nan raised her eyebrows.

'What?' said Alfie.

'I don't want to know.'

'I—'

Nan held up her palms. 'I don't want to know!'

Now Nan watched Alfie from the corner of her eye.

'Things are going my way for once,' he said.

LILY:

Hey

ALFIE:

Hey

LILY:

How are you?

ALFIE:

Good. Thinking about last
night

LILY:

Me too

ALFIE:

I really enjoyed it

LILY:

Me too

ALFIE:

☺

LILY:

About that

ALFIE:

I know, how are we gonna
tell Jack?

LILY:

About what?

ALFIE:

Me and you
He has to find out
eventually

LILY:

We're not

ALFIE:

Why?

LILY:

Last night was a one-off

ALFIE:

Was it?

LILY:

Just so we're on the same page
Jack can never know
It would really hurt him
Don't say anything, OK? 😖

ALFIE:

OK

LILY:

Promise?

ALFIE:

Yes

LILY:

We spoke this morning
We had a long chat
We sorted things out

ALFIE:

Really?

LILY:

I don't want to split up with him

Are you OK with that?

Alfie?

I just realised maybe I do love

him after all

ALFIE:

OK

LILY:

It was definitely fun

I'm really glad we got to know

each other

I don't regret it

But I woke up

And I kind of knew

ALFIE:

OK

LILY:

It happens, sometimes

Two friends

Hormones do hormonal things

No need to make a big thing of it?

ALFIE:

Sure

Glad to help out

Or something

LILY:

Maybe it was our weird way of
becoming friends?

ALFIE:

Maybe it was

LILY:

Jack can't know

ALFIE:

I know
You said

LILY:

Great
So we good?

ALFIE:

We good

LILY:

Honest?

ALFIE:

Yes

LILY:

Thanks Alfie
Really appreciate it

JACK:

Dude

Just wanna apologise about

ditching you

ALFIE:

It's OK

JACK:

Me and Lily had our first big argument

Whatever you said to her at Jōnetsu

it turned it around

So thanks bro

You're the best

ALFIE:

My pleasure

JACK:

And now you two are actually friends

I never thought that would happen

Everything fell into place

28

'You will not believe the weekend I've just had.'

Maya sat at the head of the table, wafting her fork around, bits of rice toppling off the top. An anaemic chicken thigh sat on her plate, flooded with watery yellow sauce. Her hair was tied up in a bun. She wasn't wearing make-up. Since when had Maya not worn make-up? She had spots all over her forehead and cheeks. Were there always so many? She looked . . . younger.

'OK, so everything had been going really, really well. At the Clacton gig I sang on three songs in the set, and after we finished I asked if I was in the band and Luke said yes. I was over the bloody moon. Since then, I've been going to the weekly rehearsals. Learning more songs. They booked more studio time in December and he invited me. Finally, I was gonna get to record our song! He said he was drawing up the contracts! The other two were being a bit moody, but you know, I thought they were always like that. And then he applied for this showcase. This battle of the bands thing. And they accepted him. It was this whole "festival" thing happening in the Water Rats in Kings Cross. Like, there was gonna be music industry people there. This was their chance to get a really good manager. It was like, all coming together.'

'Woah! Sounds amazing!!' said Samira.

Samira was there! She rested her chin on her palm, her long ringlets swinging round, brushing Gwen's fingers. Gwen's cheeks were red, hair tied back, barely enough to make a ponytail, both hands on the edge of the table, the corners of her lips turned up in a smile, loved-up, with the person she actually liked. Argh! When you knew, it was obvious!

Jack caught Alfie's eye, looked at Lily and gave him the thumbs up.

Maya gathered herself. 'So anyway, we got there, parked the van, loads of time to unload and soundcheck, but it was all a bit on edge, you know. Mikey and Olly were being really short with me, Luke went all cold. Barely talking. Like, the rest of them: freezing me out. I just thought, you know, *It's a big day, he's nervous, they're nervous. I'm nervous. What if we're spotted? What if we get a label? This could be the beginning of the rest of our lives! Interviews, posters, photoshoots, websites, music videos . . .* God, I'm so stupid, it's ridiculous!'

The table was silent, everyone focused on Maya. Apart from Alfie. He felt wretched. All he could do was stare at his plate. His potatoes had been boiled to mush. Three manky chickpeas sat in the middle of a puddle of sauce.

'It was such a weird atmosphere. Everyone from Luke's party just transplanted from Theydon Bois to this sweaty pub, plus these weird old music industry people who everyone had to suck up to and everyone was desperate to impress. I really, really, needed a drink and no one was drinking, not even Olly, that's how seriously he was taking it. Then, I lost Luke. Literally. He was nowhere to be found, Mikey and Olly had no idea where he was. I decided to go to the shop and I saw him . . . on the pavement . . . vaping with the singer of this all-girl punk band . . . She was the fittest person I've ever seen, all petite and slight, this demon tattoo on her collarbone, all edgy, all sexy. I'd spent two hours getting ready and felt fat and frumpy just looking at her. He was laughing and joking and touching her arm, and she was all over him, shoving her barely-existent tits in his face. Shameless! It made me wanna puke! I walked past and he didn't even notice me! He didn't even look up! My blood was boiling! Thank God Gwen showed up. We had this big heart-to-heart in the alley. She said, *Go speak to him.* I went back inside, Luke was on the stairwell, and I grabbed him and said, *What the fuck is going on?'*

Gwen's hand shot out and squeezed Maya's.

'He just like, looked at me. *Maya. I don't think this is working out.'*

'What?' said Samira.

'Seriously?' said Lily.

'I was like, *Excuse me?* He was like, *Us. The band. The gig.* I was like, *Say what?* He said, *I'm afraid so. I've been meaning to say this for a while. It's been on my to-do list.'*

'To-do list?' said Lily.

'Cold!' said Samira.

Alfie shook his head. Of course it went wrong with Luke. It always went wrong. There was no such thing as a happy relationship. He picked up the stale chocolate brownie on the other side of his tray and took a small bite. No, that was disgusting too. Everything was disgusting.

'Cold as ice!' continued Maya. 'He said, *Maya, I am attracted to you, we had a lot of fun and all that, but I don't think we have a future, long term. We tried you out, but after some consideration, the boys don't think you're the right fit.'*

'He sounds like some manager at a job interview!' said Samira.

'Exactly!' said Maya. 'But then he stuck the knife in: *They're getting a bit sick of you. We're all chill and you're intense. You're always trying to take over. Is Twisted Dreamland my band or yours?*

'I was like, *That's just who I am, I'm passionate*! He said, *Passionate … or crazy? The knife in the football? Remember that? I'm sorry, Maya. I think we were more of a holiday thing.* I was going, *You invited me to do this! You welcomed me with open arms!* He just shrugged! Unbelievable! I told him, *You have to fucking credit me with "I Wrote Your Name in the Stars". If you release it, you have to. Otherwise I will hunt you down and make your life a misery.* He's like, *You see. This is what I'm talking about.*'

'He'd been planning it for a while,' said Gwen. 'He'd obviously promised Olly and Mikey that he'd do it before, he just didn't have the balls. He left it to the last second.'

'I'm such a sucker!' said Maya. 'I fell for it. The looks! The charm! The smile! He's totally selfish! He told me what I wanted to hear and when he got bored he just … moved on. It was Ovi, Part Two!

'I'm just so happy Gwen was there to take me home and be my therapist, otherwise I might have stormed onstage, grabbed Olly's bass, and smashed it into Luke's face.'

Samira put her hand over her mouth. 'Did he sing your song?' she said, eyes worried.

'I wasn't there, was I? Knowing him, yes. Probably sounded amazing. God, I hate him!' Maya looked like she was about to cry. 'And the worst thing is, he's right. I *was* pushy. I *did* get intense. I basically forced myself into his band so I could piggyback on their talent! I thought it would solve all my problems!'

No one knew what to say. Maya just stared at her barely-eaten lunch. Gwen rubbed Maya's arm. Lily got up and hugged her from behind. Samira put her hand on Gwen's. They sat there in silence, mourning, contemplative.

'Alfie called it,' said Maya, her eyes welling up. 'He spoke to Luke's ex. He knew Luke was a player. And what did we do? Laugh at him.'

They all looked at Alfie, kindly, but Alfie just stared at his food. He was starving. Nothing was edible. Everything was disgusting. *Life* was disgusting.

'What is the point of going out with anyone?' he said suddenly.

A couple of tables away, Raheem stood up. He waved at Alfie. Alfie pretended he hadn't seen.

'Alfie! I'm paying you a compliment,' said Maya. 'You said it in a really clumsy, inappropriate way, but you were right, I should have listened!'

Why should he care about Maya's stupid sob story?

'There's never a happy ending, is there?' he said. 'Jōnetsu were right. Everything's twisted!'

'Alfie. What are you on about?' said Maya.

Alfie covered his face with his hands.

'Yo! I need to talk to you,' said Raheem.

Alfie's breathing was fast and shallow, his legs shaking.

'Oi! Alfie! I need to talk to you!'

'Why?' said Alfie. 'What's the point of talking? What's the point of doing anything?'

'Is he OK?' said Raheem, turning to the others.

'I think he's having an existential crisis,' said Maya.

Alfie grimaced.

'Alfie, what is it?' said Gwen.

Alfie shook his head.

'Dude, talk to us!' said Jack.

Alfie picked up his brownie, squeezed his thumb and forefinger together and watched the crumbs fall onto his tray.

'Listen, Alfie,' Raheem said, 'I don't know what's happening, but I'm gonna say this really fast: you know I play in that amateur league thing? We're down two players, and we're desperate, so can you come and join us?'

Alfie looked up at Raheem, and gave him a cold, angry stare.

'Ooo-kay,' said Raheem. 'When you've made a decision, let me know – thanks, bye.' He hurried off.

'I think we need to change the subject to something lighter,' said Maya.

Everyone nodded.

'Tell us about Jōnetsu!' she said.

'Yeah, dude, it was quite the eventful night!' said Jack. 'Right?'

'Yeah, Alfie tell us about Jōnetsu,' said Samira.

Everyone nodded, apart from Lily, who looked at the floor. Some boy was rapping somewhere to their left, some girls groaning at a joke behind them.

'Yes! Everything! Every last detail!' said Maya. 'I want to live it vicariously! I made such a big mistake not going! I can't believe I missed the gig of the century for Twisted-lame-Dreamland.'

'You want to live it vicariously?' said Alfie.

'I'm so annoyed I didn't go! I wanna know how amazing it was!'

Alfie looked at Lily. Lily shook her head.

'You wanna know how amazing it was?'

Lily was glaring at him with panicked eyes.

'So much!' said Maya. 'So, so much!'

No, why *should* he be quiet? Maya told everyone everything! Lily betrayed her boyfriend! Why should she get to be happy while he was slowing dying inside?

Alfie took a breath. 'Me and Lily went together because we were the only ones who hadn't bailed. We decided to patch up our differences and try and be friends. It was going well but then *she* tried to bail and we had a massive argument. Lily saved me from being beaten up by kissing me, and then we made up.'

Jack was suddenly frowning. Lily looked down at the table.

'Jōnetsu was amazing but I missed half of it cos Lily got chucked out for crowd-surfing. Then I found her. She told me that she and Jack had had an argument and I thought that meant they'd split up. Then we told each other we fancy each other.'

Alfie felt the full attention of the table.

'And then ... we *slept* together. I lost my fucking virginity and thought I was falling in love with Lily, cos I'm a sensitive romantic dumbass idiot! Then Lily decided she wanted to get back with Jack and dumped me and told me never to tell Jack. I'm a disgusting, unlovable loser and I *hate* myself.'

He pushed his tray away, and folded his arms. Jack had turned white. Lily was aghast.

'So. Yeah. I win in the awful weekend competition.'

Life went into slow motion. Maya muttering 'Oh my God.' Samira's smile, half upset, half enjoying the drama. Gwen's confused frown. Jack's angry stomp out of the lunch hall. Lily chasing after. Then Alfie sitting alone on a toilet, in a cubicle, until the end of lunch break.

29

At the end of the day, Alfie didn't leave through the front gate like the rest of the school. He walked out into the back playground, skirted round the Astroturf, along the green metal railings that demarked the edge of the school, stopping at the corner. Below him was a patch of grass, dotted with empty picnic tables. He chucked his bag over the fence, then hauled himself over and onto the pavement. He ran past the leisure centre, down an alley and out onto the busy Hendon Way, where he paused, hands on his knees, panting.

Dammit! Avoiding people was hard! He took out his phone. *No, don't turn it on. Stay off grid. Go for a walk.* When everyone had gone, he could sneak into his flat.

Shit! Alfie remembered. His interview. Today. At five. He needed to change. But what if Jack was outside their block, waiting? Jack, his sisters and mum, arms folded, blocking the entrance, holding baseball bats! Could he go as he was? He *was* in a suit. He was in A1, for god's sake. School-age kids are allowed to be in uniform, right? What were you supposed wear, anyway? Would they give him a Coffee Boss T-shirt? Ugh. Stress. He should bunk. No-show. All he wanted to do was hide.

He crossed the road via the underpass, with its grotty green tiles and mouldy autumn leaves, and walked towards the enormous junction where the Hendon Way sloped up high, soaring above the North Circular, following the pavement into the spaghetti-like mess of walkways and slip roads. Six lanes of traffic below, six lanes of traffic above, the roar of the engines hurting his ears. He hurried onwards, past weather-beaten concrete pillars, over the canalised River Brent, just a little dribble of water, an upside-down trolley in the middle of the stream.

He stood, gripping the railings, catching his breath, feeling queasy. The scrape of a shoe made him jump. He turned. Jack and Lily. Argh! This was on her way home! She'd probably gone all girly and apologetic and grovelly and told him she loved him, and the whole thing was forgotten!

Jack stood still, mouth hanging open in an O. Lily whispered into Jack's ear before stomping past, leaving them alone.

Alfie braced himself for a smack on the head, for his body to flip over the railings and into the canal. He'd be found in the morning, face down. Dead.

'Dude . . .' said Jack.

No. That was the whole joke, Jack *looked* mean but he wasn't, he was a gaming nerd, he was a wimp, that's why Alfie was so frustrated that he'd got a girlfriend before him, that's why Lily got annoyed when he was like, *Wherever you go, I'll follow!* He didn't deserve it!

'Dude!' said Jack.

He wouldn't beat him up cos he didn't have the balls!

'*Dude!*'

Jack's eyes looked anguished. Suddenly, Alfie wanted to hug him. He was his best friend! He loved him!

'I'm sorry!' he shouted.

Jack's chest heaved up and down. 'What were you *thinking*?'

'I don't know!'

'You don't know?'

'I thought it was over!'

Jack shook his head.

'I thought you'd split up!'

Jack gripped the railings. They both watched the trolley.

'She hit on me, man! She totally hit on me!'

'She said you gave her signals. You were the one hitting on her!'

'No! Maybe. We hit on each other! It all got weird.'

'I love her, Alfie! You're my best mate!'

'I know! I'm sorry!'

A dirty nappy bobbed along the water until it bumped into the corner of the trolley.

'It didn't mean anything!' said Alfie. 'Really! Nothing. I'm an idiot. I fall for everyone! I get all romantic and carried away and it's all inside my head and it's nothing to do with reality!'

He waited as a couple passed, the woman in a headdress and a black puffa, a man in a suit and new-looking Nikes.

'You left me, man! You dumped me! I had no one to hang out with! No one to play *Football Manager* with! I was jealous! Crazy jealous! She stole you!'

'What about Maya?'

'Not the same. Not the same at all!'

The nappy shifted, following the side of the trolley, before lodging itself against the front wheel.

'You promised to hang out with me!' said Alfie. 'Then Lily always got in the way! Like in Camden. It was meant to be us, hanging out, and you spent most of the time on the phone to her. And when I told you about Gwen, I asked you *not* to tell Lily, and you did. You said *Football Manager's* for losers. Which means you think I'm a loser. You took me for granted. Putting me down. You say you're interested in my girl issues but all you do is offer patronising advice. I've been really angry with you. Maybe I *wanted* to hurt you. Maybe I wanted revenge.'

It was too painful, so Alfie walked and Jack followed. They emerged from under the motorway, jumped across a slip road, and into the Brent Cross car park. They stood in an empty parking space, in between a black people carrier and green hatchback. It was quieter here, they didn't have to shout.

'Why didn't you say something?' said Jack. 'You never say shit! It pisses me off!'

They both jumped as an engine sparked behind them.

'I find it hard. Saying how I really feel,' said Alfie.

Jack scowled.

'Maybe I did you a favour,' said Alfie. 'I made her realise that she loves you! Just like you said. Everything fell into place!' Alfie watched Jack's face hopefully. 'You're the only boy at school I get on with. Our flats are next door and our bedrooms share walls! We're supposed to be best friends! There has to be a way to repair this.'

'Do you know what "trust" is, Alfie? Does the word "trust" mean anything to you?'

'Of course it does!'

'Trust is like ... my sister's money tree plant ... Give it light ... Keep it dry ... Keep it safe from pests, it grows ... Get one tiny thing wrong ..' Jack shook his head.

'What you trying to say?'

'I'm saying you took my money tree plant, and watered it ... with toxic waste!' Jack's eyes spasmed with sorrow. 'Things can *never* go back to the way they were!'

'Why were you going to hers then?'

'She wanted to talk. Fine, I'll talk. I was explaining to her what I am explaining to you ... She was grovelling. It was pathetic.'

'Dude! She was grovelling because she cares!'

'Can I trust a word she says? Can I trust a word anyone says? Ever? Again? I pay for your Oyster. I buy you lunch! And then you do *this*?'

Alfie placed his hands on Jack's shoulders. 'C'mon, man! You're gonna go to university with her. You're gonna get married! You are gonna have hundreds of little Jack-Lilys! She's totally yours! She's a great girl. She loves *you*, man! She loves you like *crazy*! You can come back from this. You *can*!'

Suddenly, Jack punched him, hard on the temple. Alfie collapsed to the ground. Jack cried out in pain, cradling his fingers. Alfie rolled onto his back, his hand over his eye.

'Maybe you're right, Alfie. Maybe I screwed up our friendship. But what you just did?' Jack stared at him. 'You hate yourself? Everyone hates you too. Maya, Gwen, Lily. Me. What the hell happened, man?'

30

Coffee Boss was busy, customers huddled round cramped tables full of paper cups, the queue so long it stretched back into the main concourse. Alfie stood at the opening to the bar, where a broad-shouldered boy frothed milk, a girl in a headscarf and red lipstick poked and tapped at the till, and a harassed-looking woman with bright pink hair bustled around the back bar, yanking the pie iron open to check on a toastie, then squeezing some syrup into a blender.

Alfie waited. His armpits were damp, his shirt creased. He checked his face with his selfie camera. His eye was puffy and red.

'Can I help you?' said the boy, placing a paper cup on the counter, an Uber Eats sticker stuck onto its side.

'I'm here for the interview?' said Alfie.

'Magda!' shouted the boy.

The pink-haired woman looked up. Her sad eyes were lined with mascara, and her skin was extremely tanned. She said something Alfie couldn't catch. The broad-shouldered boy pointed. 'Wait!' he said.

Alfie stood by a little counter containing napkins, straws and milk. Eventually, Magda arrived, clutching a ring binder to her chest. 'Nowhere to sit!' she said, sighing tragically as if it was the latest thing to go wrong in a day where everything had gone wrong. 'We'll just have to do this standing up.'

'Magda!' called the girl with the headscarf.

'Sorry.'

She hurried back behind the bar, filled the food processor with syrup, ice, coffee and almond milk, blended it, and poured the mixture into a large transparent plastic cup. She was back in the flow, and Alfie had to wait another fifteen minutes before she returned.

'OK!' she said, when they finally sat down in the alcove round the corner. 'Why the hell do you want to work *here*?'

'Um ..' said Alfie, his cheeks hotting up.

'I forgot to print your application. If I'm honest, I forgot you were coming.' She smiled. 'So who the hell are you and what do you want?'

'Err ..'

'Don't look so scared! I'm not that bad, ask them.' She nodded towards the two servers behind her. Alfie laughed politely and scratched his head. 'What's the matter? Cat got your tongue?'

'I just ... really like it here. I come all the time. And I need a job to support my nan ... so it kind of made sense ..'

'Your nan?'

'My mum doesn't live with us.'

She frowned. 'How old are you?'

'Sixteen. Seventeen in March.'

'You come from school? Of course you do. Look at you. You're a bloody schoolboy.'

Alfie told her the name of his school.

'I don't care if you go to Oxford University! I care about Monday to Friday, seven a.m. to nine-thirty p.m. I tell them I need full-time, and they send me a schoolboy!'

Alfie thought she might cry.

'I can do weekends?' he said.

Magda frowned. 'What happened to your eye?'

'I bumped into a door.'

'I need people who are reliable. Not boys who get punched by other boys.'

'I didn't—' started Alfie, but the girl in the headscarf called Magda's name, and she was gone, back behind the counter, bending down, pointing to the till screen, tapping the keypad and shaking her head. Customers glared impatiently.

Alfie felt guilty. For taking up a seat in this busy café. For wasting Magda's time. He knew she wouldn't be back. The interview was over. He didn't deserve a job. He was literally unemployable. His whole life was going to hell.

And yet . . . and yet . . . in the depths of his heart, he wanted this job. He *needed* this job. It was *more* than just a job. Why, he didn't know, but he couldn't crumple, he couldn't. Some deep instinct took over. He got up and walked to the till. 'Let me help.'

'What?'

'I'm here. Let me help.'

'This is a bad time.'

'Just give me a chance.'

'You'll slow everyone down.'

'Maybe,' said Alfie. 'Maybe not. If I'm rubbish, you can send me home. I won't be. I promise.'

Magda checked her watch. 'Adnan!'

Adnan was the broad-shouldered boy. He was punching buttons on a magnetic stopwatch attached to the espresso machine. Magda nodded at Alfie. Adnan nodded back.

'One hour,' she said.

Alfie went back to their table, picked up Magda's binder and his rucksack, and dumped them behind the counter. Adnan handed him a cup.

'Two squirts, almond,' he said, pointing to a row of syrup bottles. Alfie hovered, barely able to focus. Adnan snatched the cup from him, held it under the squirter and pushed down firmly. 'One squeeze equals a squirt. Two squeezes for a large.'

'OK,' said Alfie. 'OK!'

Adnan worked the machine, expertly grinding, tamping, pouring, cleaning, swapping out cups and mugs, bossing Alfie, pointing, guiding, encouraging, as Alfie squirted syrup, fetched tea, shoved ice in the blender, loaded the dishwasher, emptied the dishwasher, and even stuck toasted sandwiches in the grill. Twice Adnan sent Alfie off to clear and clean tables, a tray resting on his forearms. Twice Alfie pissed off a customer by accidently spraying sanitiser on their lap. Every time Alfie hesitated, picked up the wrong teabag, squirted the wrong bottle, pressed the wrong button, his heart sank. But each time he did something right: found the right teabag, produced the right-sized cup, stacked the dishwasher correctly, a bit of him remembered, so the second, third, fourth time he was faster, he was on it. Eventually, the queue dwindled to nothing and Alfie checked the time – an hour and a half had passed. Magda told him to sit down. He was coursing with adrenaline and his legs ached.

'Now you see how desperate we are!' said Magda brightly.

Alfie smiled.

'Can you drop out of your A levels and come work full time?' she said, squeezing Alfie's arm.

'Um—'

'Let me tell you a secret. School doesn't matter. You realise this when you get to my age.'

'I, er . . .'

'Only joking!' she said, laughing. 'Jesus! Finish your schooling. Don't do what I did. End up here for life!'

'Sorry,' said Alfie.

'Don't apologise!' she said. 'I like your attitude. But you need to make sure you get some deodorant.'

'Oh God,' said Alfie, covering his hands with his face.

She pointed to his eye. 'And no more fights.'

'I didn't—'

'I have brothers, OK!' Magda folded her arms. 'What's your availability?'

'Whenever you want!'

'We've been over this. You're not leaving school.'

Alfie put his head in his hands. He had to leave time for his schoolwork. Plus there was Raheem's request. He hadn't forgotten. 'Saturday. Evenings. Two evenings a week?'

Magda frowned. 'What about holidays? Christmas is coming!'

'Every day.'

Magda frowned more.

'I will,' said Alfie. 'Every day of the holidays!'

'Christmas Day?'

'Yes!'

'We're closed Christmas Day.'

Magda laughed. Alfie went bright red.

'Listen. If I take you on, I invest in you. You go to training days. That costs money. You get a big folder like this. That costs money. Adnan trains you too. Invests his time and energy.'

'I won't bail, I promise.'

'You come for a training shift tomorrow after school. I give you an apron and a badge. You change from your uniform. You don't look like the cat dragged you in. Continue as you did today, then I book you in for training. If you are even one second late . . .'

'OK! Yes! I won't be!' said Alfie.

'And if I see you chatting to your mates, giving free drinks to your friends or giving your number to pretty girls, you are sacked on the spot.'

'Don't worry,' said Alfie. 'That will not be a problem.'

31

'Oh my goodness, what on earth happened?' shrieked Nan. She was sitting on the sofa, in her pink onesie, her hand over her mouth.

'Nothing,' said Alfie sullenly. He was desperate for a shower. Nan sprung up, ran her hand down Alfie's face, grabbed the medicine bag from the bathroom and rubbed some cream into Alfie's cheek. 'I didn't have you for a fighter. I thought you were a nice boy!'

'I told you, it's nothing!'

'This is how it starts, Alfie! First they ask you to prove yourself. Then they give you a gun.'

'Nan! I'm not in a gang! It was a misunderstanding! It was my fault. It's over now!'

Nan folded her arms.

'I passed my interview and got a training shift at Coffee Boss. So relax!'

'Is that what they do for interviews? Boxing matches?'

'I've got a job! Everything's sorted! Chill, OK?'

He gave her a hug.

'You gave me a shock!' said Nan. 'I had enough of the police with your mum!'

'No. No police. It was Jack. Over a girl. His girl.'

Nan raised her eyebrows.

'It was a mistake, OK?' said Alfie.

Nan opened her mouth.

'Enough!' said Alfie. 'I've learned my lesson! End of story!'

The next day, his face was OK. A bit swollen. No black eye.

Jack had bruised a finger, maybe even fractured it. At least that's what Alfie guessed when he saw him in the lunch hall with his hand all bandaged up. He didn't talk to him, or Maya, Gwen, Lily and Samira. He sat alone, head down, eating his roast Halal chicken, only stopping to tell Raheem that he was up for joining his Sunday league team.

Raheem responded like he'd just signed Kylian Mbappé, hugging Alfie, punching the air, launching into a monologue about what kit he would need for training (on the Brent playing fields), and messaging him the link to the Google Calendar fixture list.

'You do realise I'm only doing this because my life has fallen apart and I have nothing else to do with my free time?' said Alfie.

'In every crisis is an opportunity,' said Raheem. He pulled out a chair, the legs grinding on the battered parquet floor, and sat down so close to Alfie his knees were pressing into Alfie's thigh. 'So it's true, then?'

'What?'

'First – I saw you saving a seat for that spotty Greek vampire girl. Then I see you chirpsing her mate. *Now* . . . they're saying . . . that you, Jack's girlfriend and four guys from a heavy metal band . . . had a backstage orgy!'

'What? No!' said Alfie. He picked up his half-eaten chicken slice and put it back down.

'The word on the street is Jack took your skinny-undergrown-ass and whooped it from here to the big Tesco's.'

'He did not!'

Raheem reached out to touch Alfie's eye and Alfie batted him away with his hand. 'I know what this is about! You did one of your Satanic rituals. You got a cauldron. Candles. Slaughtered some sheep! Cast a sex spell to make her sleep with you!'

'I am not a Satanist!'

'Yes, you are! Bat-blood drinker! Animal sacrificer! Wife-swapper!'

Alfie laughed. Raheem's nose was a few inches from his face.

'What?' said Alfie.

Raheem raised his eyebrows.

'OK!' said Alfie.

He told Raheem the whole story, his thing for Maya, his thing for Gwen and then his thing for Lily, and how they all went wrong. At the end, Raheem had his left hand cupped over his mouth, his eyes bursting wide, shaking his right hand, making a clicking sound with his fingers.

'Bruv!' said Raheem. 'I've got a new name for you ... Loverboy! The boy who looks for love in all the wrong places!'

Alfie stuck up two fingers. 'My name is No-Love Boy. Alfie "never talking to a girl again" Boy. Celibate Boy. Gonna-be-a-monk Boy. Single-for-the-rest-of-his-life Boy.'

After school he went home, showered, changed, sprayed himself with an obscene amount of Lynx. He checked his phone and saw a message from Gwen.

GWEN:

What the hell's happened to our
friendship group?

ALFIE:

I destroyed it

GWEN:

Are you OK?

ALFIE:

No

GWEN:

You wanna talk?

ALFIE:

No

Just wanna be by myself

GWEN:

Alfie don't isolate
I'm here if you need me

ALFIE:

Trust me
It's for the best

Then an email from his mum.

Alfie. This was very painful to read but I'm very
happy you sent me it. There's nothing I can say.

I take full responsibility. I'm not going anywhere.
No rush.

Love you.
Mum.

Damn! Everything was changing, everything was mad!

He rushed to Coffee Boss where Magda ushered him into the little alcove in the back and handed him a Coffee Boss T-shirt, apron, and a battered name badge with one word on it: *Trainee*. Adnan was there, fiddling with the magnetic stopwatches. The girl introduced herself as Faheema, and gave him some change bags to empty into the till.

But while the day before was manic, today was smooth. Magda sat at the breakfast bar, huddled over a laptop, making phone calls, while Alfie fetched cupcakes and cookies, made smoothies, loaded and unloaded the dishwasher and rinsed out blenders with an elongated bendy tap which sprayed out water like a power shower. Faheema taught him to restock the fridges and teas, and at the end of the shift, clean the bar and mop the floor. Magda didn't say anything about Alfie's performance, but she took his bank details and went over his availability.

'You go to church?' said Magda as Alfie put on his coat.

Alfie shook his head.

'Good! Because this is your new Bible.' She handed him an enormous binder, stuffed with glossy pages in full colour. 'Every detail about every drink. What it is, what goes in, how to make it, what it tastes like, why people should drink it, where the beans come from, which farms, the names of the farmers, the names of their wives and children, and what they like for breakfast. You need to know it off by heart, OK?'

It was almost as large as his chest.

Magda laughed. 'The look on your face! You're adorable. Put it in your bathroom. Read it on the toilet.'

The day after, Alfie had his first football training. Raheem had made the squad out to be old and unfit, but they were mainly men in their twenties and thirties who'd been released from the academy system. The coach was a guy called Phillip, with a massive stomach and permanent limp, who once had a contract with Chelsea.

Alfie told him he was a midfielder and Raheem piped up with, 'He goes by the name of Loverboy,' which made Alfie furious.

'Popular with the ladies, is he?' said Phillip.

'He wishes,' said one of the older guys.

'Why we playing with children?' said someone.

'Needs a haircut,' said another.

The others laughed.

'Just call me Alfie,' said Alfie. But it was too late. The nickname had stuck. They wanted to take him down a peg. They muscled him off the ball and tackled him unnecessarily hard. Alfie was rattled, overhitting passes and giving it away too easily. Raheem said it was just a bit of fun, but they all seemed to take it very seriously.

Halfway through though, something clicked. He received the ball, a big guy hustled him from behind, Alfie turned, the big guy floundered and Alfie sprinted free. He *could* still control the ball. He *could* still pick a pass. This was why he liked football! For twenty minutes he was everywhere, passing, tackling, bossing things. Then, just when he'd decided he was better than all of them, he crashed. Exhaustion. He could barely run. Raheem crunched into him, sending Alfie sprawling.

'You're wheezing like an old man!' shouted Phillip.

Everyone laughed.

No one said, 'Well done,' at the end but Phillip gave him more forms to fill out, committing him to the team, including a safeguarding form for Nan.

Coffee and football. The only two things that kept Alfie alive. That made his deep, deep sadness bearable.

Adnan taught Alfie how to pour an espresso. Pack too much coffee into the group head, and the espresso pours too slow, and tastes bitter. Pack it in too loosely, and it comes out too fast, and tastes watery and weak. Get it just right and it's sweet and fruity. On his third shift Alfie tasted so much coffee he couldn't get to sleep until two a.m.

Faheema taught him the strange system of abbreviations for the drinks and the special way to write them on the cups. She tested him on smoothie ingredients, making him recite them like a times table. She hovered behind him while Alfie took customers' orders, impatiently jabbing at the till when Alfie couldn't find the right item.

His old obsession with Arsenal came back, along with the wild euphoria and sickening gut-punches as the goals went in. Raheem came round, both of them watching every match on a dodgy livestream, just like Year Seven. At lunch, Alfie sat with Raheem and *his* friends: Abdul, Waheed and Jasmine. Raheem and Abdul supported Arsenal and Jasmine and Waheed Tottenham and Liverpool, so they spent most of the time taking the piss out of each other's teams. At least he had Raheem. At least he had people around him. He didn't look like a *complete* loser. They wouldn't be able to see how sad he really was.

And even though the lunch hall was packed, he could sense when Gwen, Lily, Maya and Samira were in the room in the same way that Darth Vader sensed Luke Skywalker. He'd turn to see them a few tables back, carrying on with their lives: Lily sitting with a swimming buddy. Gwen and Samira (always together now). Maya had stopped wearing make-up. She was pale, spotty and subdued.

Alfie never saw Jack. Not in the atrium to their flats, not in the lift or stairwell, not in the street and barely a glimpse in school. He arrived early, and left late. He didn't even come to lunch. Apparently he got permission to go home. The only way Alfie knew he was alive was when he played Jōnetsu, on full volume, the sounds muffled though Alfie's bedroom wall, every note filling him with shame.

One day, two weeks later, after training, he got a text message to say he'd been paid. He immediately checked his bank app, and got a massive jolt of excitement. He ran to the machine in Brent Cross shopping centre in his still-muddy kit, emptied his account and ran back to his flat.

Nan was in the kitchen, making tea. It wasn't a crazy amount, just under a hundred and fifty quid, but Alfie took the cash and threw it at her, and there was enough of it to feel like a snowstorm, a tenner landing on the top of Nan's head, another in a tea mug. Nan swore, clutching her chest in shock.

'Told you!' said Alfie. 'Told you I would do it!'

32

Phillip made Alfie sub for the next match. He spent the game warming up on the touchline, jogging up and down, shouting encouragement. It was a gritty, scrappy game, and with ten minutes to go, Phillip called his name. He loved putting on the orange shirt, number four, which made him feel like he was playing for Holland, and standing on the touchline, waiting to step on the pitch.

Alfie expected it to be rough, but it was still a shock when he got the ball, and the opposition midfielder raked his studs down his calf, sending him flying. But another part of him liked it, avoiding their lunges, working his low centre of gravity, changing direction, accelerating fast, his legs fresh. He hit one long perfect pass to Raheem, who kicked the ball hard, smacking the crossbar. It finished nil-nil, but Alfie was buzzing. Finally, a real game!

And just before he stepped onto the pitch, his mum's face had flashed across his mind. For a second, he'd wished she was watching him. And it kept bloody happening, more and more often: on the walk to school, brushing his teeth, as he tied up a bin bag in Coffee Boss. Mum-in-his-head wouldn't leave him alone. He'd told her how he felt. They were linked now. It felt inevitable, how long could he put off seeing her?

Four weeks after he had first emailed her, he opened his laptop and wrote:

> Let's meet once. See how it goes. I don't want to come to Manchester. I want you to come here. To my home. My life.

He pressed send and slammed his laptop shut. The next morning she had replied.

> I'm taking a week off from the 23rd, so around Christmas? I could stay in a hotel for a couple of nights and come and see you in the day? Maybe even Christmas Day?

Christmas! Damn! How many times had he and Nan put on a brave face? How hard did Nan try to make it special? Both pretending that everything was fine. How many times had he longed for his mum to be there? Ugh! Could it actually happen? This year? A normal Christmas? Was that insane?

> Christmas lunch. But you better ask Nan. See what she thinks.

> Alfie. I understand. I will. If it's easier, we could pretend like it's just a normal day.

> No. Don't want to pretend. I want it to be Christmas.

> Gotcha. Thank you for giving me this chance.

His mum had attached a couple of photos. Now he tapped the files, and watched the info bar fill up as the images downloaded, before expanding to fill his screen.

A close-up of her face, smiling at the camera. A pair of thick glasses. A denim jacket, her ears covered with piercings. Close cropped hair at the sides and a huge chaotic mop on top, dyed bright yellow. Alfie's curls. In a bloody Mohican. Turquoise eyeshadow, which brought out her electric blue eyes. Alfie's eyes. She still looked the same! She still looked young.

Suddenly he was holding her hand in the library. Walking down the street, trying to catch her attention. Watching her, passed out on the sofa, Nan telling him to go to his room. His ear, pressed to her chest, arms wrapped around her back. The soothing sound of her voice. Shouting, 'Muuummmmyyyyyy!' and waiting for her to appear in the doorway.

All the memories he never let himself remember. So, so sweet and so, so sad. He missed her. He missed her with all his heart.

Weeks flew by in an exhausting grind – school, work, school, practice, school, match, work, repeat. Then after three more sub appearances, and less than a week before the end of term, Alfie started a game. The other team were from Finchley, just up the road, so it made it a local derby. Alfie was excited until he stood over the ball, about to kick off, his thighs wobbling with nerves. He thought he might collapse.

The whistle blew. Their striker shoulder-barged Alfie to the floor. Twice he passed it straight to the opposition. He mishit a pass that could have led to a goal. The same striker tackled him on the half-way line, played it up to their winger, sprinted to the edge of the area, received the ball back and scored. Alfie collapsed to the turf in despair.

'What are you so scared of?' said Phillip at half-time. 'Bunch of mummy's boys! You're making them look like Barcelona!' He kicked the turf. 'Too much respect! They don't deserve it!'

Alfie was surprised when he was kept on. But in the second half, something changed. Maybe the opposition got tired. Maybe it was Phillip's words. Now he skipped over challenges, leaving bigger, heavier players behind. His sixth sense kicked in – he knew where the opposition player was going to hit it before he did, intercepting passes and breaking up attacks. He got the ball off his defenders and carried it into the opposition's half. He started to enjoy the fact he was the annoying small player with the big curly hair who made the other players want to bash him.

Ten minutes before the end, he crossed it to Raheem, who hit it cleanly off his forehead. Their defender sliced the ball off the line, and it fell to Alfie. Without thinking he struck it, it flew to the side, curled in a glorious arc and into the top corner of the goal.

Alfie exploded with delight, ripping off his shirt and whirling it around his head. Raheem jumped onto his shoulders, screaming 'Loverbooooy!' at the top of his voice. They collapsed into the mud, the other players piling on top of them.

When Alfie stood up he saw Maya on the touchline. She wasn't smiling or cheering, just had her hands in her pockets. She was wearing tracksuit bottoms and a black puffa jacket. He remembered her encouraging him to play football. She'd been really insistent. Was she remembering that too? He couldn't move. Like she'd frozen him with her eyes. His stomach twisted. His heart thudded. What did she want? What was she thinking? Was she zapping him with a psychic laser beam? *Go away!*

Wham! Someone smacked the back of his head. Alfie turned. Raheem stood in front of him.

'Wake up, Loverboy! Back to it!'

The other team was about to kick off. Alfie jogged back to his half, but when he turned around, she had gone.

That was the last game before the Christmas break, so Alfie could make good on his promise to Magda. Christmas Eve, Boxing Day, New Year's Eve and New Year's Day – he was gonna work them all. Double pay. He'd give all that to Nan, too. Ovi was having another fancy dress party. He'd renamed the group WhatsApp from *Ovi's Petrifying Party* to *Ovi's Santa Surprise*. He had a ten-foot Christmas tree, had hired a photo booth and a karaoke machine, and was hyping it so hard that Alfie muted the group. It was pissing him off. That wasn't his life any more! He made sure he worked the same evening, so if anyone asked him why he wasn't going to go, he had an excuse. No one did, though.

That night, Alfie rushed home, made himself a sandwich, threw on his Coffee Boss T-shirt and apron and ran to work. Magda (did she ever leave?) asked him if he minded closing up by himself because Faheema had to catch a plane. Alfie agreed. He felt good. He liked the calm Friday evening energy. The Christmas decorations were up, a thirty-foot silver Christmas tree in the central quad. Golden diamonds hung down from the ceiling, and shop window mannequins were draped in tinsel and Santa hats. He even had a special nametag, *Alfie* emblazoned on a Christmas star. It was the first shift where he felt like he knew what he was doing, trusted to close up by himself. Thirty minutes before close, he stood, hands resting on the bar, feeling like a king of his own mini-kingdom.

Faheema appeared, pulling a rattling suitcase on wheels. She parked it and held out her arms.

'Alfie. You've saved my life. My mum booked us plane tickets to Lahore and got the times wrong.'

'Ho, ho, ho, just call me Santa Alfie.'

She laughed and gave him a massive hug, squeezing him tight.

'I owe you one. I mean it,' she said. She held on for ages. Alfie blushed bright red. Then Faheema bustled off, her luggage clacking, Alfie smiling, dazed, out of it, staring at the empty space where she'd just been standing.

'Can I have a caramel latte please?'

Alfie turned to see Maya.

'Hi.'

'Hi.'

She was ready for Ovi's, in a short dress and a pair of huge lace-up knee-high leather boots. Instead of a coat, she wore a big black hoodie with the hood up. Her lips were shiny black and she'd drawn a black star on her left cheek. Ugh. She looked beautiful. Why was she here? What the hell was she doing?

'What size?' he said.

'Medium, please.'

'Cream?'

'No, thank you.'

'Have in or takeaway?'

'Takeaway, please.'

'Do you have a Coffee Boss card?'

Maya opened her bag and dug around. Alfie saw tissues, make-up, an apple, a bottle of water, a Santa hat. Her personal stuff. Alfie was back in her room, surrounded by her mess and clutter. He wanted to hear her moan about her dad, while opening a Tupperware box and giving him leftovers. He wanted to sit on her carpet and watch a movie until two a.m. on a school night. He felt so sad! They used to be so close. He used to be a part of her life. It used to be so easy. It wasn't that easy with anyone else. What the hell was happening? It was supposed to be over! All she was doing was buying a coffee!

She found her card, and handed it to him. Alfie scanned it, rang up the drink on the till and told Maya the price. Maya paid with her phone.

'Thank you very much,' she said, repeating the same thing when he gave her the drink.

They hadn't had a proper conversation, one-on-one, for half a term.

'You ... er ... not doing fancy dress tonight?' said Alfie.

'*No way!*'

'Is Ovi gonna let you in? Without a costume?'

Alfie waited for an explanation. None came.

Damn her! Coffee Boss was *his* place! Why did she have to come in here and mess with his mind! Alfie realised he was gripping the counter so hard that his knuckles hurt.

'OK! Well! Have a good night,' he said.

'You too,' said Maya, hurrying out of the café and away.

Alfie was discombobulated. As soon as he got home, he took out his phone and went to Lily's Instagram. He saw it immediately, the third post on the grid – from Luke's party – Maya's song with Luke, which Lily recorded. The caption: *So proud of my friend xx.*

He pressed play. There was Maya, blurry and small, lit purple and blue, in her strapless red dress. 'I Wrote Your Name in the Stars' starting with that catchy riff, Luke and Maya singing alternate lines, Olly drunkenly plucking his bass, Mikey's head banging, smashing the drums. Even with the bad recording and people talking, her voice cut through, strong but vulnerable, before the heavy, grinding chorus, Luke screaming, Maya dancing. She glowed onstage, like some hidden spotlight shone only on her.

How had he not realised how good she was? She could write songs! She owned the stage! In all that time hanging out with her, he hadn't actually seen her perform! What kind of best friend had he been?

He wanted to message her. He wanted to encourage her. He hated the thought of her sitting at home, beating herself up, doubting her dreams. This wasn't some big romantic fantasy of the future, like he'd had with Lily and Gwen. This was real. He. Missed. Maya. Badly. Genuinely. He really, really cared for her. Human, warts-and-all Maya.

Jesus Christ! Gwen was right! He had been in denial. All his feeling, all his desire, it was all still there. It had never gone away.

33

Alfie had trouble getting to sleep. He was pissed off when he heard his alarm. He hauled himself up, turned it off, and saw his notifications. The first one was from Nan.

NAN:

You're a dark horse

Mum called me today

Said you'd been emailing

She's coming round for Christmas lunch!

Then three missed calls. One from Jack. Two from Gwen. He checked his voicemail. Nothing. He sat there, staring at the screen. A call. Gwen. He watched her name until she rang off. She messaged immediately.

GWEN:

Alfie where are you?

I know you read this message

Please reply

A minute ticked by, then a ping. A message from Jack! No words, just a photo. A large latte with extra whipped cream.

JACK:

Guess where we are?

This time Alfie replied:

ALFIE:

WTF?

JACK:

R u working?

ALFIE:

Why?

JACK:

R u working? Soon?
Please tell me you're about to walk
into the cafe?

Jack. Gwen. Why were they together? Were they pranking him? Were they trying to humiliate him in some new, original way?

He made himself a coffee, ate some cereal, showered, sprayed plenty more Lynx all over his body, and put on his Coffee Boss T-shirt and stuffed his apron into his rucksack. He had to start work in forty-five minutes. Surely they wouldn't still be there – would they?

A knock at the door made him jump. Another one. Another. Someone shouted his name. Alfie opened it. Jack, Gwen, Samira and Lily were standing outside in the hall.

'I told you!' said Gwen. 'I told you!'

Gwen and Samira wore fake elf ears and Lily a huge, half-black, half-white curly wig.

'Ha, but look!!' said Jack. 'He's obviously *on his way* to work!'

'But he wasn't *actually there* though, was he?' said Gwen.

'He's blatantly on his way out. If we'd stayed a little bit longer like I said we should—'

'Money. Now,' said Gwen.

'I'm very confused,' said Alfie.

'They had a bet,' said Samira. 'If you would be at home or at work.'

'I bet work,' said Jack.

'And I said home,' said Gwen. 'And now he owes me five pounds.'

'None of this would have happened if you'd actually answered your phone,' said Samira.

'How do you even know I work there?' said Alfie.

'I literally watched you apply,' said Gwen.

'And Maya saw you there last night!' said Lily.

Maya! What had she said to them? And why the hell was Lily here?

'You could have just asked the barista,' said Alfie.

'That woman with the pink hair? She was terrifying!' said Lily.

'She's my boss! She's nice!' said Alfie.

'So are you going to invite us in or what?' said Samira.

They all pushed past Alfie, giggling, taking off their shoes and coats and piling them up on the mat in the hall. Gwen and Samira wore matching elf tunics. Lily had a white spotty dalmatian-style dress – she was Cruella de Vil. Jack wore green tracksuit bottoms and a T-shirt with baubles stuck to his chest and some tinsel round his neck.

'He's a Christmas tree,' said Lily.

Everyone laughed.

Jack walked pensively to the balcony and looked out over the drizzly view. The girls watched him expectantly. Jack? In his flat? Lily in full costume on the sofa? The room was suddenly tense. Alfie braced himself.

'Well, this is weird,' he said.

'You're telling me,' said Jack.

Lily, Samira and Gwen exchanged glances.

'Go on then,' said Samira to Gwen.

'Why me?'

'You said it yourself, you wanted to tell him,' said Samira.

'I feel really self-conscious,' said Gwen.

'You weren't self-conscious last night!' said Samira.

'I know, but I'm in Alfie's living room and he looks stressed and all of you are listening!'

'What is going on?' said Alfie. 'Bunch of Christmas weirdos!'

'A lot of stuff happened last night!' said Lily.

'A LOT of stuff,' said Samira.

Gwen put her face in her hands.

'And then we all woke up together and decided we had to tell you!' said Lily.

Alfie frowned. 'Were you sharing the same bed?'

'No!' said Gwen.

'We stayed at Lily's,' said Jack.

'She has sleeping bags,' said Samira.

'I'm not wearing fancy dress. I do actually have to go to work,' said Alfie. Maya had told them she'd seen him at Coffee Boss. What happened next? What did they want to tell him? He was filled with dread.

'We were dissecting Ovi's party and we came to the conclusion that the missing piece was you,' said Samira. 'If you were there it would have been perfect.'

'My partying days are over,' said Alfie. 'I've retired. It's just me and my rocking chair.'

'You have a rocking chair?' said Samira.

'No! It was a figure of speech!'

'Well, you need to come out of retirement,' said Lily. 'Last night had more drama than the Ovi-cheating-on-Maya party. More than the Alfie-bust-up-with-Luke party, more than the—'

'The-concert-in-Brighton-that-shall-never-be-mentioned-again,' said Samira.

'Exactly!' said Gwen.

The others laughed. Alfie felt annoyed at her for bringing it up.

'You can't shock me,' he said. 'I've seen it all.'

'Gwen came out!' said Lily.

Alfie's mouth hung open.

'Lily, *I* wanted to say it,' Gwen said.

'You were stalling!'

'I was working up to it!'

'Can't you see? The boy has places to be!'

'I was working up to it! You stole my thunder!'

'You got plenty of thunder last night though, didn't you?' said Samira.

OK. Maybe this wasn't about him and Maya. It was still big though.

Alfie grabbed his phone from the table. 'Jeez, you guys. Get your shoes on. Let's walk and talk.'

They all crammed into the lift, standing too close together, and Alfie felt better when he pushed open the fire door and the cool drizzly air washed over them. He and Gwen led the way, back to the North Circular, up the winding footbridge they'd crossed before when she told him he was a catch.

'You actually did it?' said Alfie.

Gwen nodded. 'I sat down and told my mum.'

'Your mum?'

'Yeah!'

'I thought you meant . . . to the people at the party.'

'Them as well. I didn't plan it. I just did it. Before I went out. I did what you said. I went, *This is me and there's nothing you can do about it.*'

'Seriously?'

'Yeah!'

'And what happened?'

'She cried. Freaked. Got pissed off. Then she calmed down.'

'Oh.'

'Then she said this annoying thing, that she was worried that life would be harder for me than it would be for other people.'

'Oh. Weird.'

'Then she cried again. Then she said she loved me. We had a big hug. She said she was sorry for not spending time with me.'

'I can't work out if this is good or bad.'

'Both! I thought it'd be a lot worse. I thought the world would burn. But they didn't make me homeless. Or disinherit me. Or murder me.'

'OK . .?'

'It's still pretty awkward, I reckon my stepdad knows cos they were talking in the kitchen for ages before we went out . . . He's the sort of person who thinks gay girls just haven't met the right man yet. But I kind of feel my mum was more on my side than I thought she would be … And then I decided to kiss Samira in front of the Christmas tree and everyone went nuts and we had a whole celebration.'

'Really?'

They were up on top of the bridge. The North Circular rose up and swooped down, behind it towered the Wembley Stadium arch, closer now.

'Some people were surprised. Some of them kind of knew. Worst-kept secret, kind of thing. Turns out … if everyone is paying attention … and it's positive attention … it can actually be quite fun.'

'What about Ovi?'

'He was lapping it up. He was dressed up as Father Christmas. He kept saying, *Finally I can say there was girl-on-girl action in my living room!*'

'Cringe.'

'It was funny at the time. And, Alfie … I'm only saying this cos what you said helped. Gave me a nudge. Just took a long time to actually pluck up the courage.' She took his hand and squeezed it. 'Much, much better than avoiding things.'

Ouch. Avoiding things. Like he'd been doing with Maya? Alfie shook his dead. *Come back to the moment.*

'You're the happiest I've ever seen you,' said Alfie.

'I am?'

'And the loudest.'

Gwen laughed.

'I'm sorry I isolated. I was really, really sad. But I should have stayed friends,' said Alfie.

She squeezed his hand again. 'You should have.'

'Oi, keep off her, I know what you're like!' said Samira,

skipping forward, linking her arm through Gwen's, both girls giggling.

Alfie felt relieved as they walked through the car park around the edge of Brent Cross to the bus station, where rows of bright red double-decker buses were parked in a line. Gwen and Samira sat down at a bus stop. Now they would go. No drama with Maya. Phew.

'We're going into town,' said Jack. 'Christmas shopping.'

'Did you not wanna get changed?' said Alfie, looking at Lily's wig.

'We're in the Christmas spirit!' said Lily.

'Um. OK. Thanks for stopping by,' said Alfie.

'Did you tell him?' said Gwen to Jack.

Alfie's stomach lurched.

'You were hogging him!' said Jack.

Tell him what? There was something else?

'Have you got a moment?' said Jack.

'Hurry up!' said Samira. 'Says there's a bus in four minutes.'

Jack led Alfie a few metres to the side. They stood by a battered fire exit with a sign saying *M&S Colleague Entrance*. Alfie scraped the concrete with his sole, kicking away a cigarette butt. God. One-on-one with Jack. Was he gonna tell him all about how much he'd ruined his life?

'So . . . you're speaking to me?' said Alfie.

'I am,' said Jack.

'Do you still hate me?'

'Not as much as I used to,' said Jack. 'I've gone from hundred per cent hate to . . . forty per cent weird.'

'I am genuinely sorry. I will always be sorry—'

'Listen. I'm not gonna lie. You think you went into hermit

263

mode? I went into solitary-confinement-high-security-prison mode. I was proper bitter and twisted.' Jack ran his hand through his hair. 'Sorry. I'm pretty hungover ...' His eyes went distant. 'I spoke to a counsellor, didn't I?'

'What?'

'At school.'

'They have those?'

'Alfie! Yes! She helped. She made me do stuff like ... scream into cushions.'

Alfie nodded. 'Did you really need a counsellor to do that?'

'Yes! We talked as well. You should try it. She helped me see stuff. Like after I got a girlfriend I became a bit of a dick and took you for granted. I could have stuck up for you more when Lily was rude. And I got a bit clingy and intense with her too. I turned into a bit of a pushover. Basically, they helped me understand why you and Lily might have been pissed off at me. And why she might have got freaked out at the L-word. It made me realise that if I handled things better ... the whole thing might never have happened.'

'Dude!'

'Yeah!'

'Thank you. For saying that.'

Relief flooded through Alfie. He was making up with Jack!

'And then last night ... me and Lily got back together ...'

'No way!'

'I know! I wasn't expecting it ... She told me she'd had a couple of things with guys at her swimming club. You know. A few dates with this one guy. I was like, *OK, he's gonna have stupid muscles and abs, me and her are definitely over ...*'

Jack's coat was open and the baubles swung and knocked into each other, clicking and clocking.

'And then it just happened. We realised . . . we wanted it. We missed each other.'

'Dude!'

'Yeah!'

'Dude! This is great news!'

'I know! It is. It's really great.'

Alfie felt elated. Maybe he and Jack could be friends again!

'I just want you to know. I don't want to go out with her. I don't even fancy her any more. The whole thing was a passion killer.'

'Alfie, I know.'

'Jack! Bus!' shouted Samira from the stop.

'Coming!' said Jack.

'If you ever felt we could . . . I'd love a *Football Manager* sesh?' said Alfie.

'What do you think I've been doing for the last two months?'

Alfie laughed.

'Sorry I was so rude about it.'

'It's OK. I mean . . . we're still neighbours,' said Alfie. 'My door is always open.'

Alfie stuck his hands in his pockets and scraped his trainer on the pavement.

'It's not just the game. It's being with you. The banter. The jokes.'

Jack nodded.

'There's no one else . . . who's known me . . . since I was yay-high . . .' Alfie held out his hand flat to just below his knee. 'I miss having a friend like that.'

'Yeah. I know. Girls complicate everything!'

'You're telling me!'

Jack smiled. 'I miss it too,' he said.

Alfie smiled.

'Part of me does want to be friends again … part of me is forty per cent unsure? Maybe I'm not quite ready. But I might be. In time.'

'OK. I get it.'

Jack held out his fist. Alfie bumped it.

'Jack! Bus!' said Gwen. 'Plus you owe me money, don't think I've forgotten!'

A double-decker had opened its doors and a long queue was boarding. He'd reconnected with Gwen. Made up with Jack. Phew.

'*They* miss you too,' continued Jack. 'That's what they were talking about last night. Missing you being around.'

'Who?'

'Gwen. Maya.'

'*Maya?*'

Alfie's stomach lurched.

Jack hesitated. 'Gwen coming out and me and Lily getting back together isn't the reason we came to see you.'

'Really?'

'Not the main one. It's hard to explain. I think you should speak to Maya.'

'What the hell happened last night?'

'It's hard to explain!'

'I told her I couldn't be friends with her. Cos she rejected me. It was all too painful.'

'But do you still have feelings for her?'

'Why are you asking me that?'

'Jack!' shrieked Lily. 'Bus!'

'And another thing – do you have a girlfriend?'

'Do I have a girlfriend?'

'Do you?'

'No!'

'You sure?'

'Of course I'm sure!'

'Listen, Alfie. You have to speak to Maya. She likes you, Alfie. Honestly, she does.'

34

Alfie hung up his coat in the tiny Coffee Boss alcove.

He still had feelings for Maya. He'd just been told she liked him. He should be happy and hopeful. So why did he feel so sick? Why did he wish it wasn't happening? He liked his new life. Things were simpler being single. He didn't need any more stress!

And what if Jack got it wrong? Last night Maya was cold and distant and didn't answer his question. What if she had only said she missed him cos she was drunk? That's the sort of thing she would do, let's be honest. A stupid late-night drunk drama, it had to be. Alfie came up short on every level. She'd remember that as soon as she sobered up. He didn't want to go back to the bad old days.

And what the hell had happened when she watched him at the match? What the hell happened in Coffee Boss, last night? Maybe Raheem was onto something. Maybe she did a Satanic animal sacrifice ritual to make him fall under her power. Cos she was lonely and sad and wanted to have loyal, lovestruck Alfie hanging on her every word. Like a dog. Like Jack used to be with Lily. He would never get over her, that much was clear. Couldn't they just leave it at that?

'Smile, it might never happen!' said Magda. She reached forward and pinched his chin.

'Ow!'

'Why are those lovely eyes looking so sad, eh?'

Alfie winced, shook his head.

'I don't need sulkers today!' she said, striding out of the alcove and taking position behind the bar. It was the last Saturday before Christmas and the shift was mental. Many shops had launched last-minute early Christmas sales and blocked out their windows with bright red banners proclaiming big discounts. It was boiling, the heating on full-blast, tense shoppers in winter coats packing the concourse, parents pushing buggies with bulging shopping bags hanging off the handles. The queue to Santa's Grotto stretched all the way to the Coffee Boss entrance, kids shouted, babies screamed, 'All I Want for Christmas is You' played every fifteen minutes.

Everyone wanted coffee. Everyone wanted cake, croissants, cookies, gingerbread, brownies. A permanent cluster of customers stood at the end of the bar, waiting impatiently for their drinks. The moment a table became free, at least two people leaped forward to take it. It was like Alfie had jumped into a raging river and the current was taking him wherever it wanted – *order, payment, beep, the panini is ready, can I have some tap water please? Do you do have hazelnut milk? Can I swap this for a gingerbread one?* Forget Theydon Bois, the undead were *here* and the staff were fighting a losing battle: Adnan was on the espresso machine, Alfie and Magda on the back bar, both of them clearing the floor when they could, but it wasn't enough, it would never be enough, there were too many customer-zombies, for every single one they served, two more appeared.

After two hours, Alfie broke. His handwriting became illegible and Adnan called the wrong names. Alfie dropped a hot panini: gloopy cheese and buttery ham scattering across the floor. He grabbed a cookie with his hand instead of tongs, and the man complained. He gave out the wrong change. He added coffees to orders that no one had asked for. The card machine wouldn't connect and he picked it up and slapped it down in frustration, which made it stop working. Magda spent five minutes rebooting it, which made the queue longer, and the customers angrier. No, the zombies weren't the problem.

Magda pulled him aside and led him into the alcove, where they stood by the rumbling dishwasher. 'What is wrong with you today?' she said.

'Nothing.'

'You're normally my favourite.'

'I'm sorry.'

'I don't want *sorry*. I want Alfie. You've been miserable and moody all shift. Your work is a catastrophe. What's going on?'

'Sorry. Sorry for saying sorry.'

Magda watched him. 'Are you hungover?'

'No!'

'I don't believe you.'

'I don't drink!' he said, his eyes becoming moist.

Magda leaned on the dishwasher. 'Is everything OK at home?'

'Yes.'

'Anyone ill?'

'No.'

'Dead?'

'No.'

'Beating you?'

'No!'

'Grooming you?'

'No!'

'Help me, Alfie!'

Alfie just looked at the floor. Adnan stuck his head around the corner and called Magda's name. Magda waved him away with her hand.

'Is this ... about a girl?' said Magda.

Alfie shook his head.

'A boy?'

Alfie shook his head again.

'It is. It's a girl!'

Magda stuck her head outside and surveyed the shop floor before turning back to Alfie.

'It is a girl ...' he said. 'I thought it was over ... My friend told me she still likes me ... and it's totally messed me up.'

Magda nodded.

Alfie looked her in the eye. 'I can't stop thinking about her, Magda! I'm terrified! I wanna run away and hide. But I have to find out if it's true! I feel like I'm being ... ripped apart!'

'OK, thank you for telling me!'

'I'm sorry.'

'Stop saying sorry!' Magda eyed him carefully. 'Go on then. Bugger off.'

'What?'

'Go. You're hurting more than you're helping.'

'You sacking me?'

'No!'

Magda laughed.

'Go and sort it and come back tomorrow with a smile.'

'Really?'

'Yes.'

'Thanks, Magda.'

He spontaneously hugged her, before letting go, feeling awkward. He put on his coat and collected his bag and felt Adnan and Magda watching as he walked out of the back of the café and into the car park. He crossed a slip road and sat on a grassy verge, his butt freezing, and called Maya.

No answer. He tried again. And again. No answer. He walked to her house. Lights off. No one was in. He walked and walked, through the cold, desolate Hendon Park, the leafless trees, the grimy underpass by Hendon station, all the way to Café Delish, pressing his face to the steamed-up windows. There she was, spooning some tuna onto a baked potato. Her face was flushed, her hair tied back. Maya's dad exited the kitchen holding a large plate of sausages, bacon, eggs, mushrooms, chips and toast, which he handed to Maya. Alfie pushed open the door and strode inside.

'Hey, Alfie! You just missed your nan!' said Maya's dad.

'It's OK, I'm not looking for her.'

'Oh. There's no match. Postponed?'

'I'm not here to see you! Sorry. No offence?'

Maya's dad laughed. He turned to Maya, who placed the plate in front of an old man wearing a flat cap.

'I'm working,' she said.

She walked to the bar, picked up the milk jug and washed it out under the tap.

Alfie took a deep breath in. 'I'm not leaving until I talk to you!' he said.

Everyone stared. An older man doing *The Sun* crossword. A group of Romanian men crowded round a small table. A young couple sitting opposite each other, two empty, ketchup-smeared plates in front of them. Maya put the jug down with a clang, and looked at her dad. He shrugged. Maya ushered Alfie into the kitchen, while Maya's dad said something to the Romanian men and they all laughed.

'They're laughing at *us*,' said Maya.

'I don't care,' said Alfie.

She rolled her eyes. She was standing next to a giant hot plate covered with caramelised onions, sausages and bacon, while Radio 2 played on a little digital radio on the counter.

'I've got the worst hangover ever, so can you make it quick, please?' she said.

She was staring at the grey lino floor, grubby from the day's work. She couldn't even look at him. Ugh! This was torture. Alfie took a deep breath in.

'OK, then. I'll make it quick. Jack told me to speak to you. He said that you like me.'

Maya's mouth hung open in shock. 'The absolute bastard!'

'Jack, Gwen, Samira and Lily all came round to my flat, specifically to tell me!'

'Oh my God! I told them not to! Ignore them! They were drunk. They misheard me. They don't know what they're talking about.'

For a second, Alfie thought he'd got the wrong end of the stick. But her grey eyes looked sad, hesitantly flickering between him and the floor, giving him the courage to continue.

'They wouldn't have come to my flat for no reason,' he said softly. 'Please tell me what happened.'

'So you can gloat?' sniffed Maya. 'Rub my nose in it? Make me feel even worse than I already do?'

She opened the fridge, removed a Tupperware box of chocolate brownies and opened it. 'Need sugar,' she said, and stuffed one in her mouth. She offered one to Alfie. He took one.

'Please? Maya?'

'Fine! If it'll make you go away,' she said, mouth full.

Alfie's thighs were shaking with nerves.

'The Luke thing totally messed me up, OK? And then Twisted Dreamland got a manager. From the competition. They're getting support slots. There's all this hype. It's so demoralising. I'm freaking out cos he's promising me he'll credit me with our song but I don't trust him and I don't want him to steal my talent. It's all so depressing. I'm not going out. I haven't even dated. I've just been ... really low, OK?'

She swallowed the brownie.

'And then last night it was the first time I'd been out in ages. I just wanted to have some fun and forget about my problems. I even thought about getting off with Ovi. As a one-off. To numb the pain. And then I saw you in Coffee Boss and it triggered the hell out of me! I had this massive realisation!'

'Why?'

'You're blossoming, Alfie. You're so much more confident! You're playing football! Do you know how happy I felt seeing you do that? You've got a job! You look ... You look like *you* now. You look really hot! It's like you've learned to love yourself or something ... I was like, *Woah! He's changed!* Not that I thought you were unattractive before—'

She thumped her fist into her chest.

'Seeing you with that girl. It stabbed me in the heart. Cos I knew I blew my chance. Cos you told me who Luke really was. And I ignored you. I thought you didn't like me and then I found out you *did* but I made this big whole speech about how you came up short. I was just super-angry with you cos you didn't kiss me when you had the chance and only told me how you felt when it was much too late! And from the moment I said it, I bitterly regretted it! I feel terrible about being so cruel, and it was because of my stupid temper! You're *way* better than Luke. You're not just hot, you're ... kind. Gwen was singing your praises about how you listened to her and gave her good advice and she's right. Even Lily was talking about how you looked out for her in Brighton. You're sensitive and caring. I miss you sharing your insecurities with me. I miss sharing mine. You're such a good listener. You're also really fun. You're also really funny. When you're around I feel happy and relaxed. I never felt that with Luke. So many reasons! There's a big Alfie-shaped hole in my life ... and I just feel even *more* awful cos I pissed it all away with my bullshit!'

Maya tugged at a large roll of blue catering tissue paper, tore off a sheet and wiped her eyes.

'Last night – I was like, *crying* about it. And Gwen was trying to comfort me, Lily and Jack and all of them were like, *Girlfriend or not, Alfie has to know, he might feel the same way, he was so into you.* I was like, *Noooo! No way! He hates me! I was such a bitch. Trust me!* The only good thing was my meltdown was at one a.m., so at least I didn't ruin Gwen's coming out.'

Maya stuffed another half of brownie into her mouth.

'So there you go,' she said. 'Gloat, if you want to. Rub it in, if you want to. You were right, I was wrong. You got the last laugh.'

She looked exhausted. Her cheeks were flushed. Her forehead was full of little bumps. She had dark patches under her grey eyes. Alfie could feel his heart thudding in his chest.

'What do you mean, seeing me with *that girl*?'

'Alfie. I saw you. That Coffee Boss girl! I'm sure you'll be really happy together!'

'What?'

'She was rubbing herself against you. You got all flushed in the face, like you were loved up.'

'She wasn't rubbing herself against me!'

'I was standing right next to you!'

'No! That's Faheema! No, no, no, no, no!' Alfie laughed. 'Did you actually think she was my girlfriend?'

'Yes!'

'I don't fancy her.'

Maya was frowning, staring at Alfie.

'I work with her! I did her a favour. She hugged me to say thank you. But she held on for a while and I felt embarrassed. She's really nice but all we do is chat at work. That's as far as it goes. She taught me how to mop the floor.'

'You sure?'

'Yes!'

'You really, really sure?'

'Yes! Jeez, Maya.'

'Are you sure you don't fancy her a little bit?'

'No!'

Maya folded her arms. 'I really thought you two were in love.'

'Well, we're not.'

Maya looked at him, as if she was trying to decide whether to believe him or not. 'OK, so that's a bit embarrassing,' she said. 'Doesn't really change anything. I know you've moved on, though.'

Alfie felt like he'd been carrying a very, very heavy weight, and now that weight was gone.

'What if I said I still like you?'

'What?'

'What if I said I want to go out with you.'

'Excuse me?'

'And listen. You didn't mess up, you gave me a chance and I blew it! *Anyone* would have gone with Luke. What I did at the gig was out of order too. You had every right to be angry. And what about Lily? How dumb was that? I totally win on the dumb front.'

Alfie ran his hand through his hair, his mind whirring, wired on adrenaline. 'And maybe I wasn't ready for you,' he continued. 'Maybe *we* weren't ready to be with each other. Maybe you had to stop going for dumb guys and I had to stop being such a scaredy cat and grow up and love myself so that we could be ready, now!'

'Ready for what?'

'*This.*' Alfie grabbed Maya's hands. 'With Gwen and Lily, I wanted it to be so much more than it was . . . I was so messed up by you and me not happening . . . I tried to numb the pain with them . . . Gwen and Lily were just a fantasy in my head . . . me and you, it's always been deeper. Why are we standing here now? Why are we holding hands? Why does you looking at me from across a field do things to my heart? Still! After all that crap!'

She looked him in the eyes. He didn't look away.

'You hurt me so much, I'm not gonna lie. You broke my heart. Really.'

'I'm sorry, Alfie. I'm so, so sorry.'

'It's OK.'

Maya was crying. 'I'm so, so sorry. I didn't mean to hurt you so much, I really didn't.'

'I'm sorry for almost ruining your gig.'

'Pah! Twisted Dreamland! Bunch of losers!'

'Hey! How about *you* like yourself a bit more? You're just as good as Luke.'

'Shut up!'

'I just watched that video again! You're so good! I feel so stupid that I didn't realise quite how good you were! You have to perform, Maya! Do drama school. Start a TikTok channel. Become a goth pop star. You don't need to piggyback off Luke's talent. You've got tons and tons of your own. Whatever you want. Do it! I'll be in the front row, cheering you on!'

'Alfie. Stop it.'

'Luke and Ovi are wrong! I still love that you stabbed the football. I still love that you're super-passionate. I just love . . . being around you. I know this sounds weird, but when you get super-intense . . . I get super-chill. Sounds contradictory but it's true. I do. There's a big Maya-shaped hole in *my* life. And if we do have a chance – a second chance – I'm willing to risk it. All over again. I wanna do it properly. I wanna do it right.'

'Alfie. Wow. Jesus. Wow!'

She yanked another load of blue tissue and wiped her eyes. When she was finished, Alfie took back both her hands.

'Are you still pissed off I came round?' said Alfie.

Maya sniffed. 'No.'

Alfie took a deep breath in and exhaled slowly. 'Are you pleased I came round?'

'Yes,' she said in a small voice.

He gazed into her pale grey eyes. She ran her thumb in circles around his palm. The same invitation he felt on the sofa back in the summer. It was different now. Less scary. More solid. No questioning. No doubt. Alfie pulled her towards him. She let go and held up her hands to say *stop*, and looked inside the café to make sure no one was looking.

'My dad's out there . . .'

'Who cares!'

'He might walk in.'

'Let him.'

He leaned forward and kissed her. For a second she went to push him away, then she let him, then she threw her arms around him, pushing him into the counter, kissing him back.

'I knew. After you and Lily. You'd done something bad and stupid and dumb but . . . I felt really jealous,' she said. 'Really, really jealous. I've been in denial.'

'Me too. Total denial. For months and months.'

They kissed again, Maya placing her hands on his cheeks, sensual, slow, passionate.

'I'm not gonna break your heart,' she said. 'I'm gonna take care of it. I promise. I'm so, so lucky to have it.'

Maya breathed in and out, her breath shaky, her body trembling.

'I love you, Alfie.'

'I love you too.'

Maya smiled. They kissed, gently, sweetly, everything disappeared, it was them and only them, and Alfie was happy, so, so happy.

'This is so unexpected,' said Maya.

'You're telling me!'

'I never even thought—'

'It's been the maddest day.'

'I know!'

Alfie ran his hands through his hair.

'There's more. Really, the Gwen coming-out stuff. Jack and Lily. This. Us! *And*... I found out my mum is coming. Christmas Day. For lunch.'

'What?'

'Yeah.'

'Your mum?'

'Yeah.'

'Your mum is coming for Christmas lunch?'

'Yeah! I found out today!'

'Your *mum*?!'

'She kept emailing. She wouldn't let it go. She really wanted to see me.'

'Oh my God!'

'She's been clean for three years. She does Narcotics Anonymous. She's done rehab, the lot. She wants to make amends.'

Alfie told her about the emails and his mum's new life in Manchester, the whole saga.

'Why the hell didn't you tell me?'

'I'm telling you now.'

'After six fucking months!'

'It took me ages to get my head round it. And what am I gonna do, spend the rest of my life hating her? At the end of the day ... she's my mum.'

Maya put her hand over her mouth. 'I'm so gutted that I wasn't there to share this with you. I should have been there to share this with you. Oh, Alfie . . . you've actually got a chance . . . out of the both of us, you have a chance . . . to actually have a mum!'

Alfie nodded. 'I know!'

'Have you got her a present?'

'No.'

'You need one! A peace offering. Peace and goodwill. Start off on the right foot.'

'I'm still not exactly feeling peaceful. What if I get triggered? What if I do a you, and attack her with a bread knife?'

Maya laughed. Tears ran down Alfie's cheeks. Now Maya pulled some tissue from the big blue roll and wiped them away. 'Buy her a present. Now. Seriously. Go.'

'Maya!'

'What?'

'You can share it!'

'What?'

'Come on Christmas Day!'

Maya rubbed her forehead.

'I just had this picture. In my head. Of you sitting at the table with a stupid paper hat. From a cracker. You don't even have to say anything. I'd feel so much better.'

Maya closed the brownie box.

'I'm bricking it, Maya. If you were there . . . it would mean so much!'

'I'm supposed to go to my uncle's,' she said. 'We're gonna drive to Essex. There's gonna be like, twenty people. They built a charcoal oven in the garden. My dad's been cooking for days . . .'

'Oh! OK. Screw it. Dumb idea. I'll be OK.'

'I'll be sending positive vibes!'

'Yeah. OK. Thank you.'

Maya stood there, smiling in her apron, her mascara running. She put her hands to his cheek and kissed him.

They were interrupted by a cough.

Alfie took a step back, knocking the Tupperware box off the counter, sending the remaining brownies skidding across the floor.

'You'll both be paying for those,' said Maya's dad.

'How long have you been there?' said Maya.

'Long enough.'

Maya's dad shook his head. It took a couple of moments for Alfie to realise he was laughing.

35

Alfie jumped straight on a bus to Brent Cross. Nan was easy to buy a gift for. He saw a pair of Nike trainers in the sale, white with a pink swoosh, the last size left was hers, size three, she had tiny feet. But what about his mum? He loitered in the perfume department in Fenwick's, testing all the samples on his wrist, but they were all too samey, too smelly. He gazed into the window of the jeweller's, where every shiny ring and chain was a hundred times what he could afford. All the old anger came back. She didn't deserve expensive jewellery! She didn't deserve shit!

He ran up to a big clothing chain and picked up one of the T-shirts he'd seen earlier. The front was decorated with a picture of a very old man with a Mohican pushing a Zimmer frame, punching the air. It read: *Old punks never die.* He knew she would like it.

He took a picture of it and sent it to Maya, along with the one of his mum.

ALFIE:

What do you think?

MAYA:

ALFIE:

Is your dad OK with earlier?

MAYA:

You owe him £10 for the brownies

ALFIE:

Seriously? You ate most of
them

MAYA:

You spilled them on the floor

ALFIE:

I wouldn't have done that if
you hadn't taken them out
the fridge

MAYA:

Joking! 😂 He let us off

ALFIE:

Great

MAYA:

C'mon, Alfie. You're the one guy he
wouldn't mind me kissing
He thinks the sun shines out of your arse

Alfie spent two hours talking to Maya on the phone before bed.
He woke up buzzing. He showered, dressed, and walked to
work, bounding into the café.

'Good?' said Magda.

Alfie gave a cheesy thumbs up.

'I'm not gonna ask you the details. This is a family
establishment.'

Alfie laughed.

She leaned in and whispered, 'I'll still pay you for the full shift yesterday.'

Adnan made him a spiced caramel latte, and handed it to him.

'Thanks, guys,' said Alfie, blushing. He was on it, ringing up orders, fetching food, pressing the timer on the oven, fishing paninis out with tongs, pressing wash on the dishwasher, refilling the milk, ripping off receipts, fixing the card machine, shouting orders across the back bar. All staff were allowed a free 'lunch' and Alfie scoffed his cheese-and-ham sandwich in the alcove in less than a minute. Later, he even got to cover for Adnan and made a flat white all by himself. The milk wasn't velvety enough, and the head too thin, and Magda remade it, but he was still elated that he even got the chance.

Then, when he left, he called Maya.

'We're having a terrible Christmas Eve,' she said.

'Why?'

'I was inspired by what you said. I tried to ask my dad if I could do some extra acting courses on Saturday. Guildhall musical theatre or something.'

'What happened?'

'What do you think? We had a massive fight!'

'Maya!'

'We both get so triggered!'

'Are you OK?'

'Kind of. I told him your opinion. I said, *Alfie thinks I'm amazing and I have to do it.*'

'Oh. What did he say?'

'Not a lot.'

'So my arse has run out of sun, then?'

Maya snorted.

'Can't you do both? Work at the café and do classes on the side?' said Alfie.

'That's much too sensible.'

They both laughed.

'I realised something, Alfie. He's scared. He's scared of me not surviving in the real word and getting into student loan debt and just being poor. He's got this business which earns us money and gave me a secure foundation and he wants me to have it too. He loves me ... but he just doesn't get the artist thing.'

'I wanna see you.'

'Not a good idea. It's got even weirder. He's decided to repaint the bathroom.'

'On Christmas Eve?'

'I know! I really wish you were here though.'

'I wish I was too ...'

'I miss you.'

'I miss you too!'

'I miss you so, so much!'

On Christmas morning, Nan cooked Alfie scrambled eggs and smoked salmon. Afterwards she ushered him into her room, where she had laid out a freshly ironed school shirt onto the bed.

'What's that for?'

'I thought you could dress up smart.'

'And wear my school uniform? And look like an accountant? She's got a Mohican, for Christ's sake. She's not some smart business woman.'

'What about Maya's dad's suit? As you haven't given it back yet. I hung it up in your room. How many months has it been?'

'I am not dressing up as the Joker for Christmas Day.'

Nan was wearing a blouse and some pinstriped trousers. 'This isn't just any old Christmas Day though, is it?'

Alfie gestured to his jeans and his Jōnetsu hoodie. 'I want her to meet the *real* me.'

He gestured at the tree, tall, plastic and silver, dressed up with tinsel and baubles, the presents underneath.

'I got her a gift. That's enough.'

Alfie was so nervous that all he could do was lie down on his bed. At ten he locked himself in the bathroom, put the toilet seat down and sat on it. Nan busied herself in the kitchen, knocking a few times to check if he was OK. At half-past ten, Alfie threw up, spewing thick pinky liquid, full of bits egg and salmon. He flushed the toilet, and brushed his teeth, praying that the fan would blow away the smell, just as the buzzer sounded. He could hear Bailey careering out of the bedroom, barking loudly. Hands shaking, he opened the bathroom door.

Standing in the hall was Maya, holding a big Sainsbury's bag. Underneath her puffa jacket she wore a black dress with lace sleeves, and big, thick-soled shiny boots. She had glitter around her eyes and her lips were glossy.

'Surprise!' she said nervously.

Bailey leaped up, paws on her legs, barking, tail wagging. Maya smiled and cooed, trying to stroke her. Nan's eyes flicked between Maya and Alfie, her head clearly whirring. Bailey wouldn't calm down, running in circles, her paws slipping and sliding.

'Well!' said Nan eventually. 'He's been threatening to bring

287

a girl round for months! I didn't expect it to be Christmas Day! Without any notice!'

She looked at Alfie pointedly.

'If it's a problem, I'll go—' said Maya. 'I wanted to support Alfie. I got a bit . . . carried away. I should have messaged.'

'I need some warning if there's gonna be guests!' said Nan.

'Blame me. I invited her,' said Alfie.

'Did you stop to think that someone has to cook for her too? Does your mum know about this?'

'I'm sorry! I just . . .'

Nan put her hands on her hips. Her gaze was steely.

'I come bearing offerings?' said Maya.

She reached into her bag and took out a large Tupperware box and opened it. It was full of golden brown cookies. 'Melomakarona. Greek honey cookies. A-ma-zing. We have them every Christmas. My dad made them!'

Nan peered at them, frowning.

'Really. I don't want to intrude. I'll go if you want. Am I intruding? Alfie?'

'Nan?' said Alfie.

Nan puffed her cheeks and blew out. She put the lid back on the box and turned to Maya. She squeezed Maya's arm. 'Just checking you're not imaginary.'

'Nan!' said Alfie.

She stepped out into the landing. 'Any angry boyfriends waiting to punch him?'

'Nan!'

'I'm real. No angry boyfriend,' said Maya laughing. 'Unless Alfie's angry with me?'

Alfie beamed so hard he thought his cheeks would snap.

Nan pressed her hands on her chest. 'Did she just call you her boyfriend?'

'Yes,' said Maya. 'She did.'

'And no,' said Alfie, 'I'm not angry.'

Nan watched them smile at each other.

'I'll get an extra chair from my bedroom . . .' she said.

'Thanks, Nan,' said Alfie.

'Thanks, Nan,' said Maya.

'Yeah, yeah, yeah,' said Nan, wandering into the kitchen. 'You're lucky I always buy too much food . . .'

'Come on,' said Alfie, gesturing to his room. Maya sat down on Alfie's bed and Alfie closed the door.

'When I woke up this morning, I knew I had to come. I said to my dad, *I don't care if you're still angry with me, I'm going.*'

'What did he say?'

'I explained. I told him about you and your mum. Hope you don't mind?'

Alfie shook his head.

'You are the most important person to me in the whole universe and I'm getting my priorities straight and I know it's a bit impulsive but I just—'

'I thought he didn't like me any more.'

'We kind of talked it out. His little girl is gonna leave soon and deep down he knows I'm basically gonna do what I want. He's sad about it. But he wants to end the fights.'

'Really?'

'I kind of compromised. I told him I'll work for him as much as I can and not be such a bitch. But it might not be forever. And I'm gonna do one class. Even if it's just a summer camp.'

'You made up?'

'Yeah . . . I guess we did . .'

Alfie was still beaming.

'And you don't have to worry. When I told him about *this* . . . he was delighted. He's friends with Nan, remember? And he's known you a long time too. He knows your mum coming over is a big deal. He's really, really happy for you. He invited you round for the Boxing Day derby so . . . yeah . . . the sun is still shining . .'

Maya kissed Alfie on the lips. 'Although it might not be, when he remembers *that*.' She nodded to the purple suit, hanging up on the handle of Alfie's wardrobe.

'Errr . . . At least my nan got it drycleaned.'

Maya laughed. 'He's forgotten. He'll be fine. It's all good.'

Alfie lay back on the bed. 'I'm so happy you're here . .'

Maya stroked his forehead. 'So am I.'

He sat up. 'Oh shit! I don't have a present for you. I've been so wrapped up in Mum and—'

'Hey. Doesn't matter. I don't either. We weren't expecting each other.'

'I won't forget next year.'

'So you think there's gonna be a next year, do you?'

'Yeah. I do.'

Maya beamed. She kissed him on the lips. They lay down next to each other.

'Still feeling scared?' she said.

'Yes. Scared. Happy and scared.'

'Listen. I've been thinking about a plan. If today goes well, maybe you can go for a walk, just you and your mum, and I can catch up with your nan. Or if it's all too much and things go full-on *EastEnders*, me and you can just excuse ourselves and can hide in here. Or go to the park. Or run away to another country. But only if you want to. I was also thinking, we should have a signal. Wink at me if you want to go for a walk with her. Nod your head if you want to hide in your room.'

'I really, really love you,' said Alfie.

'I really, really love you too.'

Maya snuggled up next to Alfie, hugging him, stroking his arm. The buzzer suddenly rang, long and slow and loud. Bailey went nuts, barking hysterically. They heard Nan lift the receiver and buzz someone in. They stood, hugging each other tightly, pressing as hard as they could, neither wanting to let go.

Someone knocked, five, strong raps. Bailey barked wildly. Alfie's fingers slid into Maya's. Hand in hand, they stepped into the hallway, just as the front door opened.

Acknowledgements

Massive thanks to: Laura Hestley for reading and feeding back on many drafts of this novel; my agent Caroline Montgomery for her unwavering support; Georgia Roncaglia for superb notes; King-Wey Hii for her friendly, sharp and enlightening sensitivity read; and my editor at Andersen Press, Chloe Sackur, for her rigorous, astute and invaluable input.

Finding Phoebe

Gavin Extence

Longlisted for the Branford Boase Award

Phoebe is autistic. She prefers to stay in her comfort zone:
walking her dog, writing fantasy fiction, surviving school.
When her best friend gets a secret boyfriend, Phoebe
reluctantly agrees to cover for her. Before long, Phoebe's
dealing with all sorts of things she'd rather not, like
deception, fashionable jackets, and the bewildering politics
of the school chess club. As events
take a seriously unexpected turn,
Phoebe realises there's more to
her than she ever imagined . . .

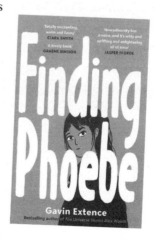

'Totally enchanting,
warm and funny'
Ciara Smyth

'Witty and uplifting and
enlightening all at once'
Jasper Fforde

Not My PROBLEM

CIARA SMYTH

*Winner of the Waterstones Children's Book Prize for Older Readers
and the Laugh Out Loud Teen Book Award
Shortlisted for the Children's Book Ireland Awards,
the Irish Book Awards and the Polari Prize*

When Aideen agrees to help ambitious class swot Maebh
Kowalska deal with her crazy workload, she doesn't expect
to end up reluctantly pushing Maebh down the stairs. With
this, Aideen becomes the school 'fixer': any problem a student

has, Aideen will sort it out, from
stealing confiscated mobiles to
breaking into parties. But Aideen's
own life is a mess. Spending
more time with the uptight (but
annoyingly cute) Maebh, Aideen
starts to wonder: can every
problem be solved?

'Smart, well observed and
highly entertaining' *Observer*

DARKHEARTS

JAMES L. SUTTER

David used to be in a band with his best friends Chance and Eli. Now the band, Darkhearts, is super famous – and David's out of the band and back in high school, brooding over everything he lost out on. Then tragedy throws David and Chance back together. Chance is everything David is not: a swaggeringly drop-dead gorgeous rock god. And yet spending more time alone with Chance, David has to admit he actually misses being with his old friend – and maybe he feels something more. Can you mix music with love?

'These boys and their love story filled up my heart'
Amie Kaufman

OPTIMISTS DIE FIRST

SUSIN NIELSEN

Ever since tragedy struck her family, Petula has learned to see danger everywhere. She's determined not to let her guard down, even if this means allowing herself to be ruled by anxiety and grief. Then she meets Jacob. Strikingly tall and confident, he's survived a different kind of disaster and still come out smiling. At first Petula is repelled by his outgoing optimism, but even she can't deny their chemistry together. But optimism is blind – and so is love. What will happen if Petula gives in to both?

'Hilarious, heart-warming and beautifully unexpected'
Lisa Williamson

'Nielsen writes with sensitivity, empathy, and humour'
Kirkus, starred review